"What?" Trace a **affair?"**

"I'm not sure I could c_____
having had one."

Julie's honesty was touching, but her statement fell into the room almost explosively. He tried to lighten the moment when he saw her cheeks start to color. How many women still blushed? he wondered. "We could always have one now."

He gave her a few seconds to stare at him wide-eyed, then he laughed. "Just joshing you. I mean, sure, I'd love to, but under the circumstances, it wouldn't be wise."

Not when someone was trying to kill him. Not when he might have to leave at the drop of a hat. He had limits, and taking advantage of a woman was a hard line for him. He had few hard lines left, and not crossing them was all that kept him from feeling he was simply scum.

Then she stunned him. "What makes you so sure it wouldn't be wise?" she asked pertly as she slid off the bar stool. She headed for the bathroom, saying she'd be back in a minute to work on the story.

For the first time, Trace wondered if he'd wandered into a new kind of quicksand.

* * *

Be sure to check out the rest of the Conard County: The Next Generation miniseries!

* * *

If you're on Twitter, tell us what you think of Harlequin Romantic Suspense! #harlequinromsuspense

Dear Reader,

Much to my surprise, when I finished writing a Special Edition that will be published in a few months, I found one of the characters was haunting my waking thoughts. Julie Ardlow had captured my mind and heart, and demanded her own story.

The next book on my list was Romantic Suspense, and Julie wanted to be right in the middle of it. So here she is, outspoken, beautiful and with a heart that doesn't count the cost when it cares. She thrusts herself into a situation that could get her killed, and she does it to protect her friends. In the process she becomes involved with a wounded spy—a real spy—and finds that his heart has nearly shut down.

Well, Julie won't stand for that.

In the odd way of the publishing world, this book is a sequel to the Special Edition to be published soon. I tried not to give away much, but if you want Ryker and Marisa's touching story...well, it's coming soon.

Hugs,

Rachel

CONARD COUNTY SPY

Rachel Lee

HARLEQUIN® ROMANTIC SUSPENSE

Recycling programs
for this product may
not exist in your area.

ISBN-13: 978-0-373-27986-9

Conard County Spy

Copyright © 2016 by Susan Civil Brown

Printed in U.S.A.

www.Harlequin.com

Rachel Lee was hooked on writing by the age of twelve and practiced her craft as she moved from place to place all over the United States. This *New York Times* bestselling author now resides in Florida and has the joy of writing full-time.

Books by Rachel Lee

Harlequin Romantic Suspense

Conard County: The Next Generation

Guardian in Disguise
The Widow's Protector
Rancher's Deadly Risk
What She Saw
Rocky Mountain Lawman
Killer's Prey
Deadly Hunter
Snowstorm Confessions
Undercover Hunter
Playing with Fire
Conard County Witness
A Secret in Conard County

Visit the Author Profile page at Harlequin.com for more titles.

For all my readers who help bring Conard County to life, and many thanks to Ashley Granger who volunteered the use of her name for a character. Hope you're pleased, Ashley.

Prologue

The hotel room was opulent, befitting an important man, one on a diplomatic mission for his country. But there was not a diplomatic discussion taking place within its confines. Deadly business was on the table.

The gray-haired man sitting near the window in a very expensive tailored suit looked at the dossier in his hands. He appeared to be extremely fit and when he moved, did so with fluid ease.

The man who faced him was decades younger, dressed in much less expensive garb suitable to a government clerk. He was also a little nervous, no matter how calm he tried to be. He was the cover for the people helping the older man. They both knew it. They both also knew it could end badly for this young man if this meeting became known to the wrong people.

The gray-haired man had a lot of experience judging people, and he knew that this one knew only what he needed to in order to complete this task. "So this is the one who betrayed me? Trace Archer?"

"Yes, sir," said the other. "We told you that several months ago."

"Where is he now?"

"We sent him on his way to recuperate away from here. We're tracking him."

"So you know where he is?"

The younger man nodded. "What he did put you in great danger, General. My superiors understand."

"My man did a poor job of taking him out in Bulgaria. It will be harder here."

"It will be cleaner here. You know we value you highly. But if something happens to him on his trip, no explanations will be needed from anyone. That's how we all want it."

The general put the dossier aside and went to stand at the window. "In Ukraine, the situation is very delicate. Now it is even more delicate because of this man."

"I know."

The general doubted the younger man knew even that much or had any real understanding of the complexities here. He was simply doing his job. "I will not trust this to anyone else. That failed last time. So this time you will get *me* close to him."

The younger man hesitated. Apparently this had not been in his brief. "General, the risk…"

"There will be no risk. I am here on a diplomatic mission, yes?"

"But that won't protect you if…"

"There will be no *if*. This man has threatened my life,

my family, everything I have worked for. I must know he is taken care of, see it with my own eyes."

After a moment of hesitation, the younger man agreed. "As you wish." Clearly he had been told not to disagree with the general.

"I would expect no less. I have worked with you for many years, first from my position in the Russian army, and now in Ukraine. You owe me."

"Yes, sir."

The general smiled for the first time. "Soon we will resume our mutually beneficial relationship. Once I remove the traitor."

Chapter 1

Trace Archer hesitated on the porch. The address was correct, but he hadn't been expecting such a large house. It rose two stories on a street that would be shady in the summertime, but on this cold March night boasted leafless branches. Probably close to a hundred years old.

In fact, he didn't know what he had been expecting and wasn't remotely certain what he was doing here. And even though an old friend lived here, he doubted he'd be welcomed.

As he was standing there hesitating, a woman popped out the front door. Covered by winter clothing, her figure was obscured, but in the porch light he couldn't miss the long, shiny auburn hair, and when her gaze settled on him, he could tell her eyes were an unusual green, undimmed by the poor light.

"Well, hello," she said, pausing.

He must be at the wrong place. John Hayes had shown him a photo of his wife once, and Ryker Tremaine had married her after John died. This woman didn't match the photo at all.

"Sorry," he said automatically, shifting a little to ease the everlasting pain in his arm and hand. "I must have the wrong house."

He couldn't mistake the appreciation in her eyes as her gaze swept over him. He wasn't sure what she was appreciating, considering that, like her, he was wearing a heavy winter jacket.

"I wouldn't be so sure," she said. "I don't live here. Who are you looking for?"

"Ryker Tremaine."

"Right house," she said, then before he could respond she turned and threw the door open. "Hey, Ryker, you've got a friend out here."

"Bring him in," came a familiar but muffled voice from inside.

The choice taken out of his hands, Trace followed the woman inside, entering a warm, pleasant foyer. Gleaming dark wood surrounded him and a staircase led directly upward. It made him feel like a puzzle piece that didn't fit the picture.

"I'm Julie, by the way," the green-eyed woman said, stripping off her gloves and offering her hand. "Julie Ardlow."

Trace shifted uneasily. He still wasn't used to all the limitations of his injury and had to make a conscious decision to offer his gloved left hand to shake hers. He saw the way her eyes widened, then saw comprehension dawn. Well, it wasn't as if he could hide it indefinitely.

Then he heard heavy footsteps from the back of the

house, and Ryker appeared. Trace experienced a sense of shock. In all the years he'd known Ryker, never had he seen the man look this relaxed, and right now he had a faint smile around his mouth. As he saw Trace, that smile vanished, and he once again looked like granite.

"Well. I'll be damned," Ryker said.

"I can leave," Trace replied. "I was just in the area…"

"No," Ryker said slowly. "No. Julie, you still need to run?"

Julie looked between the two men. Trace could almost sense her calculating whether that was a dismissal or an invitation to stay.

"Yeah," she said finally. "School tomorrow and all that. See you, Ryker. Nice meeting you, whoever you are."

"Sorry," he said. "The name's Trace."

She cocked her head a little, smiled slightly with a mouth that seemed to beg for a kiss, then headed back out the front door. Neither man moved until it closed behind her.

"I heard you were sidelined," Ryker said. "Didn't expect you, though."

"No reason you should. I wasn't expecting to show up here, either. If it's a problem, I'll leave."

Ryker shook his head a little. "I'll tell my wife you're here and make some coffee. Just…no lies, okay? There've been enough of them."

Trace didn't have to imagine those. He lived them. But he did wonder what lies the man was expecting. Between them, there didn't need to be any. When Ryker waved him into the living room, he unzipped his jacket partway with his good left hand, then sat on the battered burgundy gooseneck chair.

Seldom had he ever felt more out of place. What had brought him here, anyway? A desire to find out if life after the job was possible? Ryker seemed to be making it, but then it hadn't been that long.

This whole house smelled of baby, he noted. Powder and sour milk. He almost smiled thinking of the huge transitions Ryker must be going through. Nothing about this would resemble being a field operative.

At last Ryker returned with coffee for each of them. "The baby's been fussy the last couple of days. A cold. My wife's going to try to catch some sleep, so it's just us."

That was fine by Trace. The devil of it was, he'd brought himself here and now didn't have a damn thing to say.

"How bad is it?" Ryker finally asked.

"I won't be working in the field anymore." The least of it in some ways. Being crippled was harder to deal with than a change of jobs.

Ryker settled on the couch and crossed his legs loosely. "Sorry, man."

"Not so sure I am." This visit was pointless. He honestly didn't know what he'd expected to find here in Conard County, Wyoming. Answers to questions about a future he was having trouble facing? He needed a shrink for that, not an old friend. Maybe he should just congratulate Ryker on his new life and get the hell out.

"You going to be staying in town for a while?" Ryker asked.

Was that a suggestion he leave? Trace couldn't tell, but then Ryker had always been difficult to read. "I wasn't planning to. I just wanted to drop by."

Ryker nodded slowly, still watching him. "Where will you go next?"

"Damned if I know. Does it matter?"

A faint frown flickered over Ryker's face. Then he sighed. "Yeah, Trace, it matters. Word I get about you isn't good. We haven't always seen eye to eye, you and me, but I'm hearing things. You got trouble on your tail?"

"I'm not sure. No one's sure."

Ryker stood up then, and now there was no mistaking his reaction. "You brought that trouble right to my door? To my wife and baby?"

"I've been careful. No one knows where I am right now."

Ryker paced three steps quickly before turning and stabbing his finger at Trace. "You came here. Who told you how to find me?"

"Bill."

"Bill. Damn it all to hell."

Trace stood up, battling to ignore the savage pain in his right arm. "Consider me gone. No one knows I'm here."

"I know and Bill knows. That's one too many. Why the hell did he tell you?"

"I don't know. I'm just rambling."

"With a tiger on your tail?"

"Nobody knows that for certain. And frankly, I don't believe it."

This was a side of Ryker that Trace wasn't used to seeing. Usually the man went into overdrive to help a buddy. Now he was in a different mode, a lion protecting his pride. This had been a huge mistake. He put his coffee down. "I'll leave now, R.T. Gone tonight."

"But to where?"

"Who cares?"

Ryker scowled at him. "I do, damn it. They shouldn't be cutting you loose like this."

"I'm a liability now. Obviously." Nothing like facing the cold, hard truth.

Ryker shook his head. "Sit down, drink your coffee and shut up. I need to think."

An eternity later, Ryker settled and faced him again. "You got a number of IDs? Some that they don't know about?"

"A few. I've been using different ones everywhere I go."

Ryker nodded. "Use one of them tonight. Check into the motel on the edge of town with it. Stay low."

"And then?"

"I'm going to talk to the sheriff here."

Everything in Trace rebelled. "You can't tell him…"

"I can tell him enough. He's a good man to have on your side. But one thing you are most definitely not going to do is come back to this house. Got it?"

"Yeah." Trace practically snapped the word.

"Stay tonight. I'll see you in the morning."

"I'll leave."

Ryker shook his head. "Trace, you're hanging in the wind. You can't do that until you die. So shut up and get that room. We'll talk again tomorrow once I figure out some things."

Julie Ardlow decided not to head straight home. Instead she went to Maude's City Diner and ordered a latte to drink while she went over her kindergarten students' pictures. The exercise was designed to do two things: associate a printed color name with the actual hue, and work on fine motor skills by drawing inside the lines. Each child's first name had to be crayoned at the top. Beyond that, she didn't care how much they added their own inventions to the simple picture, but she often enjoyed them.

The papers all said *ball* and *purple* at the top. As long as the ball was purple and was reasonably neat, she didn't care what they colored the other items or how much they added. The kids seemed to enjoy it, and she had a stack of self-sticking stars and smiley faces to decorate each one with. At this point in the year, most were engaged in simple reading, so she measured their progress, especially in fine motor skills. A big improvement over the beginning of the year.

And they all made her smile. The boys' drawings were often decorated with simple rocket ships or planes. The girls' with flowers or smiling stick figures. Not always, though. Tommy Wells had added what looked like a snake or a dragon to his. Gloria Chase, defying stereotypes as usual, had drawn a big boat on hers.

When she finished with them, she pulled out another stack from her bag. Word matching this time, simple ones they had all learned to read aloud, drawing a line between the ones that matched in separate columns. Following directions, pattern recognition, reading, and…in one case, one student's work indicated some clear dyslexia. That had been brought to the school's attention, and Jason was getting extra help. She gave him a big smiley face and a gold star anyway. She never wanted to discourage a child.

She felt a cold blast of air behind her and heard the bell over the door ring. She looked over and saw that guy she had met at Ryker and Marisa's house earlier. Something about him awoke her sexual radar, but she didn't know why. Maybe because he was new to town? It had been a few years now since she had last felt the desire to even date. And over a decade since her only serious relationship.

He had the kind of face that would probably fit in anywhere, yet still had a strong appeal. Dark hair, eyes a medium brown, a good jaw. And the steel she had once seen in Ryker. Except this guy looked as if something was seriously wearing on him.

When his gaze scraped over her, she knew he recognized her, but he started for another table with his coffee anyway. Unable to resist, she waved him over. Somebody new in town. He probably wouldn't be here long and he knew Ryker, which made him safe enough. She wouldn't mind a little diversion.

His reluctance was obvious as he crossed to her booth. "I'm interrupting," he said immediately, nodding at the papers spread in front of her.

"A welcome interruption," she replied. "No point having your coffee all by yourself. Grab a seat."

Again, that hesitation. What was with this guy? Usually men didn't resist her invitation to coffee. Not that she asked many of them. She'd spent her entire life in Conard County, and she knew all the men. No interesting stories there. She figured she was going to end her days a spinster because she was already bored with the limited local selection of available bachelors.

He slid into the booth across from her, and she didn't miss his wince.

"You're in pain," she said bluntly.

"Yeah. Injury."

"I'm sorry."

He didn't answer beyond, "It happens. So you teach?"

"Kindergarten."

"Lots of smiley faces there." Which brought a faint smile to his face. "You make them color inside the lines?"

She hated that question. "It teaches fine motor co-ordination. These children are all learning to print the alphabet and their numbers. It's a good exercise, staying in the lines. But no, I don't make them do that all the time." She eyed him. "You play inside the lines?"

"Depends," he answered.

Why didn't that surprise her? Julie thought wryly. Ryker clearly hadn't expected to see him, and since they knew each other… Well, she'd already discovered Ryker didn't always play inside the lines. "Will you be visiting for long?"

"That remains to be seen. I may leave in the morning."

"A rolling stone, huh?"

"At the moment."

Julie studied him frankly. It was clear to her that this man had been through some kind of wringer, and he seemed tense, as if holding still wasn't comfortable for him. The pain? Or something else? "I gather you know Ryker, but did you ever meet his wife, Marisa?"

Trace shook his head. "I haven't had the pleasure. She must be something to have settled him down."

"She's something, all right. She's also my lifelong best friend."

He got the warning, she saw with satisfaction. She had no idea what Ryker had done before he arrived in this town, just as she had no idea what Marisa's late husband, Johnny, had done. All she knew what that it had caused Johnny's death, and she didn't want this guy and whatever secrets he bore to put Marisa in danger.

"So who do you work for?" she asked, pulling her papers together. She could finish the word-match problem later.

"State Department."

Ah, she'd heard that before, from Johnny and Ryker. She wasn't half buying it, but she knew better than to say so. "A lot of traveling?"

"Quite a bit."

"Traveling for vacation is one thing. Traveling all the time for work is another. I don't think I'd like it."

"Depends," he said. "When you stay in one place long enough, you get immersed in a different culture. Lots of new perspectives."

In that instant, she decided she liked this man. That was an intelligent outlook. "You know, I went to Jamaica a few years back, and I was on a tour bus."

He arched a questioning brow and waited.

"There was a couple from this state, sad to say, who started badgering the tour guide about Jamaica's drug problems and whether they were worse because of the race of most Jamaicans."

She watched, waiting. For an instant Trace seemed to freeze, then he just shook his head.

"Yeah," she agreed. "For the first time in my life, I wished I were from somewhere else. I stopped to apologize to the guide when we disembarked. My point is, as ugly people, they probably didn't get any new perspectives."

"Not everyone does," he agreed. "Some people never leave their comfort zones."

"I imagine you do."

His brown eyes narrowed slightly. "Often. Why?"

"Just a casual response to your comment about different perspectives." She summoned a smile and decided to back off. This guy was what Marisa had once called *a box of secrets*. Just like Johnny and then Ryker. Since he wouldn't be around long, it didn't matter, and it sure wasn't courteous to try to discuss things that might make him uneasy.

Secrets. She almost sighed. She'd grown up in a town where almost nothing was a secret for long, but she'd seen the toll Johnny's secrets had taken on Marisa. Now there was Ryker, and she sometimes wondered but never asked how he and Marisa had crossed that bridge. All she knew for certain was that they had somehow.

Still, the idea of a guy with secrets was out of the ordinary, something new and shiny in a town she loved but sometimes felt was apt to bore her to extinction.

Except for her students. She looked down at the papers in front of her and reminded herself that they were all the newness and shininess she needed. With them, nearly every day brought wonderful surprises.

"I love teaching kindergarten," she remarked, swimming out of the shoals into safer water. "Kids that age are so fresh, and everything is new and wonderful to them. They often astonish me and remind me that life can be magical."

"No bad stuff?"

She looked at him again. Was this guy jaded, or was something else going on? She couldn't imagine. "Well, occasionally I have a child who knows things far beyond his or her years. Things no child should have to deal with."

"But you can help?"

"Sometimes."

Then he smiled, a genuine smile, the first he had given her. It made her feel a sexual tug all the way to her core. "That must be a great feeling." He edged out of the booth. "It's been a pleasure, Ms. Ardlow. Can you point me in the direction of the motel?"

She hesitated, then thought, *Why the heck not?* "I can lead you there if you want to follow. It's on my way. Just let me gather up my papers."

"You want another coffee?"

She glanced up and found him still smiling. "Sure, latte with two sweeteners. Thanks."

"I'm getting some to take with me. No problem."

She watched him walk back toward the counter where Maude, the diner's owner, glowered as usual. The man had an easy stride, as if he were in great shape except for that arm of his. Curious.

Then she gathered her papers into her folders and slid them into her backpack and wondered if she'd ever learn any more about Trace. Ryker probably wouldn't tell her a thing. That man was a serious clam. Not that it mattered. Trace would probably be gone with the morning sun.

She collected her coffee from Maude, who gave her an extra frown, probably because she was associating with a stranger. Julie replied with a broad smile. Annoying Maude was the easiest thing in the world. Sometimes Julie even enjoyed doing it.

Trace pushed the door open with his back, his good left hand holding a tray with three coffees of his own. She guessed he wasn't planning to sleep tonight. She bit back an offer to help, sensing it wouldn't be welcome, then stepped out into a night that ought to be hinting at the approaching spring but instead seemed to be warning that more winter waited around the corner.

She pointed out her car, then went to climb into it. Trace needed a couple of extra steps, putting the coffee on top of his car while he opened the door, then reaching in to settle the tray on the passenger seat. He'd had some practice at the juggling act, she thought as she wished her car would hurry and warm up.

She pulled out of the parking space and waited for him. Soon he was behind her, and she led him down the main street to the edge of town, where a truck stop brightened one side of the road and the La-Z-Rest Motel sagged on the other side. She tapped her brake lights a couple of times and saw him flash his headlights once in response before he turned into the motel.

She continued her way along an unnecessarily circuitous route to her apartment. It had been out of her way to lead him to the motel, but she was glad to do it. He struck her as an interesting man.

Too bad he wasn't staying. She could use a little adventure.

At the motel, Trace checked in under the ID of Tom LaCrosse and soon had a room, paid for in cash. Once he'd dragged his duffel inside, he popped two of the pain pills the doctor had prescribed. He took them only when he didn't need to drive and felt it was safe to doze a bit. Tonight was safe. Tomorrow, who knew?

Regardless, the three coffees he'd just bought would keep him from getting too drowsy to wake up.

He ditched the winter jacket, thinking that he had to find a coat easier for a man with only one working hand. He was adept enough at buttons now and could zip up his pants, but that damn jacket was a pain. Getting the zipper to work with only one hand after he'd opened it all the way defied him, but pulling it off over his head didn't work, either. That procedure left him sweating and too close to passing out.

The pain of the gunshot wound would ease with time, he'd been told, although he'd never get the function back in his hand. Not all of it. He'd reached the point where he didn't care if it ever worked right again if it would just shower him with the mercy of not hurting as if it were caught in a meat grinder.

Shed of his clothes, he climbed into the sweat suit he preferred for sleeping and turned on the TV at low volume. He guzzled coffee and waited for the meds to start their work. A few hours of milder pain would be welcome, but nothing completely erased it.

Ryker hadn't exactly surprised him, now that he thought about it. The man was out of the business, he had a wife and child to worry about, and he could hardly want someone like Trace showing up.

But the thing was—and this bugged the devil out of Trace—nobody at the agency was sure that he might be in trouble. All the intelligence networks, all the people gathering every little tidbit, could come up with only one thing: someone had tried to find him under his real name. Something only a few people should know. The secrecy around him had somehow been pierced.

So who and why? It might be nothing. But it left him, as Ryker had so succinctly put it, blowing in the wind. The agency wanted him to keep moving until they learned more, so he'd been doing exactly that, until he was utterly tired of it.

He shouldn't have come here. Ryker was right about that. Whether someone was after him didn't matter. If there was even the slightest chance, he should never have risked exposing Ryker's family. Maybe the pain was affecting his decision-making, because this was a dumb one.

But as the buzz from the meds began to hit him and he stretched out on the bed, another part of him was glad he'd come. He'd enjoyed his eyeful of Teacher Julie. He wondered if she had any idea how that claret sweater brought out the red in her hair and the green in her eyes. Or if she even guessed how it had revealed her breasts as she'd leaned forward against the table.

Maybe not, but he'd appreciated every single minute of the view. Still, she was not for him. How much sweeter could you get than a kindergarten teacher who lived in a world of smiley faces and foil stars? She deserved the kind of man who would stay for the long haul, and he was no stayer.

Even if they found out no one was after him, he still wouldn't be right for that woman. He didn't want to cast his shadows over her bright little faces and shiny stars. Everywhere he went, he cast shadows. He knew that.

He just hoped he hadn't cast one over Ryker.

As the pills set him free enough to doze, they also set his imagination free. Images of Julie Ardlow swam in his mind's eye, images of undressing her, sensations of touching her, exploring her. The unparalleled moments of entering her hot, wet depths and claiming her.

Just dreams. Sometimes dreams were all a man had left. Sometimes they were the last safe place he could go.

Chapter 2

Ryker yanked him out of sleep in the morning with a phone call. Groaning as he awoke to searing pain yet again, Trace reached for the phone beside the bed and answered it.

"Yeah."

"It's me," Ryker said. "Meet me in thirty at the sheriff's office. It's just up the street from the diner."

"I need coffee." He needed more than coffee, but these days caffeine was the only thing that kicked his brain into something resembling a normal gear.

"Okay, then, I'll bring it to you. How much and how do you like it?"

"Three or four, black, strong."

"In ten, then. What's your room?"

Trace struggled for a moment to recall. "Four."

"Ten minutes."

Then Ryker was gone. Slowly Trace pushed himself upright, biting back groans and facing the nearly impossible task of getting dressed. Well, Ryker was bringing more coffee. So he popped another pill and started the laborious job. Shorts. Jeans. Shirt. He simply stared at the god-awful jacket. Not even enough time to shower. That was Ryker. That was the job.

Socks. Boots with Velcro closures. Damn, sometimes he felt old.

Ten minutes later he heard the knock. Rising, he opened the door, wide-awake and hating it. Ryker stepped in, carrying a cardboard tray with four tall coffees.

"Trying to hurry me out of town?" Trace asked bluntly as he plopped on the bed and reached for one of the cups.

Ryker spoke very quietly. "Cell phone?"

Without question, Trace rose and got the phone from the pocket of his jacket. He didn't say a word as Ryker pulled the back off of it and removed the battery and SIM card.

"Later," Ryker said, "get a new phone. A burner. That one is about to head out of town on the next truck that leaves the lot across the street."

Trace understood, and he didn't like what he understood. If the right person had that number, they could have been listening to what was going on in this room at that very moment, at least until Ryker pulled the phone apart. "I've been getting fresh burners all along." Because he wasn't a total idiot, although he had to admit every time he'd gotten one, he'd had to use his debit card, even if only at an ATM. Hell, if the worst case proved true, he might as well have kept his original phone. "What about yours?"

"My cell is still at home. We're going to send this one out of town this morning. Just in case. Anyway, everybody else may be kicking you to the curb, but I'm not."

That jolted Trace, and he looked over as Ryker took the only chair and reached for a coffee. "Why not?"

"I talked to Bill. Are you on meds?"

"I'm still waiting for it to hit."

"Okay. Does it help?"

He met Ryker's dark gaze and saw something very like the sympathy that had been missing last night. "Yeah, when I take enough of it."

"Probably not often, knowing you."

"Not when I can avoid it. What's going on?"

Trace could feel the buzz coming, so he finished his coffee and reached for another before sitting on the edge of the bed again.

Ryker sighed and sipped more coffee, then leaned back and crossed his legs at the ankle. "I told you I talked with Bill. I was going to rake him over the coals for giving you my address, but it turns out he gave it to you for a reason."

Trace sat up a little straighter, suppressing a wince. "What reason?"

"Apparently he thinks there's more going on than you've been told and that you desperately need an ally."

Trace felt his heart accelerate. "That's news to me." Important news. Something to give his full attention to. "Did he say what's happening?"

"No. He doesn't know." Ryker blew a long breath and glanced at his watch. "A few more and then we go. No, he doesn't know, but he was unhappy about it. He thinks they've cut you loose and don't give a damn."

"I was right. I'm a liability." Instead of just wondering, now he knew, but he was damned if he knew why. So much was becoming clear, and he didn't like it.

"My guess is you've passed your expiration date because of your injury, and they're more interested in catching the tiger that's on your tail than whether you survive it."

"Or alternatively, they have a reason not to stop the tiger. I've heard of it."

"So have I, but I've never known it to happen."

"Me, neither, but that doesn't mean it doesn't happen. You know how much butt-covering goes on." And secrets. Secrets that only a handful might ever know. Those secrets could be good for the country, essential even, but they could also cover up more nefarious activities.

A sense of betrayal began burning in him, but this wasn't the time to let it take over. Trace forced it down, trying to clear his head, suddenly wishing he hadn't taken the pain pill. It wouldn't help at all, not right now. What good would it do him to ease his hand when his brain would be in low gear?

"We've got some time. Bill never told anyone he directed you to me, and I talked to him on a scrambled line this morning."

"You have one?" Trace hadn't expected that, given that Ryker had hung up his spurs. That technology was doled out very carefully.

"Better believe it. When I resigned, I still had a lot of useful stuff in my brain. They want to pick it occasionally. Think they're going to trust the phone company with that? Or that I would? Hell, we don't even let the NSA eavesdrop on our lines."

But another thought had occurred to Trace and it

made him sick. "I got your address on an unsecure line. I'd better leave now. I don't want your family at risk."

"Well…" Ryker's eyes twinkled unexpectedly. "The conversation I had with Bill this morning wasn't exactly as straightforward as I reported. We talked sideways on purpose. I gave Bill a helluva lecture about revealing my whereabouts, and I told him I'd sent you on your way this morning. So *if* anybody was listening, I sounded p.o.'d, Bill sounded apologetic and loosely explanatory, and in theory you're already on the road. We're gonna need to get your car out of town along with the phone, though. You okay to drive?"

"Yeah." Trace started smiling. His head was getting into the game again. He guessed he'd been missing a sense of purpose. And it felt good not to be alone for the first time in a few weeks. "You wouldn't happen to know of a junkyard a few hundred miles from here?"

"Well, I do happen to know just the right guy to get a car towed a long, long way."

An unreasonable curiosity dragged Julie off her usual path to the elementary school and past the motel. Trace's car was still there, but probably wouldn't be for long. Then she got a jolt as she saw Ryker exit the room with the guy. What was going on?

Down the street a way, she pulled over to the curb and watched her rearview mirror. For some reason Ryker dashed across the state highway into the truck stop parking lot. A few minutes later he dashed back. She saw him wave toward the center of the town, then jog up the street to where his car was parked.

What the heck? It was like a scene out of some spy movie, she thought, almost laughing at herself. Why in the world would Ryker park up the street instead of in the motel lot? Shaking her head as questions percolated in her mind, she started to put her car in gear. As she looked to the side she found Ryker pulling up beside her. He was lowering his window, so she touched the button to lower hers.

"Julie," he said.

"Ryker. What…"

He interrupted her. "Whatever you just saw, forget it. Completely. Curiosity and the cat. You read me?"

Astonished, she gaped at him, feeling her head bob agreement. "I never saw a thing," she said when she could find her voice.

He smiled. "Good. Just keep Marisa in mind."

Then he pulled away, leaving her with more questions than ever. Eventually she pulled out, remembering that twenty-two children would be piling into her classroom very soon. But she didn't want to think about those kids.

She wanted to think about what had just happened and what it might mean, and why he was concerned about Marisa.

No matter how many times she told herself to just forget it, as Ryker had warned her, the questions kept percolating in her mind. Somehow she had to find out what was going on.

Determined that she would, she entered her classroom smiling.

Ryker had told Trace just last night to lie low. Walking into a busy sheriff's office hardly struck Trace as staying low. It actually seemed quite high-profile. His nerves began to crawl.

No names were exchanged. The wizened woman at the dispatcher's desk, who squinted at them through a cloud of smoke that issued from the illicit cigarette dangling from one corner of her mouth, merely jerked her head toward the back.

Trace followed Ryker down a hallway to an open door that had the word *Sheriff* stenciled on the frosted glass top. Inside a man with a burn-scarred face sat behind the desk, his khaki uniform neatly pressed. He spoke without rising.

"Hey, Ryker. Close the door." Then his gaze settled on Trace, taking him in. "Sit down," he said to both of them, "and tell me what all the cloak-and-dagger stuff is about."

Trace tensed. Some things were not to be revealed under any circumstances, and certainly nothing about the situation he was in. Operational security could be compromised inadvertently. "Maybe I should just go," he said.

Ryker clapped a hand to his shoulder. "Maybe you should, but we're going to discuss other options here. Sheriff Dalton worked undercover for years with the DEA. I think he might have some understanding of what we could be dealing with here, and I'm sure he doesn't expect either of us to reveal anything we're not allowed to." Then Ryker returned his attention to the sheriff. "Gage, you know I worked for the State Department. So did my friend here."

Trace watched in amazement as understanding dawned in the sheriff's gaze. "Yeah, I know all about that," the man said, and somehow Trace believed he did. Reading between the lines.

"Well," Ryker continued, "Trace was badly hurt, and he's been cut loose. Our main concern is that he may have a tiger on his tail."

Gage's sharp gaze flashed back to Trace. "Well, and here I was starting to get bored with domestic disputes and traffic accidents. Winter's a bad time for accidents."

Trace said nothing, but his nerves stopped crawling. The sheriff had figured it out and knew not to say too much. Ryker had been right. And was that a possible solution Gage had just mentioned?

Trace decided to take over. After what Ryker had told him, there was no longer any doubt in his mind. "I need to get out of town. I need to be gone. I don't want to put Ryker and his family at risk. Then there's this Julie Ardlow. She asked me to sit with her at the diner last night for coffee, after I met her at Ryker's house."

"And she knows something is going on," Ryker said heavily. "I warned her off."

"You're new around here, Ryker," Dalton said. "Let me assure you that Julie takes *no* as a challenge. She's not going to leave it alone."

"Unless I leave," said Trace, standing. The buzz of the drugs made him a little light-headed. "My phone's on its way to…where?" he said to Ryker.

"A semi that was going to Denver."

"Okay. Then I'll ditch my car somewhere between here and there, get another and take a different direction."

"You can't keep running," Ryker argued.

Trace simply shook his head. "I'll get what's coming to me, whatever it is, but it's not going to land on someone else's head. I never should have come here."

"Sit a moment," Dalton said mildly. "While I do admire your scruples, fact is, you're in my town and that makes you my headache, at least briefly. So what do you know about this tiger?"

Trace sat slowly, ignoring the pounding in his arm,

taking care not to let the meds make him clumsy. "Until this morning, I wasn't even sure there was one. Vague… gossip, if you will. Ryker made a call and it appears trouble is stalking me, but that's all either of us knows. Not who, why or anything. Which makes this a nearly unsolvable problem."

Gage nodded slowly, rocking back in his desk chair. It squealed a protest. The only sound in the room. "Many years ago," he said slowly, "I had a problem like that and I didn't know it. A car bomb intended for me killed my entire family. I survived. Only one itch saved me from cutting my own throat. I wanted to find the SOB who'd ratted me out."

Trace nodded. Gage's experience didn't shock him, because he'd seen it in his own unsavory world. "I get it. But for me it's not too late to protect everyone else."

"Maybe not. No way to know, but I was driving at something else. You need to start thinking real hard. You'd be surprised how different some things can look in light of new information."

Trace knew he was right. It could. It might. Something might reveal itself. But he wasn't about to sit here while the guy closed in on him and his friend. He needed to clear out. "I can think on the road."

"Or maybe we can make it seem you're on the road."

Trace shook his head. "I appreciate it, but I've been taking care of myself for a long time in situations like this. I can take care of myself now, without endangering anyone else." That was the most important thing. It always had been.

"You can't possibly know that," Ryker said. "You're assuming a sniper's bullet at fifteen hundred yards.

What if it's a bomb? What if other people get unavoid-ably involved?"

"Like what happened to my family," Gage remarked. "Best you stay around people who know what's going on. Who might be able to help. Like I said, I admire your scruples, but they don't necessarily protect any-one. And not everyone has them."

Trace sat in silence, staring down at his still-gloved, destroyed hand. They were right. He didn't want to admit it—he wished he'd never set foot in this town—but they were right.

He'd been a damned fool to ever come here, but he hadn't really believed he was in trouble. Not when he arrived here, simply because a colleague he knew lived here. The threat had been so vague that it seemed im-probable that anything would happen. Someone looking for him under his real name? Could have been anyone and probably meaningless. He figured the suggestion of a threat had been used to shunt him aside until his medical retirement came through. He'd become useless, mainly because of the pain and the meds, and frankly no one wanted to see him hanging around like a reminder of what could happen to any of them. He'd known he made his coworkers uneasy.

But this? The burn of betrayal was returning, light-ing a fire deep in his belly. The sheriff was right about one thing: he wanted to know who'd put him in this po-sition and who was after him. He wanted those answers more than he wanted to preserve his own messed-up life.

He sighed. "I took my pain meds this morning. I'm not at my best. I need more coffee."

"Three didn't do it?" Ryker asked.

"This is strong stuff. That's why I hate to take it."

Dalton surprised him by rising and limping over to the door. He opened it and leaned out. "Hal!"

"Yo?"

"Get me six tall and strongs, black, from Maude's. Double time."

Then he limped back to his seat, and with every one of his careful movements, Trace felt a twinge of sympathy for the sheriff. Evidently he hadn't escaped all the effects of the bomb that had killed his family.

"That'll tick Velma off good," the sheriff remarked when he'd settled again.

"Velma?" Trace asked.

"The smoking volcano at the front desk. She makes us coffee every morning. We all pretend to drink it so as not to offend her. Might as well swallow thickened battery acid." Gage waved a hand. "Her coffee is infamous. Enough about that. We'll pump some more caffeine into you, and when you feel ready, we'll get into some detail about what, if anything, Conard County can do for you, if you'll let us."

Trace shook his head, trying to absorb this. "Why should you help me? You don't know me from Adam."

"I have some inkling about the service you've been providing to this country," Gage said quietly. "I get freaking frosted when people like you get cut loose. I don't like the stench, and I want to clean it up. Besides, you're Ryker's friend, and his wife means a whole lot to folks around here."

That was when Trace realized he'd walked onto a different planet.

The coffee arrived within ten minutes. Trace drank the first as fast as he could without burning his mouth and throat, then started on another. The two other men took their time chatting about how another storm was about to blow in and how everyone hoped it would be the last of the winter.

Trace listened with only half an ear. Ryker had given him enough information to fly with this morning, and as the coffee drove away the fuzziness the meds caused in his mind, it slipped into high gear. He'd hated the last weeks of running from an invisible threat that might not even exist. Well, now he was pretty certain it was real. Not knowing who or what made it pretty hard to take evasive action, but at least there was a reason for what he needed to do.

As a field operative, he'd seen enough of the underside to know that sometimes assets were more important than operatives, that his employer would protect some of them at any cost. He'd never known personally of a case where an operative had been hung out to dry, but it didn't exceed his ability to imagine. It became even easier to imagine when the operative, namely him, had become useless. Yeah, they'd do it all right. If an important asset demanded Trace's blood, nobody would intervene.

He looked up, interrupting the conversation without apology. "My phone's on the road. The car needs to be, too."

Ryker checked his watch. "Very soon. The driver of the truck I put your phone on was just walking inside to order breakfast when I spoke to him. He's probably just finishing up. Or maybe just pulled out of the lot. But you're right."

"I'd better get to it, then."

"Hold it," said Dalton. "Give it five."

"Why?"

"Because Ryker told me earlier we might need to get rid of your car. I've got a couple of guys who should be here any minute. So you think they've got a tracking device on your auto?"

"I don't know. It's unlikely, but I never looked for one. Besides, phones are easy to track. But if they're tracking both, then we don't want them to get too far apart."

"Why in the devil would they want to track you when they've cut you loose?" Gage nearly growled.

"Because," Trace said, "I might be a peace offering." Dead silence answered him.

The burn was growing. He'd spent a long time preoccupied by his recovery and rehab, and hadn't been paying much attention to a lot of things. When they suggested it might be best for him to hit the road until they figured out if he was at risk, it had made perfect sense in the morphine-induced haze.

He'd gotten off the morphine to milder stuff, meds he could mostly control with coffee, but he hadn't really thought about the entire setup. He was a field operative, for heaven's sake. Living at risk didn't seem strange or unusual to him. Being on the run had sometimes been part of his job. It had never occurred to him that the agency might just want him to be far away when fate overtook him. Plausible deniability was stamped all over this.

He looked up again as a tall man entered the office without knocking. His bearing, his gaze… Trace would have bet the guy had a special ops background. To the casual eye, it wouldn't show. To the experienced eye, it was unmistakable.

"Hi, Seth," Gage said. "I'm not going to introduce you."

Seth half smiled. "I wouldn't expect it. What do you need?"

"I need you and Wade to wreck a vehicle for me. Make it bad but nonfatal."

"Easy enough."

"Well, I'm not done yet," Gage said. "We need to do this fast. There's a cell phone on a commercial truck headed for Denver. I need the crash to occur about one hundred and fifty miles from here, close to that phone. Maybe twenty or so miles ahead of the truck." He looked at Ryker. "Whose truck?"

Ryker rattled off a license number and a description.

Seth nodded. "Got it."

"Leave the vehicle, leave the plates on it. One of you can drive an official car so neither of you get stopped for speeding on your way out, okay?" He pointed to the wall. "Grab the keys for number sixteen. She's gassed and ready to go." Then he turned his attention toward Trace. "Your keys?"

Trace stood, shoving his good hand into his jacket pocket and pulling them out, handing them over. "Might be smart to lose these in the snow, too."

Seth smiled faintly. "Will do. Which car?"

"Virginia plates, dark blue."

"See you in a few hours," Seth said and departed.

Trace began to see a little humor in all this, out of place though it was. "Who was that masked man?"

Gage chuckled. "Hang around here for a while and you'll find out." Then he leaned forward, reaching for his coffee. "We've got one more immediate problem. Julie Ardlow."

Julie Ardlow. Trace thought about her, of course, but what really chapped him was that he'd lost control of everything. Oh, he knew he wasn't at his best with pain pills in his system, and he seriously considered throwing them away. But each time he started to, he was forced to admit that he couldn't yet. The pain could keep him from thinking clearly even more than the meds. At least those he could fight with coffee.

But he was usually the manager of operations like this. The one who laid out the plan and directed it. Instead, he was along for the ride, and he didn't like it. He approved of the sheriff's actions. They were the same thing he would have ordered himself in a similar circumstance. But instead he'd been forced into the position of passenger.

What good would it do in the long run? Maybe he should have gone on his way with a sharp eye out and hoped to run into the tiger. Problem was, from the instant Ryker had reminded him there could be collateral damage, he'd been trapped.

But trapped in what? He couldn't spend the rest of his life in this small town waiting for the guy to find him. Yeah, he'd been blowing in the wind, and Dalton and Ryker had helped to give him a landing spot, but for how long? How long could he stand it? What if others in this town might now be at risk? Ryker had worried about it, justifiably.

All he knew was he had to find a way to get on top of this, take charge again. Or get the hell out very soon.

After school and a meeting, Julie drove by the motel and saw that Trace's car was gone. So he had taken off. That kind of saddened her. Someone new would have been nice to get to know.

So she swung by Ryker's place as the early winter night began to fall, saw that his car was gone but Marisa's was there, and she decided to pop in. Maybe she could satisfy her curiosity about Trace a little more, then put it away.

Marisa was awash in crying baby and dirty diapers and looking worn out. Julie stepped in immediately, taking the three-month-old into her arms. "Sit. Let me deal for a few, Marisa. What did the doc say?"

"Just a cold." Marisa smiled weakly, her lavender eyes showing little sparkle. "Why isn't this in all the congratulatory cards?"

"Because no one would ever have a kid if they knew," Julie retorted. "Anything special you have to do?"

"Suction out Jonni's nose from time to time so she can keep nursing. Something for the fever. Believe it or not, she does sleep sometimes."

"Hah." Julie's laugh was mildly sarcastic. "Not enough from the looks of you. Where's Ryker?"

"He ran to the store. We're about to burn through the last of the diapers."

Julie paced with the baby against her shoulder, hating to hear the little snuffles between cries. At least there was no coughing. "So what did you think of that friend of his?"

"Friend?" Marisa's brow creased. "Oh, he said someone stopped by last night. Did you meet him?"

"Briefly. What was your impression?"

"I didn't even see him," Marisa admitted. "Jonni fell asleep, so I did, too."

Well, so much for curiosity, Julie thought. "I guess he didn't say much about the man?"

"Just that he used to know him. Apparently he was in town for only one night."

Julie didn't know whether Ryker had been withholding or if Marisa just wasn't interested enough to be curious herself. Probably Marisa was just too dang tired. It didn't matter anyway, since Trace had moved on.

Disappointment filled her again, but even as it did she told herself not to be silly. What was disappointing? That a guy who'd barely left a footprint in town had already departed?

Sheesh, was she getting desperate or something?

But no, there'd been something in his brown eyes that had reached out to her. Those eyes had stuck with her. Then that crazy scene at the motel this morning.

Was Ryker keeping secrets again? God, for Marisa's sake, she hoped not. "Why don't you grab a nap? Unless this kid is going to starve in the next hour, I can walk her and change her."

"She won't starve. We just finished a feeding."

Julie eyed her. "And she's still awake? Good heavens!"

"Poor baby is miserable," said her miserable mother. Marisa rose and touched Jonni's forehead. "She's a little cooler. An hour, no more, okay?"

"An hour," Julie agreed, although if she could get the baby to sleep longer she'd give Marisa more than that.

Marisa disappeared into the bedroom and closed the door, a great sign, Julie thought. She *was* going to try to get some sleep, although how anyone could sleep with this racket escaped her. Babies seemed to have a volume out of all proportion to their small size.

But as she paced from kitchen, through foyer to living room and back, eventually Jonni did fall asleep. Little twitches and occasional snuffles replaced the heart-rending cries.

Eventually she heard the side door in the kitchen open. Probably Ryker. She stayed in the living room so that inadvertent sounds wouldn't wake the baby. A minute later, Ryker appeared, his jacket unzipped.

He smiled at her and the child. "Marisa?" he whispered.

"Asleep, I hope."

"Think you can come into the kitchen and pace? I want to make some coffee."

"I'll wait until you've started it. I gather peace is hard to come by right now."

He laughed silently. "Understatement." He stepped closer. "You're going to have to keep some secrets, though. Will you?"

"Not from Marisa."

"Not from Marisa. Just from everyone else in town."

"That I can do. I've been practicing my skills almost since I learned to talk."

Rocking side to side to provide a soothing motion, she waited and enjoyed how good it felt to hold a sleeping infant. Baby smells, warmth, soft little noises and cute little movements. Heavenly.

Ten minutes later, the baby still slept. Ryker returned with two mugs of coffee, followed by Trace.

"My, my," Julie murmured, her heart quickening. "Somebody's got some explaining to do."

Chapter 3

Trace left his jacket hanging open, set his coffee on a table, then eased into the gooseneck chair again. He stared at Julie and the infant and felt guilty as hell. This wasn't right; nothing about this was right. Now they were dragging an innocent woman into the middle of this and he decided that the smartest move might be to catch a bus for Seattle in the morning.

Then he remembered, yet again, Ryker's warning about collateral damage. He wanted to pound his fist on something to express his frustration with the way this was going. Maybe he ought to just shoot himself before this went any further.

But Gage's words surfaced. The only thing that had kept Gage from cutting his own throat was a desire to catch the rat. Oh, he could *so* identify with that. Plus, he had a feeling that if he gave himself over to this guy, some people who had set him up might not learn a lesson: not to cut an operative loose and leave him to his fate. There were other people, people he worked with, respected and liked, who might suffer the same fate. Assuming, of course, that all of this was about an asset being after him, and he had no idea who that might be.

Galled by it all, he sucked down more coffee and waited for Ryker. His hand burned like fire in a forge and felt as if a blacksmith were hammering it. Just a little longer, he promised himself. Then he could take a couple more of those pills. Right now he needed his wits, every last one of them.

It was Julie who broke the silence, her voice quiet. Her question surprised him and made him wonder how much she had already been told and how much she had guessed.

"So," said Julie, "did Fiona see Trace arrive?"

"Fiona?" Trace asked immediately.

"Nosy neighbor," Ryker answered. "No. It's dark out there and that's why I came by the side door. Trace had his head covered and ducked. If Fiona saw anything at all it was me pulling a week's worth of diapers out of the SUV, and that pretty much occluded her view of the kitchen door."

"Okay. Well, I'll be the first one she asks if she's curious. What do I tell her?"

"Nothing," Ryker said flatly.

"Nothing isn't a good answer for some people. Relax, if necessary, I'll deal with that woman." Julie smiled. "This is fun."

"No," Trace said. "It's dangerous and I shouldn't be here."

Ryker shook his head once. "You're sounding like

a one-note fiddle. Wherever you go, others will be at risk, so it might as well be willing participants who know what's going on."

Trace scowled at him. Damn, he hated being boxed in.

Julie spoke again. "So let me guess. The so-called State Department doesn't only have jobs that lead to an exciting life of world travel and fancy parties."

Neither Trace nor Ryker answered her.

"Oh, come off it," Julie said. "Johnny died. What kind of fool do you take me for? No, don't answer that. Don't answer anything. Just tell me why you're cutting me in. Then tell me how you're going to keep Marisa and Jonni out of it. Because frankly, that's all I really care about now."

Trace admired Julie's spunk. Right now she looked like the epitome of womanhood, an infant rocking on her shoulder, her long hair flowing down her back, a delightful body encased in a green sweater and black slacks. And all she was worried about was the safety of her friend and the baby. Not herself. He wondered if he needed to be more emphatic. "We're talking deadly danger here. I am not exaggerating. You should want to be as far from me as possible."

"Kinda hard when you're in my best friend's house," she retorted. She looked at Ryker. "Start talking and then tell me what we're going to do to protect your family. I am not leaving here until I know."

Ryker smiled faintly. "Gage was right about you. He said you take no as a challenge."

"Is that why you're talking to me? Because right now, I need some filling in. So Trace here is in danger and is worried about everyone around him. For some reason he's not leaving town. I assume the reason is a good one. So…what can I do to help?"

"We need to disguise him and stash him somewhere."

Julie shook her head a little. "Stashing someone in this county isn't easy. He needs to hide in plain sight." She looked at Trace. "Tell me you don't know how to do that."

Astonishment grew in Trace. This woman was talking like an experienced operative. Where was this coming from? "Yeah, I know how to do that."

"Cool," said Julie. "Change of hair color would be good unless you can grow a beard fast." She ran her gaze over his face. "Glasses can fool facial recognition software, too."

Ryker started laughing quietly. "Where's this coming from?"

"I studied a bit of theater in college. The biggest problem we have is Trace's arm. That'll be hard to conceal when he can't use it. Can you wear a sling? I can wrap it up so it looks like an ordinary injury."

"I don't know if I could stand it," he answered frankly. "But it's worth a try." He decided to let go for just a few minutes and let this woman take the lead. He was beginning to enjoy the way she was just diving in, dealing with the problem presented to her, without demanding explanations. She'd assessed the situation amazingly well and was working with it. No faint heart, this one.

Still rocking the sleeping baby gently, she continued. "He can't stay here. Period."

"Right," Ryker agreed.

"But he can stay at my place. All we need is a cover story. So, Trace, you're an old college friend of mine, you got hurt in a skiing accident, and you're visiting me for a few weeks. You can use my spare bedroom."

That was the instant when he came dangerously near an eruption. All that kept him from giving in to the sudden blast of anger was the sleeping baby. Keeping his voice low and level, he said, "I will *not* put you in that kind of danger."

"You're the one in danger," she answered. "And if you were so all-fired worried about the rest of us, why didn't you just keep moving?"

"Now, wait…" Ryker began.

He shut up when Trace interrupted, "I tried to. When I arrived here, I had no reasonable belief I might have someone after me. Now that I know, of course I'm worrying about everyone else. But Ryker and your friend the sheriff pinned me here, at least temporarily."

Julie glanced at Ryker. "Really? This is a story I want to hear someday, but first we have to get Trace out of this house. As soon as the baby wakes, I'm going to the store for what I need. Ryker, you bring Trace over to my place in the wee hours when all sane people will be asleep. He's going to be my old flame until you two figure out something that works better. And that's my final word. I don't want him within a mile of Marisa and this baby."

Jonni woke abruptly, and her crying resumed. Ryker took her immediately, rocking her and talking to her. Trace was amazed. Never in all the time he'd known Ryker had he thought such soft, soothing sounds could issue from that man's throat.

"I'm off," said Julie. "Bring Trace around three a.m."

Ryker nodded. "Thanks, Julie. See you then." He headed toward the back of the house with the unhappy baby.

But Trace couldn't leave it alone. He stood and faced Julie. "You don't want to get involved in this, Julie. I'm not kidding about the danger. You could get killed."

She looked at him, her smile completely fading. "Some things are worth risking your life for, Trace."

"Not me. Least of all me."

She frowned. "Is that how you feel? God, that's screwed up. See you at three."

He stood without another word to say as she donned her jacket and left. His arm reminded him he was still very much alive, but he wasn't sure that was a good thing. Why should Julie think so?

He had no answers. All he knew was that the people who should have been protecting him had thrown him to the wolves, and a man who could have justifiably kicked him to the curb to protect his family had decided to stand with him.

But the biggest mystery of all was Julie Ardlow. Something in her gaze had told him she didn't think this was a lark, that she grasped how dangerous it might be.

Why should she do this for a stranger?

Just before 3:00 a.m. Ryker pushed his car out of the driveway and onto the street. Helping as much as he could, Trace sat in the passenger seat at an angle with one foot over the brake and steered the car as Ryker pushed it down the street a few hundred yards. When it rolled to a stop, Trace manipulated the lever into the park position. Then Ryker climbed in beside him, started the car and headed away.

"Fiona?" Trace asked, remembering the nosy neighbor. That would explain pushing the car this far before starting it.

"I suppose there are all sorts of valid excuses I could use, having a sick daughter and all, to explain what I'm doing at this hour, but actually I'd rather not explain squat. Less explaining is better, as I'm sure you know."

"Absolutely. Anyway, I'm more concerned about Julie. That woman has the instincts of a field operative." Just enough of them to create additional problems, anyway. Worse, with every step he seemed to be drawing a new person into his hell.

Ryker snorted. "Thinking about recruiting her?"

"After this? Never. Just commenting. She sure took charge and her ideas were good. But she's unstoppable."

"Pretty much," Ryker agreed. "I thought Gage was exaggerating when he said she wouldn't take no for an answer. I was almost positive that when she learned this was dangerous, she'd back off."

"I didn't get the impression she's deluded."

"How could she be?" Ryker asked. "She knows Johnny Hayes died on the job. She's hardly likely to dismiss what we told her." He turned a corner and soon a moderately sized building appeared. "I'm going to drop you on the street, assuming you can manage that duffel."

"I can manage. I don't want to draw attention to the woman. Which unit is hers?"

"Apartment fourteen, ground floor, this end of the building. I don't think she has any immediate neighbors right now."

"Good." Trace paused. "You know I'm getting out of here as soon as I can."

"I get it. But first we need to figure out what you're up against. Know your enemy, and all that. In the meantime, you can't just keep moving without knowing what's after you. So let's not argue this all over again."

Trace reflected for a few moments as the car slowed.

"The thing is, I can't stop wanting to clear out. You know why. So at least give me the space to figure out how and when."

"Of course," said Ryker, stopping the car. "No buses before tomorrow afternoon, so don't get any cockeyed ideas about cutting out tonight. You'd freeze to death. Need any help?"

"I've got it."

Trace climbed out, grabbed his duffel from the back-seat and stood beside the road watching Ryker drive away. The pavement was clear, but there were snow banks between him and the parking lot. He spied a place that had been shoveled open and walked toward it.

He wished he thought this would work out well, that he'd get cleanly away and leave everyone behind him safe, but for some reason that wish was growing dimmer by the moment.

He had to figure out who wanted him. Only then would he know how to react. And figuring that out wasn't going to be easy, because he had zero information.

Sighing, he slogged toward Julie's apartment, hoping like hell that death wasn't right on his heels.

Chapter 4

Julie opened the door and let Trace in quickly. He had a little snow on his boots and remained on the rug in front of the door, dropping his duffel to one side.

Julie spoke. "Don't worry about the snow. I track it in all winter and clean the carpet every spring. Just make yourself comfortable. You want to go straight to bed or do you want coffee? There's a fresh pot."

"Coffee sounds great, if you don't mind." He was too keyed up to even think of sleep. Besides, he'd dozed a lot at the sheriff's office, where he'd spent most of the day out of sight in a utility closet. The pills had helped, but he wasn't ready to take more yet. Right then he'd reached the state where the pain in his hand wasn't driving him nuts, as if his brain had gone on overload and refused to handle any more of it.

"I'll join you," Julie said. "Saturday, no school, no

sleep necessary. By the way, the guest room is ready for you. I made it up while I was waiting."

A guest room. He wasn't used to such nice digs anymore. "Do you have a lot of guests?" he asked her as she walked into the kitchen area with a bar and passthrough that left it open to her small living room.

"My parents," she said as she filled two mugs and returned with them. "They retired to Florida, but by July they're tired of the heat and come to visit for about three months."

"You don't mind?"

She laughed. "Of course not. They have a lot of friends up here and spend a lot of time visiting. It's not like they take over my life or anything. So you've got until July to figure out your mess."

"It had better not take that long." He scanned the room, taking in the small desk and computer, the clutter of school papers on both desk and coffee table, the decent-looking cranberry-colored sofa and two matching chairs, one of which appeared to be an upholstered rocker. "Pretty place," he remarked.

"Pick whatever seat looks most comfortable to you," she answered. "Because I'm going to get very nervous if you hover over me."

He allowed himself to relax a little as he realized that he wasn't going to spend a whole lot of time wondering what Julie was thinking because she was naturally blunt. That was a plus. This whole situation was awkward enough; he didn't need to be wondering if she was just being polite.

He set his coffee on the end table beside the chair he thought would be easiest for him to get out of, then started to pull his jacket off. He tried to do it without jarring his hand or arm too much, but rarely succeeded. The nature of the beast.

Surprising him, without a word Julie came around behind him and started easing it off his shoulders. She seemed to intuitively understand that his arm was a problem, and when she slid the jacket down all the way, she didn't jar him.

"Thanks," he said, hating the fact that he needed the help but grateful for it anyway. At least the meat grinder didn't rev up any.

"No problem," she said casually. "You want a problem, try to help a five-year-old into snow pants, boots and jacket. I do that all winter long."

As he sat on the chair, she hung his jacket on the peg by the door. "What happened to your arm?"

"Gunshot," he said. "Hand, actually."

She perched on the edge of the couch, still wearing the green sweater and slacks she'd had on earlier. "They can't fix it?"

"They did what they could, but there's a whole lot of nerve damage."

"I'm sorry."

"It happens. Life happens. As I'm sure you know."

She pulled a band off her wrist, grabbed her hair all together, then wrapped it into a ponytail, pulling it away from her face except for a fringe of bangs. Now she looked a lot younger, and he felt a lot guiltier.

"It's nice of you to do this," he said presently. "Not wise, but very nice."

She leaned back on the couch, picking up her mug, then crossing her legs at the ankles. "You can thank me when this is over for all of us. And don't judge my wisdom. I can figure out what's going on."

He started a bit. "What do you mean?"

"Ryker," she said shortly.

"Meaning?"

She sipped her coffee, regarding him steadily. "If there's one thing I've learned about that man in the last six months, it's that he'd die to protect his wife and baby. But he's not prepared to send you on your way to do that."

"So?"

"So, he'd die to protect you, too. I don't know why, and you probably wouldn't even tell me, but I get it. If he's willing to take this risk for you, then there's only one thing for me to do. Because I'd die to protect Marisa, too. Ryker's a man who feels very strong loyalties. Well, I have my own loyalties. That's why you're here."

He nodded, accepting it and respecting it. He was also very glad to know that this wasn't just a spot of excitement for her. But as soon as he had the thought, she shocked him again.

She smiled. "Besides, I could do with some adventure. I'd prefer it to be a little tamer, but that's not what's happening. Anyway, I wasn't kidding about Marisa. I will do whatever it takes to protect her and her family. Period. So get used to it, spy guy."

He stiffened, then wished he hadn't because his arm let out a shriek. "Why'd you call me that?"

"Because I wasn't born yesterday, Trace. I may live in a small town, but that doesn't mean I don't know anything about the larger world. State Department, my foot."

He didn't answer because he couldn't. One thing was becoming increasingly clear: for all Julie appeared to live in a world of foil stars and smiley faces, she faced reality square on, and she didn't buy into illusions. One smart, savvy lady.

Silence filled the apartment until he began to wonder if he was being rude. "So you knew Johnny Hayes?" he asked of Marisa's late husband.

"Most of my life."

"What did you think of him?"

"Unexpurgated or published version?"

He felt an unexpected desire to laugh. "Unexpurgated."

Her mouth twisted. "He was a charming daredevil. He loved his adrenaline. He loved Marisa insofar as he was capable of loving. But he kept walking right out that door and leaving her alone for endless months at a time. So my opinion of Johnny? Selfish. But don't tell anyone. I'd hate for Marisa to know what I really thought of him."

"I have no reason to tell anyone. I just wondered." Frankly, that would have been his assessment of Johnny, too. Always ready to take a chance until he took one chance too many. Taking risks was unavoidable in their line of work, but there was a difference between taking calculated risks and taking risks for the hell of it. Johnny hadn't been with the agency that long, but from the one job they had worked together, Trace had concluded Johnny would be sidelined before too long. There were cannons, and then there were loose cannons.

"He had a lot of years in with the rangers," Trace remarked.

"I know." Julie shook her head. "Somehow I think being part of a unit kept a leash on him. But what do I know? Nothing. Everything was secret. Anyway,

Marisa never knew a thing about what he did. All she could do was keep the faith. What I do know is that when he died, she wanted to die with him. So excuse me if I intend to see that doesn't happen again."

Trace decided Julie Ardlow was one amazing woman. Love, loyalty, determination, beauty and intelligence wrapped into a single package. Women like her didn't come along every day. Or if they did, he hadn't met them. "Believe it or not," he said, "I'm on your side in this."

She smiled faintly. "I do believe you are, Trace Whoever. I do believe you are."

She put her coffee down. "I'm heading to bed. Your bedroom is that way." She pointed. "You have your own bath. I'll see you in the morning and then we'll figure out how to disguise you. Sleep well."

He might actually do that, he thought, as he pulled out his bottle of pain meds and popped two more. Fortunately, before they'd sent him on the road, they'd given him plenty, so he wouldn't need a pharmacy for quite a while yet, and thus wouldn't betray his whereabouts. And addiction, they'd assured him, wouldn't be a problem, as long as he took them only for pain.

But tonight, at least, he figured he could safely relax. If anyone was tracking him, they'd be looking in the vicinity of Denver. Only when they were sure they'd lost him would they even consider backtracking his route.

Slowly, he rose from the chair and headed for the bedroom she had pointed out. A few hours. He needed a few hours.

Julie didn't even have to open her eyes to know the threatened blizzard had arrived. She could hear it in the rattling windows and keening wind, in a world that otherwise held no sounds. She was glad she'd gone to the store yesterday evening instead of waiting for her usual Saturday trip.

Trace. Suddenly remembering he was in the other bedroom, she popped her eyes open and stared at the ceiling. Her heart slammed as she faced what she might have gotten herself into. Danger? She believed it.

But she hadn't been kidding herself or Trace when she had told him she'd die to protect Marisa. They had been friends since early childhood, inseparable through everything, and if anyone meant as much to Julie as her own life, it was Marisa. Caring that much for Marisa by extension meant caring for those Marisa loved, like Ryker and the baby. Her friend had already suffered one of life's greatest losses when her husband Johnny died, and Julie would have done anything to prevent Marisa from enduring that again.

So here she was, involved in a web she knew nothing about, except that both Ryker and Trace had tried to warn her away, had made no secret of how deadly this game could be.

Well, she thought with sudden wryness, that was probably the only thing they hadn't kept secret. A first. Maybe she ought to acknowledge the strange experience of getting the truth out of one of those guys. Because she'd sure never gotten a lick of it out of Johnny and then Ryker. Those men swam in secrets, and Trace was evidently another one.

Rising, she promised herself she was going to get a few answers. She deserved them, after all. She'd just offered her own neck as part of their plan, and while her reasons might be different, if she was going to be at risk along with them, then she had a right to know at least something.

After her shower she dressed in a hunter-green jogging suit and pinned her wet hair to the back of her head. Storm or no storm, she was amazingly eager to begin this day. She had to work on Trace's disguise, and while she was at it she intended to pry some more information out of him. Carefully, of course. She suspected that if she pressed too hard he'd bolt like a horse headed for the stable.

She made more coffee, studied what she had on hand, and finally decided to make French toast. It was a perfect snowstorm breakfast, a favorite from her childhood. Warm, sweet and syrupy. While she wouldn't recommend it as a great way to start the day to her students, none of them was watching right now. A smile danced around her mouth. Do as I say and all that.

She had just started heating her electric griddle and whipping some eggs with milk when Trace emerged from his room. He wore a black flannel shirt, sweatpants and socks, and the black leather glove on his right hand. He glanced toward her living room window and remarked, "Great weather."

"I always loved snow days," she replied. "French toast?"

"Sounds wonderful."

"Good, because that's what I'm making. How many slices?"

"Four."

"Help yourself to coffee." She watched from the corner of her eye after she pointed out the cupboard where she had the mugs stashed and noted how very careful he was not to move his right arm. That must be some agony he was trying to avoid.

He sat on one of the bar stools, facing her across the counter, and appeared to wander off in his thoughts. She let him. Not everyone awoke quickly the way she did, and she knew an awful lot of people who didn't want to talk until they had sufficient caffeine running in their systems.

"How long is this weather going to stay?" he asked as she dipped the bread in the mixture and threw it on the buttered griddle.

She reached for the cinnamon and started sprinkling it on the browning toast. "I'll turn on the weather just as soon as I get this going. Why? You planning on hitting the road?"

That drew a reluctant laugh from him. "Does that look likely? By the way, thanks for the room. It's pleasant, far nicer than anywhere I've stayed in a while."

"Why do I imagine that's not a high bar?"

He laughed again. "You'd be right. But seriously, it's very nice and the bed is comfortable. So thank you."

She washed her hands quickly, then went to turn on the flat-screen TV viewable from both living room and kitchen. The weather forecaster took great delight in telling them the next two days were going to be miserable. Snow, blowing snow, low visibility, but hey, it wasn't going to get that cold, only in the upper teens.

She loved that guy. He could make a catastrophe sound like a trip to the circus, and this was no catastrophe. The ranchers needed the water this snow would bring, and nobody else really had to go anywhere.

While she enjoyed the luxury of a second bedroom and bath, the builders had economized by not giving her enough room for a dining area, so they ate at the bar. Trace wanted to help with the dishes, but she waved him away, pointing out that she had a dishwasher. The truth was, she hated the way pain flickered over his face when he moved, and she couldn't see any point in letting him overdo it. But when all that was done, she could tell he was getting antsy. Apparently he wasn't a man accustomed to having time hang heavy on his hands, and she didn't know what to do about it. He was, after all, supposed to be in hiding.

So she addressed the matter of his disguise.

"I picked up some of those cheap reading glasses for you to wear," she announced.

He turned to her, clearly making some kind of mental shift. "Glasses? Oh, the disguise."

"Yeah. I got them at medium strength, so I don't think they'll give you much trouble. I mean, all they do is magnify, and your eyes will look bigger, so you'll look different. Are you going to stop shaving, or do we need to change your face somehow?"

"Growing a beard would be the easiest answer," he admitted. "I've already missed two days, if you can't tell."

Well, she could, but she wasn't going to say anything about it. She kind of liked the growth anyway. In her opinion, a clean-shaven man only meant beard burn for her tender skin if she got into any heavy kissing. She flushed a little, wondering why her thoughts insisted on heading in that direction with Trace. He was attractive, yes, but as soon as his problem was solved, he'd be gone. Maybe sooner, from the way he'd been talking just last night.

She gave herself a mental shake and reminded herself she had more important concerns. *They* had more important concerns.

"You wanna give a sling a try?" she asked. "I have one left from when I broke my arm eight years ago."

"Skiing accident?" he asked.

"Nothing so romantic," she admitted. "I slipped on ice. No interesting story to tell, just an admission of idiocy."

That at least brought a charming smile to his face. "I'd have to be stupid myself to think you're any kind of idiot. Well, let's try that sling. Maybe I'll be able to stand it."

She paused after taking a step toward her bedroom. "So it's not just your hand?"

"It's mostly my hand. That's where the bullet hit and shattered everything. I'm not sure why my whole arm hurts, though. The doc said something about referred pain."

"Does the glove help?"

"All it does is keep me from disturbing strangers."

Now that was freaking sad, she thought as she continued to her bedroom. She found the sling on the shelf in her closet, way in the back. It was one of those things she hoped she'd never need again, but it had cost too much to ditch. Once, she'd lent it to a friend.

She hoped he could wear it, because it would help with the cover story. And who was she to be thinking in terms of cover stories? She shook her head at herself and tried not to think about how abruptly her life had changed in just twenty-four short hours. She was simply doing what needed doing.

The sling was big, more than enough to cover his arm from above the elbow past his hand. She loosened it completely and let him work it onto his arm. Once it was on, it was impossible to tell if his arm was in a cast or wrapped. Then she lifted the strap over his head and shoulder and began to tighten it. Soon they had his arm against his chest.

"Well?" she asked.

"It doesn't feel any worse," he answered. "That's the most I can ask for. It'll do. Great idea, Julie."

She smiled. "Good. I thought about lightening your hair, but you have too much red in yours. I'd make you look like a carrottop, and that would look so weird with your skin tone." There was a hint of olive in his complexion. "You'd look like someone needed to put a clown nose on you."

He laughed at that. "Talk about drawing attention."

"Exactly. There are other things we can do later if you want. A little putty to change your jaw. Maybe some glue to add lines to your face. Your decision. I think the beard and the glasses will be the biggest thing. That, and the fact that nobody's going to give a damn that I have an old friend visiting."

He was still moving around her small living room, as if confinement didn't suit him. She settled on one edge of the couch and let him pace. "Will Ryker be able to keep you informed if he learns anything?"

"I'm sure he will. He'll probably have to call your phone, though. Mine's somewhere around Denver, dying."

"Denver?" He had her full attention now. "Why? Or can't you tell me?"

He stopped pacing, hesitating visibly. After a moment, he sat down. "I guess you deserve to be filled in as much as I can. You're in it up to your neck now."

"That would definitely be appreciated."

One corner of his mouth lifted. "I always hated being in the dark. Unfortunately, I often was. And right now I'm pretty much in the dark, so I can't offer you much. Suffice it to say, Ryker put my phone on a truck heading to Denver yesterday, then some friends of your sheriff crashed my car somewhere along the same road."

She drew a sharp breath. "You think someone's tracking you electronically? Who would…" She trailed off as more lights went on in her mind. "Oh God. I don't like what I'm thinking." The kind of organization that could track one man that way? It couldn't be just anyone.

"Neither do I," he said frankly. "We don't know for sure—it's only a possibility, but one we can't afford to ignore."

"That's what put Ryker in high gear, isn't it? What he suspects?"

"You could say so."

She stared down at her hands, absorbing it all, then said quietly, "I don't think I like the people you work for." In fact, between this and Johnny's death, they'd be easy to hate. She never wanted to hate anyone, but she had been steadily discovering her capacity for it since Johnny died.

"Right now, I don't, either. But again, we don't know for sure. All we know is that someone is after me. Could be anyone. We simply took evasive action so I couldn't be tracked easily."

She nodded slowly and realized that the dark world she had always known was out there somewhere, a world she had so far successfully avoided, now sat in her apartment with her. She knew those jobs needed doing; she wasn't a fool. But it had never been something she wanted to participate in. Now, as he had said, she was in it up to her neck. For Marisa. For the people Marisa loved. Well, she'd just have to survive this brush with the ugly side of the world.

"I'm sorry, Julie. We never wanted you involved."

"I kind of involved myself," she admitted. Slowly she raised her gaze, trying to smile. "There are threats, and there are threats. I'd like to think that people who are working for me, for my country, aren't being exposed to them by the very people who should be protecting them."

"We'd all like to think that. And most of the people I've worked with would never dream of doing something like this. But there are always some… Anyway, maybe that's not what's happening. We'll find out."

"How?"

He looked rueful. "I'm supposed to think, according to your sheriff. He says that information can look very different in light of a new perspective, and he's right. So somewhere locked inside my head is the answer. Who wants me dead? And why? I'll figure it out."

She bit her lip, forgetting her own shock and feeling sorrier for him than she could say. Wounded, cut loose and left to his own devices. Not a pretty picture. "It must be awful, knowing someone wants to kill you."

"I've been here before."

She studied him, knowing he probably had been. It was almost beyond imagining. "You ever think about quitting?"

"I'm in line for disability retirement right now."

She nodded. "Then what?"

"Well, that's a good question. But right now I need to survive this."

Indeed he did. Rising, she went to get more coffee, seeking to settle her upset and keep a cool head. It was the only way she could be helpful now. "How's that sling doing? And can I help you with your thinking?"

"The sling is great. I actually believe it might be helping. Less blood running to my hand. As for the thinking part, I'd have to reveal…"

"Operational secrets," she interrupted. "I get it. I've heard it before. So I'm living with a ticking time bomb, nobody knows when it might go off, and I'm not allowed to know a thing about it."

"Pretty ugly," he agreed, frowning a bit. "Are you aware of compartmentalization?"

"Not exactly."

"It means nobody, absolutely nobody, is given any more information than what he or she needs to complete a job. We do that because the flow of information can be dangerous, so we limit it. For example, in all the years I've known Ryker, I couldn't tell you most of what he's done. A few ops we worked on together, yes, but nothing else. It can be frustrating at times, but you get used to it because you understand the reason for it. It protects people and saves lives."

She thought about it. "That requires an awful lot of trust, that you're being told all that you need." It was a way of life that would surely drive her crazy in short order.

"Yes, it does."

Her gaze met his as she put the pieces together. "Somebody's betrayed your trust."

"Maybe. No way to know for sure, so we're covering all bases."

She wouldn't be able to stand living like that, but here she was, right in the middle of it. Which left only one question she could ask, and she wasn't sure she wanted the answer.

"How many people want to kill you, Trace?"

He rose from his chair and began pacing again. "Let me make something clear, Julie. I never hung anyone out to dry. I took care of my assets and my operatives. They were helping me, and they deserved everything I could do to keep them safe. So a few days ago, I'd have said nobody wants to kill me. Clearly I was wrong. Somehow, somewhere, I put someone in a position that is driving them to seek vengeance. That's what I need to figure out."

She thought that'd be enough to keep anyone burning the midnight oil. She could barely imagine how many people he needed to remember, how many situations he needed to reevaluate. After a few moments, she carried her coffee to her desk.

"While you cogitate, I need to plan a week's lessons."

He simply nodded, wandering into his own thoughts again. She forced herself to pull out her plan book and tried to find the mental space that gave birth to her ideas for the coming week. It wasn't going to be easy with a caged lion pacing behind her.

The benchmarks were already laid out in her plan book, for each day and each week. All she needed to do was come up with some ideas for reaching them that would keep her students excited and not bored. She glanced over to the side and saw the stack of workbooks she'd purchased and decided that maybe it was time to introduce them. The kids liked workbooks because they provided measurable progress as they moved through them, and then when they had finished, they could take them home to show off their accomplishments. They would certainly help with her planning for the week.

Drumming her pencil on the desk idly, she stared out the window, noting that even the next building had vanished in the blowing snow. Full whiteout: a good day to be inside, even if Trace was pacing around behind her.

Or maybe because Trace was pacing around behind her. She rather liked him, little though she knew about him. He'd only told her a bit, but it had been enough to gain her respect.

She hated, though, to think of the world he had lived in for so long. Just this instance made her wonder about all the rest of it. She was sure whatever he did was nothing like the movies, and she cherished no illusions of Tom Cruise doing fanciful things as part of *Mission: Impossible*. The work was probably extremely stressful and often unpleasant.

But she wondered how he had come to this point, depending on a friend and people he didn't know. And why. He'd never tell her the why, she was certain, but the very fact that he lived in a world where someone wanted him dead was chilling enough.

He was an attractive man, though. Not a standout; women wouldn't crane their heads as he walked down a street, and that probably aided him most of the time. But he was still attractive, to her at least, and she wished she could have met him under ordinary circumstances. She'd love to get to know him better, and maybe even have an affair with him. He *did* get her motor humming, although exactly how she had no idea. Ryker hadn't affected her that way, not even once. And the few men around here that she'd dated, well…those had been a flash in the pan. The doldrums had settled in quickly. It was nice to once again feel the sparkle of attraction, even though she imagined nothing would ever come of it. He was totally preoccupied with survival, and she'd be selfish to think of anything else.

But… She smiled secretly. Maybe a one-nighter would answer a lot of other questions. As a teacher she had a reputation to think about, but she'd noticed the town tended to turn a blind eye when she dated. Folks here weren't cruel, and most weren't judgmental as long as people didn't flaunt their peccadilloes. Quiet little affairs…more than one person had whiled away a winter that way. She almost laughed, considering the truth of that. It wasn't as if all the married couples in this county were always faithful, but no one wanted to be at fault for causing marital problems. Unless, of course, it was their own marriage. Then the mess could hit the fan big-time.

The phone rang, and she reached for it. She kept the base set on her desk and cordless extensions in her bedroom and kitchen. Every time she picked up one of these phones, she remembered her mother walking around the house trailing a twenty-five-foot phone cord coil that always managed to twist and knot. Phones had come a long way.

"Hello," she answered and heard Ryker's voice in response.

"Hey, is our friend around?"

"Where else would he be?" she asked wryly. "He's wearing a hole in my rug. Do you want to talk to him?"

"Can you put us on speaker? You might as well hear this bit."

"Ooh, I feel privileged," she retorted, and heard him laugh.

He said, "She who shares the noose gets a piece of the action."

Then she punched the speaker button and said, "You're on speaker." She turned and saw that Trace had come to stand right behind her. A slight sweat had appeared on his brow, probably from pain.

"I'm here," Trace said.

Ryker's voice filled the room. "Just a small update. Mission accomplished yesterday. We tried your cell this morning and were sent directly to voice mail, so it's probably dead. Your car hasn't been towed from the accident scene yet, and probably won't be until this storm passes. State police recorded an accident yesterday afternoon, no driver or passengers around, and they traced the vehicle identification number to one of you. So, buddy, you're off the grid. At least, for now."

"That's good. I need some thinking time."

"You know, I was trying to do that last night and early this morning while pacing with my cranky daughter."

"And?"

"I realized how difficult this is going to be for you. You can probably cut off everything before the last couple of years, but that'll still leave a lot of possibilities. Like you, I don't know why anyone should be after me, but if I had a problem like yours I'd be pretty much at sea."

Trace lowered himself carefully onto a chair. "Well, I dealt indirectly with a lot more assets than you. Assuming this is an asset. And it must be, or the agency wouldn't be helping him."

Julie interrupted. "What the heck is an asset?"

Silence greeted her. Finally Ryker said, "Buddy?"

"It's no secret," Trace said slowly. "Assets are foreign nationals who help us. Sometimes in big ways, sometimes in small ways, and occasionally for a very long time. We protect them the way we'd protect our families. We'll pull them out and give them new lives if they ever get exposed."

"So why would one of them be after you?"

"Because," said Trace heavily, "sometimes things don't go according to plan."

Julie's heart lurched as she considered *those* possibilities.

"But you had some distance between you and most of the assets you were running, at least for the last few years," Ryker pointed out.

"Yeah, I did. But I was still in charge of the guys at lower levels. Who knows how one of them may have screwed up? Stuff happens."

"And we don't always hear about it when it does," Ryker said.

Julie spoke. "Compartmentalization?"

"Exactly," Trace answered. "Exactly. That multiplies the problem here."

Silence fell for a little while. "Julie?" Trace said.

"Yeah?"

"You wouldn't happen to have one of those phones that plugs into the wall, would you?"

"Actually, yes I do. It's cheap, but I keep it for when the power goes out."

"Then can we use it? Because cordless phones broadcast their signal."

Julie felt a shiver of shock run through her. The things she'd never thought about. Never had to think about. But as soon as Trace said it, she knew he was right.

"It's probably okay right now," Ryker said, "but he's right. If someone starts backtracking Trace from Denver…"

"As soon as we sign off here, I'll get the old phone."

"And disconnect your base set, okay?"

"You got it."

It struck her again that all of a sudden she was involved in a real spy story. A deadly one. An amazed cussword floated into her head, but she didn't speak it. When you dealt with little kids all day, the worst cussing you could do was *darn it*. Right now she felt a need for something stronger. The next best thing emerged. "Cusswords," she said vehemently.

Two surprised men fell silent, then Trace asked, "Cusswords?"

"When you talk to youngsters all day…"

He laughed, a real laugh. "Copy that. Okay, then. Let's switch the phones and I'll get back to thinking."

"How's the baby?" Julie asked before Ryker could disconnect.

"Believe it or not, she's a little better. Cranky, but not nearly as stuffed up. My wife is getting some sleep right now."

She noted the way he didn't use Marisa's name. They were broadcasting. For the first time, being on the telephone chilled her.

"My ear's to the ground," Ryker said, by way of farewell. "I'll keep you posted."

When she hung up, she immediately pulled the plug for the base set out of the wall and got the regular phone from the kitchen drawer where she had stashed it. *I'll bet Tom Cruise never felt like this.* At least the thought amused her. Mildly.

"I'm sorry about all this," Trace said as he watched.

"I don't know that I am," she said frankly. "Am I getting a ration of shocks and surprises? Yes. Do I hate it? No. A little shaking up is good for the soul. Anyway, I'm determined to treat this like a game I have to win, because if I really let myself think about it, I might freak."

He eyed her sympathetically. "Freak if you need to. I'll listen."

"I'm sure you will. But freaking never fixed anything. You wouldn't believe how many times a week I have to tell that to a child. Now it's my turn to take my own advice. So no freaking out. However, I see sweat on your brow and it's not that warm in here. If anyone out there is moving, it's by dogsled, and we'll hear the barking before they get here, so why don't you take something for that pain?"

"I need my head," he said, but he smiled. "Half a dose mixed with a heavier dose of caffeine, if you don't mind."

She waved a hand. "I have plenty of coffee, and if you want stronger I once splurged on an espresso machine. I can light you up, baby."

That drew a laugh from him and brought a twinkle to his brown eyes. "You light me up more than you know, and no caffeine required."

She felt her cheeks heat and headed quickly to make

that espresso. So she wasn't the only one feeling it. A warm glow settled deep inside her. She liked it.

Much as Trace tried to keep his head on his problem, Julie took up space. While he sipped the double shot of espresso she'd made for him and waited for the pain pill to kick in, he decided she was not at all what he would have expected from a kindergarten teacher. Not that he'd ever spent a lot of time thinking about it.

She'd have to be lively to some extent to deal with children of that age all day successfully. But it was more than that. *Cusswords?* He still wanted to laugh over that. But it was yet more. Most people would have wanted nothing to do with him and his dangerous problems, but she'd dived right in to protect her friends. Loyalty was a quality he valued above almost anything. She had quite a tongue on her when she chose, she didn't hold back, and her face was entrancing to watch as expressions continually flitted across it. Always having a sense of what she was feeling and thinking would be a comforting quality to him after all the years he'd spent in a world where everyone tried to conceal everything. How relaxing to be with someone who had no secrets, and who couldn't really conceal them if she wanted to.

She turned from her desk and found him watching her. "See something you like?"

He had to grin. "Very definitely."

She smiled back. "Me, too. So tell me something?"

"If I can."

"What did Ryker mean when he said the police traced your vehicle back to one of you?"

He probably wouldn't be telling her anything she

couldn't guess if she thought about it. "I have a number of identities."

"Ah. Will the real Trace Whoever please stand up?"

"Sort of like that." For once he threw caution to the winds. "My real name is Trace Archer. I don't use it very often, but that's pretty much what's on my paychecks."

"So you assume that's the real one." A smile danced around her lips.

"That same guy pays my taxes, too."

She laughed. "I've never had an alias. Maybe I should get one. Except that I can't imagine who else I could be."

"I think," he said, meaning it, "that you could be anyone you want to be." Beauty, intelligence and a quick wit, all in one package.

"If it's just about a piece of paper, probably. Changing other things about me would be harder. Do you have to do that?"

Again he weighed the question. He wasn't in the habit of talking about these matters, and every question posed the possibility of revealing something he shouldn't. "Yes," he said presently. "Sometimes I've had to. It's like being in a play, except that you can't afford to drop your character, ever. You have to live it, breathe it, even sleep it."

She chewed her lower lip, nodding slowly. "How do you find yourself in all that?"

Shock shook him. He was amazed that she'd even thought of that part of it. "It's not always easy. When you start to forget, it's time to come in for a while. Repatriation, they call it."

"What do you call it?"

"Finding my feet again."

She stood up. "More espresso?"

"Thanks, yes."

Halfway to the kitchen she stopped and looked straight at him. "How well did you know Johnny Hayes?"

Everything inside Trace congealed. She was going to a place he couldn't go, wasn't allowed to go. A place that could leave everyone who had worked with John Hayes in a deadly position if links were made. "Julie…" Then he had to lie. "We met."

"And that's all you can tell me." She frowned. "You don't want to know what his wife went through after he was killed. She never believed the official story. Never. I don't know what finally settled her down, but she's made peace with it. I'd like her to keep that peace, so lie if you have to, Trace. She's happy again, and while I'm not fond of lies and half truths, in this case they'd have my full support."

He felt awful about his evasion, something new to him. Evasions and lies were part of his job as required. But this time it bothered him, and while she'd made her position clear, he was left with a bad taste in his mouth. His world was steadily seeping into Julie's, and he didn't believe it would leave her untouched. He absolutely hated himself right then.

Halfway across the country, the clerk stood outside the hotel room door. He didn't know what was going on, but the general inside that room made him uneasy, and his job as go-between made him even uneasier. To begin with, he wasn't a spy, but a very expendable clerk. This job was making him acutely aware of that, even though he didn't know what was going down here. He just didn't like it, didn't like that these contacts had to be carried out at his low level. Even as inexperienced as he was, he understood that a kind of secrecy was being invoked here, and that he might well become the person who received all the flak if something went askew.

But he also knew he had no choice. If he disobeyed his orders, he'd become even more expendable, because from the moment he'd been ordered to meet the general and turn over the dossier, he'd begun carrying knowledge well above his pay grade. Dangerous knowledge. He was walking on plausible deniability.

Uneasy or not, however, he had something to prove here: that he could do the job. Eventually he wanted to move into field operations, and there was a possibility this task could help him reach his goal. So he swallowed his discomfort and knocked.

The door opened, revealing the general. Today the man wore a long robe and leather slippers. Apparently he had no other meetings until later.

At a jerk of the other man's head, he stepped inside and heard the door close behind him. It sounded like a vault door, and considering the information he'd been tasked to provide, he honestly wasn't sure if he'd get out of here in one piece. Although it would be foolhardy for the general to do anything to him in such a public place, in a room that was being rented by his delegation. Of course, the clerk realized that a lot of alternative explanations could be provided. The agency he worked for was good at covering things up.

"Well?" said the general.

The clerk needed to clear his throat before he could speak. "The target was involved in a car accident. We were able to trace him as far as Denver, but now he's off the grid."

"You lost him?" Fury descended on the general's face like a violent thunderstorm. "You lost him?"

The clerk compressed his lips. "Only temporarily," he said, parroting the message he had been given. "There's a bad snowstorm. We're sure we'll find him again as soon as it passes."

"How?"

"Because he needs money," the clerk answered simply. "He'll have to buy a car, rent a room, eat a meal. He doesn't have that much cash on him."

The general's face grew so red that the clerk hoped he'd have a stroke on the spot. Little as he knew about all of this, he suspected that a dead general would mean all of this would end.

Unhappily for him, the general didn't collapse and die.

"How long will the storm last?"

"Two, possibly three days."

The general nodded. For a minute or so he didn't move as his color slowly returned to normal. "You tell your officer that I want to be in Denver before the airport closes. I will want to know as soon as this target reappears."

"Yes, sir." Then he took his courage in his hands and defied the man with the truth, something he believed his boss would want him to do. The weather was something he knew about himself, although it hadn't been in his brief. "But it is probably too late to get you to Denver until after the storm. Flights are already being delayed and diverted. I will tell my superiors your wish, but I can make no promises."

"Of course you can make no promises. I know what you are. You are powerless. But I will tolerate no more mistakes." The general pounded his fist into his palm, his voice growing even more strident. "Make that clear. There have been too many mistakes. I am tired of having to clean up their mess. No more."

The clerk left the room as quickly as he dared. Outside, shaking, sweat beading his brow, he began to wish he'd never been born.

Chapter 5

Outside, the snow continued to blow, covering the world in a pristine white cloak. Trace wondered if he stood out there, if the storm would cover his sins. Then a bubble of amusement rose in him. Sure, go outside and freeze into a snowman. That would make everything better.

Julie brought him more espresso, and a cup of regular joe for herself. She sat at her desk again, but this time kept the task chair turned so she could see him. "Should I be quiet while you think?"

He gave a small shake of his head. "I've lined up the ducks in my mind. Now I'm going to just let it sit for a while and see if any of them quack."

A light laugh escaped her, and he noticed again what a beautiful woman she was. Who'd ever have thought he'd be envying kindergartners? Certainly not him.

"I've never had anyone want to kill me," she remarked. Then added, "Well, that's not exactly true. One woman threatened, and said I should have been strangled at birth."

He arched a brow. "What brought that on?"

"I reported that her son was being physically abused. Social Services agreed and removed all the children from the home. Dad liked his drink, I guess, and she was covering for him."

"Did she ever come after you?"

Julie shook her head. "Our sheriff—you met him, right?"

"Yeah."

"Well, he paid her a visit and told her that she'd better hope I never so much as twisted an ankle, because she'd be the first one they'd look at."

Trace began to smile. "I like that man."

"Most everyone does, unless they get on the wrong side of the law. He's a good man. His wife is the county librarian, and everyone loves her, too."

"There seems to be a lot of love running around this town."

"Depends." She screwed up her face. "Like everywhere else, we've got both good and bad apples. Mostly good apples, but still. I wouldn't want you to get a Currier & Ives picture, because it wouldn't be true. We've got a few families everyone would cheerfully disown, the requisite number of youngsters who get stupid ideas and the occasional really bad seed. Overall, though, it's a pretty good place to live, unless you're a hermit with privacy issues."

That made him laugh.

She smiled at him. "Anyway, we need your cover

story. Where we met, how long we've known each other, what brought you to visit me after all these years. And what name you're going by. Because sooner or later the storm will blow out and people will notice I have company. They're going to ask, Trace. Natural curiosity."

"And it'll get around?"

"To every point on the compass." She laughed quietly and shook her head. "Not a great place to be the secret agent man."

He stiffened a bit, but she moved on so easily he figured she was joking.

"Anyway," she continued, "it'll get a lot of attention because I haven't dated in a while."

Curiosity grabbed him. "Why not? You're a beautiful woman."

"Thanks. But beauty, or lack of it, has nothing to do with it." She sipped her coffee. "Boredom has everything to do with it. If you took a census of the available men in this county and selected those who are of an age that might interest me, the list would be fairly short. And I've dated all the ones who caught my attention and who were interested in me. That's the downside of such a low population. I suppose I could take a summer and haunt the singles bars in Denver…" Then she laughed again. "I'm happy with my life, Trace. Honestly. But all of a sudden a strange man is staying with me? I can already hear the gossip mill revving up. So we need to agree on a story."

With slight variations, it was exactly the kind of thing he'd done multiple times in his life. Create a character and live it. Cover stories for how he'd known an asset, why they encountered each other occasionally. Inventions that would protect the asset. Now he needed to protect Julie, from his past, from a tiger and from the talk that might make her life more difficult.

"Okay. You already suggested I could be an old college friend. But will that work? How many people here knew you at college?"

"Good point," she acknowledged. "Give me a break, Trace. I'm not used to this and it was the first thing off the top of my head."

His smile widened. "Let me show you how the pros do it."

And with that he'd probably revealed a whole lot more than he should have.

They used the bar because Julie's desk was still covered with work. She kept a piece of paper to take notes, although he warned her they'd have to destroy it as soon as they'd settled on the story.

"First is to keep it simple," he told her. "Use no verifiable facts. For example, it would be easy for someone to find out if I actually went to college with you, so that's off the table. Do you have any family around here?"

"Not anymore. A strange thing happens to people when they get into their sixties."

"What's that?"

"They hate winter. They complain about their bones aching. They move somewhere warmer. I told you my folks live most of the year in Florida. My aunt and uncle practically live next door to them. Cousins all over the map, none here."

"That's it?"

"I have a sister who fled for California with a notion about being an actress. Instead she got a different job in the industry and spends an extraordinary amount of time on location in Canada directing some TV show. We talk on the phone nearly every week."

"No one else?"

"Just friends around here."

"All of whom would reasonably expect to have heard about me if we knew each other that well."

"Ouch." She frowned. "I hadn't thought about that."

"These are the things that kill a cover story," he said quietly. Truth was, he was strangely reluctant to make one with her. He'd much rather play a caveman—as if he could with his hand—and drag her off to bed, then shout from the rooftops, "I'm making it with Julie Ardlow." Right.

It shouldn't concern him, but it did, to think that he'd be starting in this town with lies. He knew he wouldn't be here long, however matters turned out, but he felt like he was about to make a major misstep that might haunt him forever.

"We need," he said, "to stick as close to the truth as possible for a variety of reasons. Not the least of them that whatever we come up with is going to linger with you long after I'm gone. It needs to be believable, but unverifiable. How much traveling have you done? On your own, not with a friend from here."

There was suddenly a twinkle in her green eyes. "I am about to shock you."

"How?"

"I've traveled a lot. I have long summer breaks and I take a month each year somewhere else. So let's see. I mentioned the Jamaica trip. I've also been to Peru— my God, Machu Picchu is never to be forgotten. Mayan temples. Egypt, the pyramids and temples, of course. In between the years when I blow my entire savings on big adventures, I take smaller ones. I camped and hiked for a month in the Cascade Range in Oregon and Washington. I spent a few weeks in Nova Scotia. I go skiing over winter break in Colorado…"

"Stop," he said. "When was that camping trip in the Cascades? Were you alone?"

"Um, two summers ago. And yes, I went alone. I had a guide a few times for the more rugged areas…"

"Did you mention the guide?"

"Only that I had one."

"Photos of him?"

"No."

He smiled. "There we go. Spice it up a little and I have a reason to have dropped on your doorstep."

He watched her grow excited. "That'll do. I can say we've kept in touch, that I really liked you when I was out there and if you hadn't been engaged at the time…"

"What?" he asked jokingly. "No torrid affair?"

"I'm not sure I could carry that off without actually having ever had one."

Her honesty was touching, but her statement fell into the room almost explosively. He tried to lighten the moment when he saw her cheeks start to color. How many women still blushed? he wondered. "We could always have one now."

He gave her a few seconds to stare at him wide-eyed, then he laughed. "Just joshing you. I mean, sure, I'd love to, but under the circumstances, it wouldn't be wise."

Not when someone was trying to kill him. Not when he might have to leave at the drop of a hat. He had limits, and taking advantage of a woman was a bright line for him. He had a few bright lines left, and not crossing them was all that kept him feeling he wasn't simply scum.

Then she left him stunned. "What makes you so sure it wouldn't be wise?" she asked pertly as she slid off the bar stool. Then she headed for the bathroom, saying she'd be back in a minute to work on the story.

For the first time, Trace wondered if he'd wandered into a new kind of quicksand.

Julie stood in the bathroom pressing a cold washcloth to her face, easy enough to do at this time of year. The water that came out of the tap was refrigerated-by-the-outdoors cold.

But oh my. He'd alluded so casually to having an affair, had said he'd love to but that it wasn't wise. Then she'd said… She was no shrinking violet when it came to sex, but sometimes she couldn't believe her own mouth. The man was a complete stranger. An attractive stranger, but still a stranger who was running from a killer and who'd probably vanish at the first opportunity. She wasn't even sure he'd told her his real name when she'd asked.

She stared at her reflection in the mirror, reminding herself of something she'd learned long ago. In college, she'd played a lot of poker with friends on free evenings. She was lousy at it because everyone could tell when she had a good hand.

But then she'd realized that life was a lot like poker. Chance always played a role, whether in cards or life. So the best you could do was estimate the odds of whether you held a good hand, and then decide whether to bet. And when you did, you should never, ever bet more than you were willing to lose.

She'd applied that philosophy to romantic relationships after her first big heartbreak. How strong was her hand, how much was she willing to lose, was it worth the bet? And if so, how big should the bet be?

Not since her first awful mistake had she ever gone all in on a relationship with a guy. Playing cagey, she waited to see whether the odds were improving or not with each step in the relationship. So far she'd never bet more than she could walk away from, and so far she'd always walked away with her heart.

Sometimes it had gone against her grain to be so cautious. In most things, she was anything but. She loved adventure—hence her solo trips all over the world—loved new experiences, and sometimes even thought about trying skydiving. She wasn't afraid of risks. Every date was a risk. But only in dating did she calculate the odds at some level. Once burned, twice shy, as they said.

For the first time, she wondered if her own caginess about dating hadn't caused some of her relationships to blow up before they were fully born. Maybe Adventurous Julie should have come out to play, and damn the risks. She'd survived one broken heart. Surely she could have survived another.

She stared back at herself and realized her mouth had twisted with something like self-disgust. Well, if she got the opportunity with Trace, she was going to take it. He wasn't going to be around long enough for her to worry about the odds.

The only odds that should concern her right now had to do with survival. Trace was a hunted man, and he was sleeping in her apartment. Somehow that threat seemed a lot easier to deal with than dating.

Well, they wouldn't date. Nothing like that. It would

be a sheer sexual romp before he moved on. She could deal with that.

Laughing silently at herself, she left the bathroom and returned to the living room, where he was now sitting, his eyes half closed. Scrumptious, she thought. Delicious. Well worth throwing a chip or two into the pot.

But given what he was trying to deal with, she didn't think he'd risk it. He needed time and space to think. Thoughts he couldn't share with anyone. His life depended on it.

"Coffee?" she asked as she passed him on her way to the kitchen. "And I'm thinking about a ham sandwich."

"Yes to both," he answered quietly. "You okay?"

"I'm fine." And it was true. She'd walked into the middle of a deadly situation, and the more that understanding sank into her, the more alive she felt. "Latte? I'm going to have one."

"That would be great. What can I do?"

"Sit there. The most important thing you can do is rest and think."

"Thinking too hard is often a waste of energy," he remarked as she began pulling food out of the fridge.

"How so?" Turning, she found he'd risen and now stood in the doorway.

"If you think too hard about something, you can fail to make room for anything else. Overlook things. Quash your subconscious. So, like I said, I lined up my ducks and I'll wait to see."

"Sure you've got all the ducks?" she asked as she opened the package of sliced ham.

He laughed. "I hope so. Ryker was right. Something like this hasn't been simmering for a decade. I can probably trace it to something that happened in the last two or three years."

"Any way you can get more information about those, um…people?"

He shook his head slowly. "Not really. So what I'm waiting for is a ping in my neural net."

She gaped at him. "Okay, that's too science fiction."

He laughed quietly. "My brain is churning. All those connections are taking turns firing. At some point, with any luck, something I know, something I didn't think of as terribly important at the time, is going to surface. If it clicks, I'm off to the races."

"Now that's something I understand."

"A lot of what I did had to be intuitive. I had to rely on instincts, on a feel for a situation, on my impressions of someone I was working with. I didn't have time to think out every move as if it were a chess game. Too much has to happen fast when you're dealing with people. So, yes, I rely a whole lot on my intuition."

"Which is honed by experience?"

"Of course. It always is."

She pulled the bread out of her chrome bread box, a nice rich rye from the bakery. "Mustard, mayo? Or both?"

"Mayo, please. When I was in Europe, I noticed they use mayonnaise the way folks here use ketchup. On everything."

"I don't know if I'd like that. But I'm not a big fan of ketchup, either." Swiss cheese, lettuce, and the one decent tomato she'd been able to find at the grocery.

She made three sandwiches, and as soon as she passed him two, she started brewing the espresso for lattes. "Trace? Would they really put a tracking device on your car?"

"Not likely, but possible," he answered. He gave her a crooked smile across the bar, half a sandwich in his hand. "There's always a risk that if they did that and I had a car problem a mechanic would find it. For example, if they did, my wreck could cause them headaches. That device would have to be recovered or explained. I don't think they'd do it, but then I never thought any of this would happen."

She nodded, tipping two shots of espresso into a tall mug, then started steaming milk. "What about tracking devices on your clothes or luggage?"

His smile widened. "Only good at short range, like a pet's microchip, only a little better. Broadcasting a signal over a large area requires increasing amounts of power, which sooner or later makes the devices too big to hide. Hence, tracking cell phones." He paused. "You know, most tires you buy these days have a radio-frequency identification device in them."

Her head jerked up. "Really?"

"Yeah. Problem is, it only has a range of twenty-four inches, and it's designed to talk to the car's computer, to tell when air pressure is getting low, that kind of thing. It could also be used to assign a tire to a particular VIN, which might be useful to the police after the fact. But it's sure no good for tracking anyone."

"Wow," she murmured as she finished making the lattes and joined him on the other side of the bar to eat. "The things I learn. But what about these tracking devices in kids' shoes?"

"They rely on cell towers. Same with anything they might put on a person. But why put one on my personal belongings that would need a nearby cell tower to locate me? That takes time, I'm on the move, and I could move out of range repeatedly. Plus, I was already carrying a phone. Most adults do. Yeah, I changed it a couple of times, but every time I did that I revealed my whereabouts again. I had to pay for them, you see."

"But you got rid of your most recent one?"

"Right. So for now I'm a blank."

"It's not like the movies," she remarked as she picked up her sandwich. Less scary in some ways, and more scary in others.

He spoke quietly. "It *is* possible to disappear. Don't use your bank cards, your credit cards. Get rid of your cell phone. Change cars. You can vanish."

"I guess that's why the FBI still has a wanted list."

He laughed quietly. "Exactly. People can't be tracked like packages. A package moves only when a human moves it, and tracking depends on scanning its bar code. No way you can really do that with a person. We move around too much, and we can avoid doing anything that can identify us."

"So you could be perfectly safe here?" She felt her hopes rising.

"For a while. Not for long. At some point, if someone really wants to find me, they'd backtrack from my last known location."

She nodded, feeling a sinking, uneasy feeling in the pit of her stomach. "Safer if you move on, in other words."

"Probably. Again, only for a while. Sooner or later I'd do something. I'd have to, even if it's only tapping my bank account. A day labor job could cover me for that, but who's going to hire a one-armed man?"

She fell silent, eating only because she had to, thinking about this situation. Now she understood why he kept wanting to move on, but she also understood why Ryker seemed to want to keep him here. Trace couldn't live on the run forever. Eventually they'd find him again. At least in this area, they'd have some control over the situation. Strangers had a way of sticking out. Including Trace, which she suddenly realized maybe wasn't the best thing in the world.

Her stomach took another plunge, and she stopped eating. Impossible situation, and she'd walked right into it. Not that she wished she'd passed on by, and yeah, she got the part about it being dangerous. But now she was thinking how awful this had to be for Trace. He was trapped and he couldn't even see what was trapping him. Moving or staying—either one seemed like a bad option.

There were no *good* options for him. This really stank.

"It would," she said slowly, "take a really big organization to track you like this."

"Yes."

She looked at him, meeting his brown eyes. "So if they are, it has to be your bosses."

"That's pretty much a given."

"Ryker couldn't be wrong?"

Trace swallowed the last of his sandwich and washed it down with latte. "Ryker, I learned over the years, is rarely wrong."

"And you?"

"Same thing. That's why we're both still alive."

Julie returned to her lesson plan after lunch, but Trace could still feel the suppressed agitation in her.

She might appear to be concentrating on that spiral-bound book in front of her, but he didn't believe it.

So, he thought, the shadows of his world had fallen over her even more. Maybe he'd said more than he should, but he'd never forgive himself if she didn't understand just how real this game of cat-and-mouse was, if she didn't grasp that he couldn't stay hidden forever. Ryker had bought him some time, but that's all he'd gained.

Beyond Julie's head, the storm continued to rage, additional cover. In his present position, he needed to view everything in terms of cover and exposure. Julie was cover, and it sickened him. He half wished she'd throw him out into the storm.

He'd seen the look in her eyes when he'd said that rarely being wrong was the only reason he and Ryker were still alive. It was an ugly truth. Maybe he shouldn't have shared it. But he had to be absolutely certain she knew how real this was. He gave her huge points for guts, determination and loyalty, but how could she not be sitting over there asking herself whether her desire to protect her friends might be better served by throwing him out on his can?

Of course, he could always take himself out. Not that he was the best shot with his left hand, but he could do it if necessary. And there were certainly other means. So why didn't he just walk out into that storm?

Because too many people mattered. Ryker had hit that nail on the head, and he'd run up against it himself. As long as he was alive, others might be at risk. And if his employer got away with this crap, turning him out into the cold to face and help an angry killer, then others he worked with would be at risk of the same treatment.

No, he had to end this for everyone, and his death wouldn't do that. He could see the faces of people he'd worked with, people he'd come to care about. They were his only real family now. He had to protect them, too, and he could only do that by exposing this mess and proving it wasn't just his imagination gone wild on painkillers. That he wasn't just paranoid.

He had to catch this guy. No asset could have the kind of power to track him around this country without help from the Company. None. So once he was exposed, that would expose those who had helped him. The mission was clear.

He knew Ryker could protect himself and his family. Besides, if anyone had been listening to his cell phone for random conversation and heard him get his friend's address, by now they'd know Ryker had thrown him out the night of his arrival here. Had told him to stay away. Then the phone had left town the following morning.

But there was also Julie, and that pained him most of all. Ryker was accustomed to a world where he could get tail-bitten by the unexpected, and he knew how to defend against it. Julie was totally inexperienced. Good instincts, but little know-how. She needed *him* to protect her as long as he was around. She'd probably hate hearing that, when she thought she was protecting him.

He popped a pain pill and started another pot of regular coffee.

Yeah, she'd hate the idea he was protecting her when she'd dived into all this to protect her friend, and then him. She'd certainly given him cover, but that was as dangerous as the job itself. That probably hadn't crossed her mind, and he hoped it never did.

He wished to hell Ryker and the sheriff hadn't been

right about possible collateral damage. He couldn't just buy a clunker and head for the West Coast. Anywhere he went, the shadow of death followed him.

So he might as well face it here with people who'd volunteered for this mission. Even if Julie didn't fully grasp its parameters. At least he wouldn't have any explaining to do if he yelled for them to clear out. At least here the threat might stick out enough that they'd see it coming. It sure as hell would be invisible in a big town or city.

Cusswords, as Julie had called them, traipsed through his mind like a Greek chorus. Betrayal burned in his belly, but rage did as well. He was being hunted by someone who was being aided by the very people he'd entrusted with his life countless times over the years. People he'd served well. Rage? He'd like to punch holes in walls.

As he knew from experience, a fire like that in his belly could fuel him for a long time. He'd known it before when one of his operatives had been betrayed by an asset they were cultivating. He'd known it when a good asset had been discovered and killed before they could pull him out. It didn't happen often, but it happened. And when it did, Trace made sure retribution descended. *You don't mess with me and mine.* A clear, unmistakable message, however anonymous.

Now there was a new card in his deck, a truly lovely woman who didn't have the experience or training to really handle any of this. He thought again about going out into the storm. Freezing to death might not give the tiger the satisfaction he wanted, but it would solve the problem for everyone.

Instead he sat staring out that window over Julie's

head and began running through his mental list again. If it was an asset the Company wanted to appease, then he had to be a big one. An important one. One on whom a lot depended.

Just thinking about it shrank his mental list a bit more. Every asset mattered, but some were in a position to be nearly indispensable. He'd run a few. He knew of others. So who would be worth this kind of trade?

"You got any family, Trace?"

He snapped back to the present and saw that Julie had turned her chair around. God, she was pretty, and whatever she might have been stewing about earlier had been pushed into the background. Her expressive face reflected only natural curiosity.

"You won't believe it," he said. Anticipating her reaction, he felt a bit of humor leaven his gloomy, angry mood.

"Why not?"

"Do I look like I was raised by medical missionaries?"

Her eyes widened, then she laughed. "How in the world did you wind up here?"

"Different ideas of helping the world. A stethoscope in one hand and the Bible in the other didn't appeal to me. When it comes to religion I'm sort of a live-and-let-live kind of guy."

"And your parents?"

"Very deeply involved in their faith and good works. I grew up in Indonesia, India and Africa."

"Where are they now?"

"They went racing into Sierra Leone at the outset of the Ebola crisis. Unfortunately…" He shrugged a little.

"They died doing what they believed in. You can't ask for much more than that."

Her entire face drooped. "I am so sorry, Trace."

"I miss them occasionally, but I understood them. Belief is a powerful motivator. We just had different sets of beliefs about how to make the world a better place."

He wondered if he actually had, though. He'd believed in what he was doing for a long time, but lately... Well, this wasn't the time for soul-searching. Not that kind. If he survived this, he could take some time for that. If he survived this, he was going to have plenty of time to examine his sins.

"Anyway," he said, trying to bring the conversation back from the brink, "you could say I'm a typical preacher's kid. I rebelled and went my own way."

"But with the same set of ideals."

"Not quite." He smiled almost bitterly. "Not by a long shot, really. But the basic goal was the same."

"So what was it like growing up in such exotic places?"

"Kids adapt rapidly. I melded with the surrounding culture as much as I was allowed to. I developed a facility for languages, learned how easily I could be a chameleon."

"Will the real Trace Archer please stand up?" she said lightly.

"Can't do that. I took a pain pill, and anyway, you're getting the real me. What's left, anyway."

Again that shadow flitted across her face. "You need some coffee?"

"I made some, but right now I don't want to move. Pain pill is kicking in, and at this very moment the fire seems a long way away."

"Want me to bring you some?"

"Please, if you want to talk to a guy who isn't half brain-dead."

"So it burns?" she said as she poured and brought him a mug of coffee, placing it within reach of his good left hand.

"Burns. Yeah. Sometimes it feels like it's in a blacksmith's forge and being hammered on. Not all the time, thank God. But right now…hey, that hand must belong to someone else."

She laughed as if she felt it was expected, and he admitted he'd been hoping for it. He liked the sound of her laugh. She should always laugh.

He grabbed the mug, realizing he was in danger of becoming sappy.

"So you learned to be a chameleon," she remarked as she retreated to her desk chair. "How did your parents feel about that?"

"My folks were good people. More tolerant than some. When I adapted to the local culture, it was good for them, too."

"I guess I can understand that. But what about later? The path you took?"

He paused, sensing dangerous waters here. He resorted to the stock answer, even though he felt bad about not being able to share all the truth with her. "I traveled a lot for the State Department."

Her face shadowed. "I see."

And there he had to leave it. She already guessed or knew more than she should. Nor did the irony of it escape him. He was giving his cover story to his cover story. Life sometimes had a twisted sense of humor.

And thinking about cover stories brought him back

to theirs. "We never hammered out our story," he reminded her. "Nothing beyond that I was a guide you hired when you were hiking in the mountains. I need details that fit with what your friends might remember of that trip. Maybe some photos so I don't stumble about what the area looks like."

She raised her brows. "So there's some place you've never been?"

"Quite a few, actually." He summoned a smile for her benefit.

"I'll bet most of them are within the borders of this country," she said tartly. "Okay, then, get ready for the teacher to teach."

She urged him to sit in her desk chair and carried over the chair he'd been sitting in for herself. Then she opened a folder of photos labeled "Coast Range." Two hours later, he felt he had a good enough handle on what the area looked like, including some of the small towns at the foot of the mountains. She brought up a map that he memorized quickly, then told her that he would say he hadn't grown up in that area, that he was a relatively recent arrival who had brought his guide skills from the Appalachian Trail.

"It's all about not getting too specific," he advised her. "Were there any particular stories that you shared with friends that I should know about?"

"Wait, have you walked the Appalachian Trail?"

"Portions of it as I had time, which wasn't very often. Why?"

She put her chin in her hand, green eyes growing dreamy. "That was next on my list. What did you think of it?"

"I enjoyed it. It's truly challenging in places. And not

everybody attempts it without a guide. In theory you could do it alone, but not everyone is cut out for that. So you can get guides to lead small groups on hut-to-hut hikes, or even longer trips if you want."

"So why did you stop doing that and go to the Pacific Northwest?"

"Because," he said wryly, understanding that she was padding out his cover for him, "for most of the summer, portions of that trail are nearly as well traveled as a highway. I wanted more isolation. More rugged hikes."

"Okay." She smiled. "You know enough to be a guide."

"Stories?" he prompted her.

"Only one that sticks out when I was with the guide. We were off trail, off the lumber roads, which isn't easy to do. Climbing up toward a peak through complete wilderness. Then I saw some footprints. Huge footprints."

He felt a smile twitch at the corners of his mouth. "Sasquatch?"

She laughed and shrugged. "Who knows for sure? My guide studied them. He was troubled by how separated they were but kept reminding me that when a bear walks it puts its hind foot almost exactly where its front paw landed. That leads to slightly overlapping prints that can often be mistaken for a single huge, human-type print. He pretty much decided that a bear had left them. So I told my friends about it because it was fun and kind of funny. That was the only story they might have remembered. The rest were pretty ordinary, off-trail kinds of things. I got to do some rock climbing belayed by my guide. I'm pretty sure he took me to some views I couldn't have seen otherwise. And the main thing that impressed me was how much wilderness there still is out there."

He nodded. "That leaves the question of what I'm doing here."

"Oh, that's easy," she said, waving her hand as if it were of no importance. "I kept in touch with you by email. I was attracted to you, but you were professional and never crossed any lines. Then when you mentioned you'd hurt your arm in a fall, I was just brazen enough to invite you to visit. They'll believe the brazen part."

His gaze met and held hers. "Lo and behold, I was feeling that attraction, too."

He saw her full breasts rise as she drew a quick breath. It would be so easy, he thought, to reach out and touch her. To take this moment to places he had no right to go. She had visibly softened at his remark, and she had leaned ever so slightly toward him, inviting.

And only the vestige of a conscience yanked him back. Hell, he didn't even know who he really was anymore. A chameleon? She ought to be thinking about that, because it could become ultimately important to her if he were here more than a few days. He could become whatever she wanted, whatever she needed, and then leave her feeling used and tossed away.

Absolutely not. Playing those games because it was his job was a very different thing from playing them with a woman who had been drawn into his net inadvertently. He didn't want to cultivate her like some asset.

It suddenly seemed so important to him that whatever happened between them be *true*.

"Julie?"

"Yeah?" she breathed.

"I'm a chameleon. Remember that." Then he slid off

the desk chair and went back to the bar stool. Maybe he ought to take enough of those pills to knock him out. It would at least make her safe from *him*.

Julie pretended to focus on her lesson planning, even though it was complete, because it gave her an opportunity to stare in a direction that didn't include Trace.

A chameleon. That had been a warning she couldn't mistake, and she'd be a fool to ignore it. Except that she didn't believe Trace was being a chameleon with her. When he hadn't been able to speak the truth, he'd as good as told her with an obvious statement or omission.

So he wasn't trying to mislead her in some way. Why, then, had he felt the warning necessary? Because sometimes he didn't feel like he really knew himself? Because instinctively adapting to situations was something he did without thinking?

But wasn't that what most people did? The Julie she presented in the classroom wasn't at all like the one her friends saw. That her family saw. Marisa, whom she'd known her whole life, was different around Ryker. Everyone did that kind of thing to some extent.

So she wondered if he was in fact warning himself. That was possible. Whatever deceptions life had forced on him, she sensed a straight arrow inside him. Maybe that missionary upbringing.

She almost laughed as she stared down at her book without seeing it. No, she never would have guessed that two medical missionaries had raised a man who did the kind of job she suspected Trace had done. Yet his motives had been good, she gathered. He had served his country in important, essential ways. She wasn't so naive as to think spying was for other people. Everyone spied on everyone else. Intelligence gathering was important in order to know what was *really* going on in the world behind all the carefully orchestrated speeches and diplomacy. Lives could depend on it.

The fact that he'd had to become different for each person he dealt with seemed only marginally different from what everyone did without thinking. Maybe his changes were bigger, his omissions bigger, even his lies as necessary. But at heart, really no different.

Heck, she thought, she lied often enough when someone asked casually how she was doing. Imagine the shocked responses from some if she'd actually said, "I'm having a rotten day and right now I'd like to gag and bind twenty-two kindergartners." A short, muffled laugh escaped her.

Maybe she spoke her mind more often than most, but white lies, as people called them, were part of the social grease that kept society moving. And white lies were still lies. The world couldn't stand unvarnished truth all the time.

What if she'd told Martha Beringer exactly what she really thought of that hideous new dress she'd worn last week? Oh, man, the repercussions!

No, something was troubling Trace beyond the fact that he was a hunted man and had been betrayed by his employer. Something that had him questioning himself.

That ticked her off. Whatever he'd done, he'd done it in the service of his country. Treating him like this was the real crime here, and a far worse crime if it made him see his past as wasted, as a lie, as an ugly thing.

Intentions *did* matter. She firmly believed that. A person might not always get the desired outcome, but if the intentions were good…well, that really wasn't a bad thing.

Giving up, realizing that she wasn't going to solve the puzzle of Trace Archer any faster than she had solved the Rubik's Cube—and she'd never completed that—she rose.

Looking out her back window, she froze. "Trace?"

He was sitting in the armchair again, his eyes closed, but as soon as she spoke, he opened them.

"What?"

"There's someone out back moving in the storm. What should I do?"

He jumped to his feet. "Get away from the window. Damn, they couldn't have found me this fast." But still he was yanking on his jacket, apparently ignoring the pain that brought an immediate sweat to his forehead. "Lock the door behind me."

"But…"

"Just do as I say, okay?"

She pulled back into the hallway, watching him shove his feet into his boots, her heart beating so fast she felt she could barely breathe. "I should call someone."

"I'm faster."

God, she hated this. As soon as he hurried out the door, she locked it as ordered. Then she stood there, wishing she could watch out the window, but knew he was right. Even though all she could see through the whiteout was the dark shape of a person out there, anyone looking toward her window could see as much if she stood there. She shuddered, facing the reality of guns and bullets. And Trace was out there alone.

She'd felt fear occasionally in her life, but never before like this. Trace could get hurt, killed. Someone was out there in this deadly weather. A waking nightmare with no escape.

She stared at the phone, thinking of calling the sheriff, but it was probably already too late and they'd be really slow in this storm. No one had even attempted to plow the streets yet.

And then she remembered what Ryker had said earlier about the cordless phones broadcasting. Had that given them away?

Her nerves stretched as if they were on a rack, and she paced the hallway, unable to hold still. Time couldn't have moved any slower if it had completely stopped. She was ready to scream by the time someone knocked on the door.

Her heart climbed into her throat. Slowly she walked over to it and peered out the peephole. Trace.

Relief turned her knees to spaghetti, and she fumbled at the lock before she was able to open it. He stepped inside immediately, bringing a blast of blowing snow with him.

"Your neighbor," he said. "Frank Willis. His dog got out. We found him."

She sagged against the wall, watching him struggle with his boots and jacket. "Really? He was looking for his dog?"

"Given what it's like out there, what choice did he have?"

As relief washed through her, she began to feel angry. "You should have let me call someone!"

"Sure. They might get here by tonight sometime."

"My God, Trace! It could have been a killer out there."

"Then I'd have dealt with it."

His calm infuriated her, but even as it did, she realized she was being unreasonable. Why be mad at him for doing what he considered necessary? It made as much sense as being mad at Frank for hunting for his dog. Trace, she reminded herself, had experience with this. He knew what he was doing. Not that it made her feel a whole lot better.

She paced the hallway a couple of more times, trying to shake the adrenaline that had roared through her. It felt like a lifetime before her anxiety began to ease. She might enjoy adventure, but not this kind.

"You okay?" she asked when she recovered her ability to speak. He had flopped onto the chair.

"Considering more pain meds. It's been a while."

"If you need them, take them. I think you just proved that even Santa Claus with a GPS would have trouble getting here today. I'm making some more coffee. Interested?" Anything to feel useful. After that little scare, she felt purposeless. What could she possibly do except give this man a roof? Little enough.

"Yeah, it'll keep the pills from overwhelming me."

She came to stand in front of him, then asked a question she'd thought might be impolite. That didn't seem to matter anymore. "Will it get better? The pain?"

"The doc said it might. He said the nerves are trying to heal. They're raising a ruckus, but eventually they could make the right connections again. Or just give up."

"How long since you were shot?"

"Almost five months."

She shook her head and rounded the bar into the kitchen. "Regular or espresso?"

"Regular. Strong but regular."

So she threw an extra scoop of coffee into the basket and started the brew cycle. When she returned to sit on the couch, he was pouring a single pill into his gloved hand. He took it with what was left of his coffee. "Can you use it at all?"

"The hand? Some. Hey, Teach, here's a question for you. I've always been a leftie for writing, but I always shoot with my right hand. Why?"

She recognized that he was trying to restore normalcy after the scare. "Do I look like a neurologist? At best, I can guess. Cross-dominance, maybe. Or…that's just the way you learned."

He was giving her a little smile, almost as if he were teasing her. But about what? Then what he'd said struck her. "Um, do you have to shoot often?"

A chuckle escaped him. "Never. I know how, but my job is persuasion, not assassination. In my position, I'm usually armed with my wits…which seemed to have slowed down quite a bit since I was shot."

So he *had* been teasing her. "Who shot you? Could it be this same guy?"

"I wondered about that, but I don't think so. It's more likely I got caught in some cross fire than that I was a target."

She accepted his judgment because she was in no position to evaluate it. He was the expert. Hearing the coffeepot finish percolating, she went to get them both mugs.

When she returned, his eyes had again narrowed, and he seemed far away. "Am I bothering you?"

His eyes opened fully. "Hell, no. My brain seems determined to run in circles. I haven't gotten anywhere yet except to narrow down the possibilities. There are still too many."

The phone rang. For an instant Julie didn't want to answer it, but then it occurred to her that Ryker might be calling with some useful information. Instead it turned out to be her friend Ashley.

"What's up?" Ashley asked. "I'm bored with this storm already."

"Not me," Julie said honestly. "I had a friend arrive in town last night."

"Who?" Ashley sounded surprised.

"Remember I had a guide when I went hiking two summers ago?"

"The Pacific Northwest trip. I remember. But you didn't say much about him."

Julie turned and saw that Trace was listening attentively. "Well, he was cute, but not interested back then. Anyway, we kept in touch by email. When he told me he was recuperating with an injured arm, I invited him to come visit."

"Ooh," Ashley remarked, the smile in her voice coming over the phone. "Still cute? Any more interested?"

Julie laughed. "I don't know. He hasn't even been here a full day yet."

"Well, I want to meet him as soon as we can dig out of our snow caves."

"Sure. So other than boredom, how are you?"

The conversation continued in a more ordinary vein. Ashley had resorted to watching DVDs to pass the time and admitted she was kind of hoping that school would be closed on Monday. She taught fourth grade.

"Don't count on it," Julie answered. "We never have snow days."

"Hardly ever." Ashley sighed. "Well, I won't keep you. Enjoy your company."

"I am," Julie assured her before hanging up. She found Trace watching her with a faint smile.

"Cute?" he said.

She cast her mind back, then laughed. "Girl talk. Would you have preferred being referred to as gorgeous?"

"That would have been over the top."

Julie didn't think so, but didn't argue with him. Trace was a man making unimaginable mental and physical adjustments, and she just couldn't see giving him a hard time.

"You shouldn't have mentioned me," he said, the smile gone.

She sank back onto the couch and stared at him. "It's the cover story!"

"I know, but cover stories should be used only when it can't be avoided. The fewer people who know I'm here with you, the safer for everyone."

Everything inside Julie clenched as a new concern crept along her nerves. "Are you telling me I just put Ashley in danger?"

"Probably not," he said. "But how many others is she going to pass this to? New guy in town visiting you. It might have been possible to clear this whole thing up before anybody else knew about me at all."

"Well, excuse me, but I never had any training in this!"

His voice changed, growing almost gentle. "I know. I'm not criticizing. It's just a caution."

"I don't live in your world," she said irritably. "It would have been even weirder if I hadn't mentioned you to a friend and then she ran into us somehow. She'd start wondering why I hadn't mentioned you. We're talking small-town here, not grand schemes in big cities."

"I know." Lifting his hand to his forehead, almost as if he were shielding his eyes from bright light, he simply sighed. "I'm not good at this."

"Good at what?"

"Helping someone learn how to handle these situations."

"But surely you had to teach your...what did you call them? Assets?"

"That was easier. I wasn't living with them."

"How did that make it easier?"

"Because we always met for a reason, and a cover was provided. This is different."

"Well, I don't see it, Mr. Secret Agent Man. This is *my* world, and if I don't act the way I normally would, people will notice and wonder what's wrong. So live with it."

She flounced off to the bathroom, irritated, and never realized that smiling eyes followed her.

Far away, on the other side of the continent, a phone call was taking place. The clerk was still sweating bullets, even though he stood outside in a chilly wind that made the early cherry blossoms around the Reflecting Pool seem crazy. They had just begun to bloom; the crowds were small, probably kept smaller by the cold weather. Next weekend...

The thought trailed away as his superior spoke. "I'm told we don't want the asset leaving town just yet."

Relief washed through the clerk. "I said flights were already getting delayed and diverted."

"They will be very shortly. This storm is going to hit Denver hard. So much for global warming."

The clerk kept his opinion to himself. He had trouble with some of his superior's political views, but arguing him about whether one storm disproved or proved anything would be pointless. He needed to skate through this thankless job as safely and easily as possible. "The man is furious."

"Of course he's furious. He's one great big stinking pile of elephant dung because he's furious. But I guess we need him. I wish I knew what all this was about."

The clerk wavered on that. Sometimes he really wanted to understand, and sometimes he was sure that the less he knew, the better for him.

"Anyway," his superior said, "go home for the weekend. I guess we're going to send him some diversions and try to keep him in place for a few more days. Apparently, having him run around on his own is the only thing that gives certain people nightmares. We have to find the target and make sure the general is properly directed."

The clerk wished he could close his ears. "TMI," he said.

His boss laughed. "I read you. That's more than I wanted to know. But I think you're off the hook at least until Monday. I'm going to go home, too, and turn off my phone. I suggest you do the same."

"Yes, sir."

"Good job," his boss said, just before he disconnected.

Sure, thought the clerk, staring at the cherry blossoms and the perfectly ordinary people walking around him. For the first time in a while, he wished he were one of them.

Chapter 6

Morning brought no change. The storm outside still hammered the world with its fury. The news said it was unsafe to go out on the roads for any reason and that much of the state was being shut down for what was rapidly becoming called "the Blizzard of the Century." Trace watched just long enough to pick up the important bits.

"I don't believe that," Julie muttered as she scrambled eggs to go with some bacon she'd fried. "I've heard that line before."

"So there's more than one blizzard of the century?" Trace asked. He still hadn't put on the sling and was wearing yet another flannel shirt and jeans. He preferred dark-hued shirts, and this was another shade of gray.

"Apparently. And while there's lots of snow, it's not even that cold. We had colder weather last year, dangerous. Clippers don't often reach us here, but we got one last year. Nah, he's exaggerating."

"Maybe it makes people feel better about being stuck in place." He couldn't imagine why he was defending the guy. Just to make conversation? He had a feeling Julie was slightly out of sorts this morning, but he didn't know what to do about it. Maybe she was still dealing with the tension of this whole situation.

"Could be."

"I feel bad about you having to take care of me like this," he said as she served their breakfasts at the bar. The last person to do this for him had been a girlfriend years ago, and she hadn't lasted long when she realized that one of his failings was taking off on a moment's notice.

She cocked an eye at him. "Alternatives? You can't exactly get out of here and go hang at the diner or a bar, waiting for your hunter to arrive."

"Not in this weather, although it might have been preferable to dragging you into this."

"Cut it out," she said, picking up a crispy piece of bacon in her fingers. "This was the best alternative to leaving you hanging out there. I don't mind. Save the guilt, at least as regards me."

He hoped he wouldn't have to feel guilty about her at all when this was over, but he had some serious doubts. He decided to change the subject. "So how's an adventurous woman like you wind up being a kindergarten teacher here?"

"I grew up here. I love this place. As for teaching kindergarten, I wouldn't do anything else, and I've had the opportunity. I love working with those bright, curious little minds and their off-the-wall perspectives on a lot of things. They often make me see the world differently. They certainly keep it fresh. So for me, teaching is an adventure. A different kind of exploration."

He smiled, thinking he understood. "But the world traveler in you?"

"Small doses are best. I go take my little jaunt, have a great time, then come back here and get grounded again. It's my *home*, Trace." Then she paused, and he saw guilt dance across her face.

"Easy. I chose my life, too. A child of many cultures, son of none, I guess." However it sounded, it was true. He wondered if the word *rootless* applied to him. He wondered if he'd ever be able to learn to live any other way.

"Except this culture," she argued.

"Clearly. This country is my home, little time as I've spent here over the years."

He watched her eat some more eggs, then she asked, "So do you feel rootless?"

Funny her question should echo his thoughts. What was she picking up on? He usually did not reveal much about himself. "There are all kinds of roots," he remarked. "I'd sunk mine pretty deep into my work and my coworkers."

"But now they've been cut?"

He looked down at his gloved hand and tried to close his fist. Not quite. "It feels like it," he admitted. "But then…look how Ryker stepped up for me. And another guy he talked to about me. They haven't managed to cut all the roots."

She pushed food around on her plate. "What about now? Are you thinking about different kinds of roots?"

"If I survive this, I'll need to." Blunt truth. The best he could do by her in the midst of this mess.

She astonished him by reaching out and covering his gloved hand with hers. "Does it hurt when I touch you?"

"No more than usual."

She gave him a little squeeze, then let go. He wished she'd kept on touching him. Friendly touch was a rare experience in his life.

She spoke again. "I don't know how I'd feel if I lost my job. Or what I'd do. And I wouldn't even have to consider that someone had betrayed me."

She turned her head toward him and he could read the worry in her face. "What is this doing to you, Trace? Really? I know you're treating it as a mission. I gather that you're spending all your time trying to figure this out. But how do you *feel* about what's been done to you?"

"My feelings? I don't have any. I need a clear head."

"Bull," she said. "I don't mind your evasions and omissions, but don't you lie to me. Everyone has feelings, and they aren't classified."

"Julie…"

"I'm serious here. This has to rip you up. Maybe you can suppress all of that while you need to, but you can't tell me you didn't react in a million ways to this news. Maybe you ought to let it all hang out and get it out of the way."

Her words did a better job than the coffee at clearing his head. Springing up from the stool, he began pacing, wondering what she was trying to draw out of him. "How did I feel? Mad as a hornet. Betrayed. Even the desire to kill someone. But I can't let that get in the way of my thinking. Believe me, there's nothing like emotion to mislead you."

"Or lead you to the truth," she said quietly.

He pivoted sharply. "Meaning?"

"Exactly what I said. You know someone is after you. Maybe your gut has a better answer to that than your brain. Regardless, nothing's going to happen until this storm and this weekend are over, so let your gut do the talking for a little while. Experience the rage and get past it. If you need to rant, I'll listen. All I know is you devoted your entire adult life to something you believed in, and now you find that people you trusted would be just as happy to see you die. If that doesn't infuriate you, nothing could."

"It infuriated me, all right. But what good does that do? I've got a burn on to catch this guy, but other than being a propellant it serves no purpose. It sure isn't going to give me any answers."

"Are you so positive about that?" Then with a boldness he hadn't anticipated, she rose and came to him, stepping right up against him and sliding her arms around his waist. "You're not alone, Trace. Right now, you're not alone. You need to let the cork out of the bottle and let us help you. Ryker wants to. I want to. You can't just sit here marching through your own thoughts all by yourself."

Feelings? Feelings were crashing through him now, a mixture of rage at the position he was in and powerful desire to just wrap her in his own arms and forget it all. Which cork did she want him to pull? There were a couple of genies he wasn't prepared to let out of his bottle. Not now. Maybe never. He couldn't afford it.

But she leaned into him a little, and as he felt her full breasts press against his chest, the man in him responded instantly. A new ache swelled in his body, purely pleasurable. His own arms rose, wrapping around her, holding her close and savoring the moment. But just for a few seconds. He was saved by the spiking pain in his hand, called back to reality just in time.

He dropped his arms and stepped back. "No, Julie." Then he strode across the room and settled on a chair.

She stood staring at him. "No? No, what?"

"No, I'm not going to pull the cork. Running on raw emotion will get me and everyone else killed. I won't do it. Giving in to anger is rehearsing it, feeding it. It's the most dangerous thing I could do right now. Now I need to be smart, cunning and thoughtful. Later there might be a time for rage, but not yet."

He closed his eyes, waiting for her to accept his decision. This was the woman who took *no* as a challenge, according to the sheriff. He had no doubt she'd come at him another way, although he sure as hell couldn't figure out why. Was he just something new in her life, a package she wanted to open, or was something else going on?

He heard the clatter of dishes as she cleaned up from breakfast. She was angry. Well, he could understand that. But he wasn't one of her kindergartners to be coaxed into sharing things he couldn't, and shouldn't, share.

The phone rang again, and she came around to answer it. "Hey," she said. "Yeah. Here." She passed the receiver to him. "Ryker."

Oh, man, that woman was fuming. Maybe because he'd rejected her advance. Because he was sure it had been an advance, however mild.

"Yeah," he said into the phone.

"Eastern Europe," Ryker said succinctly.

"Well, that covers a whole lot of territory."

"Slightly. Anyway, I have some hacking skills. Question is where I can safely use them. Not from this house, that's for sure."

"Maybe just hold off a bit. Let me think some more. If I can narrow it, maybe we can limit the information search. Meanwhile, I'm going to ask Julie if she'll let me fiddle with her computer."

"Okay. Talk to you soon."

He handed the receiver back to Julie, who hung it up, put her hands on her lovely hips, and said, "Why do you want to fiddle with my computer?"

"To make it anonymous, in case I need to hack a secure database."

Her anger evaporated. Her hands slipped until they hung loosely at her sides. Slowly, she sat. "You can do that?" she asked quietly.

"Yes. I can make it look as if this computer is logging on from almost anywhere in the world. It's basically called VPN, a virtual private network. You could get software to do it yourself if you wanted, but I have access to some of the best. I'll only use it if I need to, and it'll give me only a narrow window."

"Why?"

"Because if I start hacking, alarms will go off. One slipup and I might get tracked. I don't want to expose you to that."

He most definitely didn't want to risk that. But his mind was already running on something else. Eastern Europe? He'd done a lot of work there in the last four years. Managed a lot of operatives who had managed a lot of assets. It wasn't the narrowest field Ryker could have given him. He'd already been thinking about it, so basically what he'd gotten was confirmation. Eastern Europe. And whomever Ryker was talking to apparently didn't know any more than that, or Ryker would have said so.

Almost absently, he reached for another pain pill, to lessen the hammering agony in his hand so it wouldn't distract him. Then he went for more coffee to keep his head clear.

Julie remained on the couch, watching Trace slip away again into thought. She shouldn't have become angry with him. She'd pushed into places she had no right to go, and he'd pushed back. She'd deserved it.

But now…the thought of making her computer so anonymous it would look like it was logging on from some other part of the world…well, she hadn't known that was possible. Oh, she'd heard of anonymous servers, but didn't realize she could become anonymous from right here.

But equally troubling was that he seemed to think he might have to hack into some seriously secret databases. She didn't like that. She understood his life was on the line, but…

Settling back, she closed her eyes, folded her arms and reevaluated her position here. She had believed she was walking into this with her eyes open. Trace was in danger. By extension, so were Ryker and Marisa. It had been easy to jump in with both feet to help in any way she could.

But now a man was sitting in her living room, talking about making her computer anonymous so that he could do some hacking. She had always hated hacking, felt it was criminal, and to make matters worse, he was probably talking about entering secret government databases.

God, she wanted to shudder. Her ethics were teetering on a knife-edge here. Some things she would never do, never approve of, and yet…here she was, watching it happen.

But Trace, she reminded herself. Ryker and he had made it clear that someone in the very organization he had worked for had helped set him up. That wasn't right, either. In fact, compared to that, a little hacking seemed minor.

"Julie?"

She opened her eyes and found Trace watching her with those brown eyes of his. Eyes that could go from warm and inviting to hard chips in an instant. "What?"

"Are you okay?"

"I'm trying to swallow the idea of hacking into a secret government database."

He smiled faintly. "It's only hacking because I don't want them to know I'm doing it." He lifted his good hand and waved it a bit. "I'm still employed by them, remember? If they hadn't put me on leave, I'd have every right to do what I'm proposing to do. If I even need to."

"That's supposed to make me feel better?" But it did, actually.

He leaned forward a little. "If this were an ordinary situation, I'd be entitled to get most of the information I might want. All that's different is that I don't want them to know if I have to look a little further than I should."

"Because…"

"Because some of *them* are involved in this mess. People I can't trust."

Well, that made sense. Perfect sense. He only wanted to get at information he would be allowed to see if he were still working. Although she didn't exactly miss the part about looking further than he should. Under these circumstances, however…

"Duh," she said.

"Duh?"

"I feel like an idiot."

"Why?" His brow creased. "Because you have some ethical qualms about hacking a database? You should be proud of that. I'm glad you have those. And I hope I won't need to look at anything I couldn't look at under ordinary circumstances. You didn't know that, but now you do. I won't be breaking any laws." Not exactly. *Need To Know* was a big impediment, but he didn't want to get into that with her.

"Okay. Then why the worry about making my computer anonymous?" That troubled her, too.

"Because I don't want your location to be traced. I don't want the trouble we're trying to avoid showing up at your door. That's the only reason. If they flag me, they'd be drawn right here. You'd be in trouble because you aren't allowed access, and I'd be in trouble because they'd find me. That's the whole of it. So we make your computer anonymous."

She nodded slowly, settling down internally. It made perfect sense. She understood now. Which left only one thing. "I'm sorry I made you uncomfortable by hugging you."

"Oh, Julie," he said quietly. "Another time I'd be telling you just how much I want you."

She caught her breath. At once, warm syrup seemed to pour through her veins, and her body responded with a deep, aching throb. "Trace?" she whispered.

He shook his head. "I could be dead soon. I'd vastly

prefer it if I were the only one. So I have to keep focused. Besides, you don't even really know me."

"I know what I want," she said, her voice growing stronger. "But if you're worried that I hardly know you, why don't you tell me more? Who is Trace Archer?"

He smiled faintly. "A guy with a messed-up hand who is on the run for his life and is sojourning with the most beautiful woman he's ever seen."

She could have felt flattered, but that wasn't her. She scowled. "Nice evasion, Archer."

He surprised her with a laugh. "Told you. Evasions. A chameleon. It's all second nature. Now why would you want to get mixed up with that?"

Good question, she thought. But she still wanted to get mixed up with him. So where did that leave her? "Tell me just one true thing that you feel it's safe to share."

"Okay. I guess I can do that." He thought about it, taking his time. "I was being truthful when I said I wanted you. I have since I first saw you. I was truthful about my parents, too."

"We've already covered that ground. Surely you know something else about yourself." Probably little he wanted to think about, but she waited anyway, giving him time. She wasn't letting him off the hook.

"In the service of my country, I used people. Yes, I tried to protect them, and they were rewarded for their help, but I was still using them."

That was brutal, she thought. She gave him marks for honesty on that. She doubted many people who'd done what he had would have failed to find a comforting rationale.

"So you have a conscience," she said.

"What's left of one, anyway. It would be easy to

tell myself that these people were all on my side, but I know better. Some saw personal gain by helping. Some acted because they hated their governments. Some just didn't care. A few *did* have the best motives. But by any traditional sense of the word, most of them were traitors, and I helped them become treasonous. Did I save lives? I'm sure. Am I happy with being Mephistopheles? Not anymore."

His choice of description hit her hard. She was sure she'd never known anyone who felt that way about himself. She ached for him. "Aren't you being a little hard on yourself?"

"You wanted truth, and that's the truth. It's what I did. I hope intentions matter."

"Intentions always matter," she said firmly, knowing it in the deepest part of her heart. "If you mean to do good and everything goes all cockeyed, you can't be blamed for having a black heart. You might have been stupid or made a mistake, but you meant well. Yeah, I think that counts a whole lot."

But it horrified her to hear him comparing himself to a Faustian demon. Which brought up another question. "What planted the image of Mephistopheles in you? Your upbringing?"

"Do we ever escape what we learned as children? I served what I believed to be a good cause. I'm not so sure I always served it in good ways. Apparently not, since someone is mad enough to want revenge."

He shook his head a little. "Enough truth for right now. I'll have to deal with my sins later. Right now, if I'm ever to do that, I need to save my life and make sure hell doesn't rain down on you and Ryker."

He paused. "And if I can, I need to make sure this never happens to another operative like me."

A chill trickled slowly down her spine. "How can you do that? Won't that just put you in more danger?"

His gaze had grown hard again. "I'm not afraid of danger, Julie. Never have been. I'm not afraid of dying, either. I just don't want to leave a mess behind me."

"Meaning what, exactly?" she demanded. "When you got here, you were willing to hit the road and hang yourself out there. You stopped only because you didn't want to inadvertently involve more people. Now what's going on?"

"The realization that I'm a blood offering. And if they'd do this to me, they could do it to someone else."

A blood offering. The words chilled Julie to her very core, and the feeling didn't dissipate as the morning wore on. Outside the storm continued unabated, but she felt as if it had entered this apartment, entered her heart and soul with its stinging ice.

A blood offering. "Trace?"

He was pacing again, his arm once again in the sling. "Yes?"

"Blood offering. As in sacrifice?"

"Exactly," he said. "I don't know for sure, obviously, but the only way to put this together is that an asset wants to take me out, and they think appeasing that person is more important than my life."

She nodded, but words escaped her for a little while, a rare circumstance for her. Finally she asked, "Everyone wants you dead?"

"I doubt it. It's probably a very small group. Maybe only one or two individuals who think they can let this all happen under the radar. Poor Trace Archer, we sent him on medical leave and he met with a terrible accident. Or something like that. This isn't the kind of activity that anyone would want to become widely known."

"I can see why. But you believe they're capable of it?" Some last vestige of the old Julie hoped he would deny it, but reality was driving home fast.

He stopped pacing long enough to meet her gaze. "Some of them are. I don't doubt it. It's a culture of secrecy, a culture of people willing to take great risks or to put others at risk. Among them have to be some who don't feel any particular loyalty to anything except their perceived mission. If a few people think this will be ultimately helpful, they won't even hesitate."

"But if they're so sure they're right, why not just take you out themselves?"

"Because this way they can deny any part in it. No tracks. Clean."

She leaned forward, put her arms across her thighs and stared at the floor. Once again it struck her that she'd led a very sheltered life.

Then she realized something else. When she'd dived into this, she'd blithely thought that Trace was the target and all they had to do was protect him and help him find his pursuer. Yes, it might be risky, and she was indeed willing to die to protect Marisa, but she hadn't thought about something else, something very important.

If they got Trace, they might not stop there. Cleaning up this operation and covering their tracks might mean they needed to erase her as well because she might know something. She might not just happen to be collateral damage.

She could very well become a target, too.

Chapter 7

Ryker called again about three in the afternoon. Julie answered.

"Hey, I'm coming over. About thirty minutes."

"You can't go out in this!"

"I need stuff for the baby. Anyway, I'm heading for the grocery. The sheriff will pick me up there and drop me off near your place. Visibility is near zero, and no one will see."

Julie stared out the window at the stormy day. "It's dangerous."

"Not in an official vehicle with chains and a plow on the front. I'll get there. Tell our friend."

Then he disconnected. She returned the phone to the cradle and found Trace right behind her. "Ryker's coming over."

He didn't answer, simply looked at the TV set where

a cheerful meteorologist was showing a growing storm and saying it was unlikely to pass through before Tuesday. Schools would probably be closed due to the dangerous conditions.

"That's Ryker," he said finally.

"Schools almost never close around here. He's nuts. He shouldn't even attempt this."

"He's probably going crazy wanting to do something about this situation. I can identify."

"Well, I'm glad you can! If something happens to him, Marisa and the baby…"

He caught her arm gently in his good hand. "Nothing will happen. I've known Ryker for a long time, Julie. He doesn't take stupid risks."

"No? You've got a killer on your tail. Tell me again about stupid risks. You, Ryker… Johnny, even. Do you ever think about anyone else?"

She watched his face tighten. He dropped his hand from her arm. Then he said three succinct words before he turned his back on her. "All the time."

"What all the time?"

"I think about other people all the time," he snapped. "I made a career of it. Do you imagine I never once thought of Marisa when I had to identify what was left of Johnny? Anyway, who do you believe I did all those things for, Julie? Myself? No, I did them for the benefit of all the people at home, people like you."

She instantly felt about two inches tall, and she wished she could take her angry words back. It was just that watching Marisa's late husband leave all the time, going off to destinations unknown as if he had no obligation at home, had left her with a bad taste in her mouth. She'd always thought Johnny was selfish.

Now she was accusing Ryker and Trace of the same thing. Maybe Johnny had been selfish, but only because he'd taken a wife. Maybe that was his true selfishness, falling in love and then leaving so often. Maybe it wasn't his job at all.

Trace pivoted to face her, and some of the tension was gone from his face. "Who were you talking to, Julie? Who were you mad at?"

"Johnny," she said, exhaling until her own tension fled. "Johnny Hayes. I watched all those years as he went traipsing off, leaving Marisa behind to handle everything on her own. I could see the excitement building in him when it was almost time to leave. He was like an addict who knew a fix was on the way. But then I had to watch Marisa grieve him. My God, his death almost ripped out her heart. Did he ever think of that?"

"Probably not," he admitted. "He was a bit of an adrenaline junkie. You alluded to it yourself. But it's the main reason I never married. Why drag anyone else into this hell? But now I've pulled you in."

"I don't think I gave you much choice," she reminded him. Slowly, she wrapped her arms around herself. "Maybe I was seeing it all wrong. Marisa loved him. He loved her. Maybe the sacrifice didn't seem that big to her until he died. Maybe it wasn't selfish at all."

"Oh, it was. Every relationship is selfish to some degree. I know plenty of guys like John who have married and raised families." He shook his head a little. "However, when you're gone a lot, those relationships sometimes suffer. It all depends on how much you're around to take care of it."

"When he was home, it was beautiful to behold," she murmured. "But…Marisa's not me. I shouldn't project

my feelings about it on her. I just know I often wondered how she could stand it. But she did."

"Different strokes and all that," he replied quietly.
"Look, Julie, if you want out of this, just say so. I never
meant to get you involved. I wouldn't have except the
sheriff said…"

"That I don't take no for an answer. He's right." She
gave a tired laugh. "You know, Trace, telling me no
is like waving a red flag in front of a bull. I know it.
Enough people have told me, and I can see it in myself."

She lifted her gaze to his. "Just do me a favor. Don't
try to protect me by cutting me out of this."

"But…"

"And don't give me the operational security argu-
ment. This operation isn't entitled to any security, in the
first place. In the second, I may already be a target, too."

His brows lifted. "No."

"As soon as they find out about me, am I going to
look like a loose end that needs some cleaning up? I
don't know, and neither do you. Maybe not. I'm just
a small-town teacher. Chances are, they'll figure you
manipulated me like an asset and I don't know a darn
thing. Then again…"

He reached out with his left hand, catching a strand
of her hair and running his fingers along it. Then he
cupped the back of her head and pulled her against him
so that she felt his warmth, his hard chest. His heart
beat strongly against her ear. Oddly, he made her feel
surrounded by safety. "I won't let anything happen to
you," he said, running his hand down her back, causing her to shiver with a pleasure that seemed to contra-
dict their conversation. "I swear it." Then he let go of
her and added in a lighter tone, "I protect my assets."

FREE Merchandise is 'in the Cards' for you!

Dear Reader,

We're giving away FREE MERCHANDISE!

Seriously, we'd like to reward you for reading this novel by giving you **FREE MERCHANDISE** worth over **$20** retail. And no purchase is necessary!

It's easy! All you have to do is look inside for your Free Merchandise Voucher. Return the Voucher promptly...and we'll send you valuable Free Merchandise!

Thanks again for reading one of our novels—and enjoy your Free Merchandise with our compliments!

Pam Powers

Pam Powers

P.S. Look inside to see what Free Merchandise is **"in the cards"** for you!

We'd like to send you two free books like the one you are enjoying now. Your two books have a combined price of over $10 retail, but they are yours to keep absolutely FREE! We'll even send you 2 wonderful surprise gifts. You can't lose!

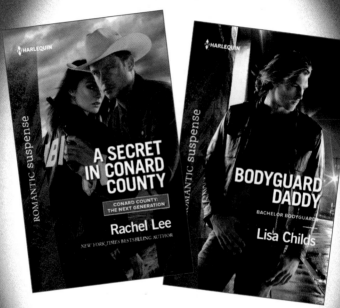

REMEMBER: Your Free Merchandise, consisting of **2 Free Books** and **2 Free Gifts**, is worth over $20 retail! No purchase is necessary, so please send for your Free Merchandise today.

Get TWO FREE GIFTS!

We'll also send you 2 wonderful FREE GIFTS (worth about $10 retail), in addition to your 2 Free books!

Visit us at:
www.ReaderService.com

Books received may not be as shown.

YOUR FREE MERCHANDISE INCLUDES...

2 FREE Books **AND** 2 FREE Mystery Gifts

FREE MERCHANDISE VOUCHER

❑ Please send my Free Merchandise, consisting of
2 Free Books and **2 Free Mystery Gifts**.
I understand that I am under no obligation to buy
anything, as explained on the back of this card.

240/340 HDL GKCC

Please Print

FIRST NAME

LAST NAME

ADDRESS

APT.#   CITY

STATE/PROV.   ZIP/POSTAL CODE

NO PURCHASE NECESSARY!

RS-516-FMH16

READER SERVICE—Here's how it works:

Accepting your 2 free Harlequin® Romantic Suspense books and 2 free gifts (gifts valued at approximately $10.00) places you under no obligation to buy anything. You may keep the books and gifts and return the shipping statement marked "cancel." If you do not cancel, about a month later we'll send you 4 additional books and bill you just $4.74 each in the U.S. or $5.49 each in Canada. That is a savings of at least 12% off the cover price. It's quite a bargain! Shipping and handling is just 50¢ per book in the U.S. and 75¢ per book in Canada.* You may cancel at any time, but if you choose to continue, every month we'll send you 4 more books, which you may either purchase at the discount price or return to us and cancel your subscription. *Terms and prices subject to change without notice. Prices do not include applicable taxes. Sales tax applicable in N.Y. Canadian residents will be charged applicable taxes. Offer not valid in Quebec. Books received may not be as shown. All orders subject to approval. Credit or debit balances in a customer's account(s) may be offset by any other outstanding balance owed by or to the customer. Please allow 4 to 6 weeks for delivery. Offer available while quantities last.

◄ If offer card is missing write to: Reader Service, P.O. Box 1867, Buffalo, NY 14240-1867 or visit www.ReaderService.com ►

BUSINESS REPLY MAIL
FIRST-CLASS MAIL   PERMIT NO. 717   BUFFALO, NY

POSTAGE WILL BE PAID BY ADDRESSEE

READER SERVICE
PO BOX 1867
BUFFALO NY 14240-9952

NO POSTAGE
NECESSARY
IF MAILED
IN THE
UNITED STATES

"You're not getting off that easily," she said. An impish idea had occurred to her, and before she could rethink it, she decided to go for it. God knew, she needed to change the mood in this place.

"Meaning?"

"Before we face the world, you need to give me a cover story."

His mouth opened a bit, and stayed open for several seconds before he responded. "We have a cover story."

"You do. But I invited you here, remember. I need to be hanging all over you like a starstruck kid. The guy hunting you will think you've manipulated me, romanced me into stupid compliance."

She could tell he was thinking about it. "It might work," he agreed finally. "But your reputation."

"Will recover," she retorted. "So get used to the idea of me clinging. In fact, I think you should take me to bed."

"Julie!" For the first time she saw him gape.

She almost laughed and was grateful to feel her mood lifting, but before she could shock him anymore, there was a knock at the door. Grinning, she went to peer out the peephole. Hah. She'd thrown an agent off balance. How many people could do that?

And what a relief not to be brooding. She wasn't the sort.

She let Ryker in quickly, and he entered with a swirl of blowing snow. "Success," he said, stomping his feet to clear his boots. "They'll come back for me when I'm ready."

"What about Marisa and the baby?" Julie demanded.

"A couple of guys are watching the house. The baby's

sleeping and I suspect Marisa has long since crashed. They'll be fine."

"Sure, and how did you explain your absence?"

He smiled at her. "Julie, you don't know Marisa very well in some ways. All I said was I needed to go out. She didn't pepper me with questions."

He unzipped his jacket and hung it on the peg. "Trace? How's it going?"

"Nowhere, basically. I've got a narrowed list of possibilities, but not narrow enough that I want to do any hacking yet."

Ryker nodded, his face settling into the granite lines Julie remembered from when he first came to this town. For his part, Trace was beginning to look as stony. Game faces, she thought. They were putting them on.

She decided to treat this as a view on something new. They certainly weren't going to be able to discuss anything inside this small apartment without her hearing it.

She settled at her desk, telling the men to help themselves to coffee, then waited. She wanted to know what they were thinking, what paths they were considering.

"Okay," said Ryker, "we took you off the grid two days ago. How long do you figure before they start backtracking? You were higher up the ladder than I was."

"Well, this storm plays into the problem. Have you been looking at the maps?"

Ryker nodded. "It's hitting Colorado hard, too."

"So I could be hunkered down in Denver, as far as they know. That's where my cell went off the grid. If I were managing this operation, my first thought would be that I had a wreck, got picked up by a passing motorist and made it to Denver or even a little beyond. With the atmospheric conditions that moved in overnight Friday, there are lots of reasons my cell might not be making a connection right now. I could have gotten out of range of a tower, for example, then been stopped dead in my tracks by the weather."

"Makes sense," Ryker agreed. "And then?"

"If they've been following me all this time, they know I occasionally hit dead zones for cell transmission. They won't be particularly concerned unless I don't show up again by, say, Wednesday. Then they might be concerned enough to backtrack my route."

"Might be?" Julie dared to ask.

"Pain meds," Trace said to her. "There've been a couple of times since my injury when I hurt so badly that I just doped myself up and stayed put. It wouldn't be the first time I stopped moving. In fact, I'm not so sure that they didn't give me all those meds to make me do exactly that. Anyway, I'm not supposed to know for certain that someone is hunting me. What's more, I'm supposed to believe that the Company is looking out for me. The real concern will arise if I don't emerge to check with them, say…Thursday."

"I'd give us a Wednesday cutoff to be safe," Ryker said.

"I agree," Trace answered. "That's not a whole lot of time to figure out who the tiger is."

Julie found this fascinating. She could hear the expertise as they spoke, the certainty that they could predict at least some of what would happen. How many times had they done things like this? She looked at Trace with renewed respect. "You can fiddle with my computer," she said.

Trace smiled. "Thanks. I guess under the circumstances, if I start hacking into those files, I should do it from someplace not too far from Denver."

"That would continue the illusion," Ryker said. "Might even strengthen it and keep them from looking backward too soon."

Julie leaned forward. "Why is time so important?"

Trace answered. "Because I haven't yet figured out who this guy is. I need to know who, at the very least, or we might not be able to protect anyone. Which got me thinking…" He turned to Ryker. "Everyone was indefinite about whether someone was after me."

"Until Thursday night," Ryker agreed. "That's when Bill let the cat out of the bag, indirectly at least."

"So maybe they weren't sure before then. Maybe it was a suspicion, which could mean this guy hasn't been tracking me for very long. Maybe he's gone off the grid for them, too."

"Now I'm confused," Julie said honestly. "Are you saying they might be on your side after all?"

"Hell no," Trace said bluntly. "All I'm saying is that until sometime last week they weren't sure what this guy was going to do. I'm reasonably certain they expected this, but they didn't *know*."

"I suppose," she said acidly, "that it counts for something that they told you to go on the road." This whole thing, she thought, would have given Machiavelli a run for his money.

Trace shook his head. "Sorry. That was pure plausible deniability at work, regardless of what this guy might do. Some butt-covering going on. The question is, are they actually going to help him find me?"

Ryker looked at him. "What's your gut saying?"

"Probably."

Ryker swore quietly. "I was afraid of that. I've been

arguing with myself for three days now, trying to find a way around it. Makes me sick."

"It makes me sick, too," Trace admitted. "And not just for myself. There's a viper's nest that needs some cleaning."

"I was hoping you'd say that, because when we catch this guy I want to use him as a broom to do a little housecleaning."

Julie felt impressed by their certainty, then reminded herself that these men had been in similar situations before. They knew what they were doing. Of course there could be no guarantees, but their skills made a good outcome more likely.

But as she listened, she had to fight to see it as an intellectual problem. From that place, this was a fascinating discussion for her. From any other place, such as her heart, it was sickening, disgusting, horrible.

"So," Ryker said, "Eastern Europe is a pretty broad area. How many ops did you supervise there?"

"Too many," Trace admitted. "I was running people all over the place."

"Well, if there's one thing that's clear, it's that at least one of your operatives screwed up somehow. The question is whether you even heard about it."

"There is that," Trace agreed. "If something blew up badly enough that some asset is this angry, then it must have been terrible. And it should have crossed my radar."

"Maybe not," Ryker said slowly. "Every operative is a filter. You know that."

"Filter?" Julie asked.

Trace looked at her. "They pass along what they think we need to know. Their screwups, maybe not so much. Or maybe they didn't even realize how badly they messed up."

"But as the guy in charge," Ryker said, "Trace could become a target for their anger, too. If some asset found his privates caught in a vise, he wouldn't stop with taking out his handler unless he had no other choice. Or maybe he'd just decide to go straight to the top. Another question. How did he find out about you? There were layers."

Trace snorted. "Some of the people we were dealing with were well-versed in intelligence operations. In fact, they were some of our most valuable assets. They could pierce those layers the same way we did."

Then Ryker dropped a bomb, at least from Julie's perspective. He asked, "What happened to John Hayes?"

Julie tensed, afraid of what she might hear, only to be disappointed.

"I don't know," Trace answered. "I got the same story as everyone else. Messy street shooting in Kiev. It's not like they don't happen."

"True, but then seven months later you get shot in your hand when you walk out of the embassy in Bulgaria. What exactly was John doing?"

"He was starting to take over handling a high-value asset. He hadn't even fully assumed the responsibility yet."

"So no link."

"I wouldn't think so. But if there was, the cover-up started early."

"Very early," Ryker said heavily. "Okay, I need to call my ride and get home. When are you planning to look into the files?"

"Tomorrow sometime. I want to do some more thinking first."

* * *

Anxiety was performing an unpleasant dance along Julie's nerves. After Ryker left, she was the one who started pacing. It had shocked her that Johnny's name had even come up, then relieved her when Trace seemed to think his death was unrelated to his current problem.

Or maybe he was just saying that. Protecting operational security still, even with his own neck in a noose. What she knew for certain is she didn't want any of this to touch Marisa. That woman had been through more than enough, and she certainly didn't need to learn that her late husband had screwed up badly.

"Trace?"

"Hmm?"

"If Johnny's involved in some way, I don't want Marisa to ever know."

"She won't hear a whisper. No reason, and anyway, I doubt he was. He's just one of nearly a dozen situations I'm thinking about."

She had closed the curtains against the night, not that anyone could see inside unless they were standing right outside the window, unlikely in this weather. She could hear the wind still blowing, and from time to time the window glass rattled a little.

"Julie? Are you okay?"

She faced him then and read genuine concern on his face. "I'm fine. Just…uneasy."

"Well, that's understandable. I'm surprised it hasn't hit you harder."

"You live like this all the time?"

"No." He sighed and passed his good hand over his face. "It's been a while since I worked at the ground level. Mostly you can imagine me as the spider at the center of a web, waiting for something to ping on one of my strands."

"You operated out of Bulgaria?"

"Sometimes." His face shuttered a little and she realized she was getting into sensitive areas. Well, she didn't care.

"So you advanced from actually cultivating the assets to managing the operatives who cultivated them?"

"Usually, yes."

"But that creates layers of removal, like Ryker said."

"It also made me more visible. While my operatives had little or no direct contact with an embassy, I actually had an office."

"Wow. That would identify you, all right."

"Sometimes I met my guys on the streets, but usually we minimized contact because I could out one of them just by showing up unless I had a really good cover."

"You ever meet Johnny?" Her heart was accelerating, aware that she was pushing him, aware that at any moment he might snap at her or shove her away. Afraid of learning more about Johnny, too.

"I think I mentioned, I did once. Before he went into the field for us. After that…" He shook his head. "The next time I saw him was to identify his remains, and I needed help with that."

"But you still think he might have been shot by accident. That you might have been shot accidentally, too."

He frowned. "Julie, without information to the contrary…"

She waved a hand, silencing him. "I get it. Or maybe I'll never get it. It doesn't matter. You lived in the shadows. All of you. I just can't imagine how hard that must be."

"In a way you're doing it right now," he pointed out.

"I guess. But I don't have enough information. Oh, I know you don't, either, but you sure have more than I do. I'm blind here."

"At the moment, so am I."

"But you're used to it. I'm not. I hate your secrets."

To her surprise, he started to smile. "I'm rapidly getting there myself."

He'd removed the sling again, and for some reason her attention settled on his gloved hand. It seemed to her that an important bridge needed to be crossed. Of course, little ever stopped her from speaking what was on her mind. "Are you ever going to let me see your hand? Or don't you trust me that much?"

His smile faded. "It's not about trust. What are you talking about?"

"It *is* about trust. You don't trust me not to be repelled. You said that's why you always wear a glove. Do you trust me even that much?"

He appeared disturbed. "Julie, what's going on here? What is it you're trying to do?"

"Trust," she said succinctly. "I trusted you enough to invite you into my home and to face this danger with you. Admittedly, my first thought was Marisa, but that's not why you're still here. But you don't trust me. You don't trust me with information, and you don't trust me with your hand. I guess I'm just an asset."

"Julie!" His tone was at once angry and appalled. "I don't see you that way at all."

"Really? Then how do you see me, Trace? A convenient roof? A handy computer? A willing aide to whatever you need to do? Because I seriously get the feeling that you have your walls as high as ever and you have no intention of letting me past your guard. Fine. But I don't have to like it. I don't think I've ever spent this many hours with anyone and learned so little about them."

And that was the core of it, she realized. The sense that she was getting only what he wanted her to see. That she would never know any more than the image he chose to project. The price of dealing with a spy, she supposed.

"I told you I was a chameleon."

"Yes, you did, but you don't have to be with me. Stop spoon-feeding me what you want me to know. Just... just...be yourself!"

His face had grown flat, emotionless. Then, without a word, he peeled off the black glove. What she saw was enough to make her draw a sharp breath. Scars everywhere, some ragged, some clearly surgical, one finger not quite properly aligned. The fingers curled somewhat, and she wondered if he could straighten them.

"Oh God," she whispered. All she could think about was how much that must have hurt, how much it still hurt.

"Good reason to keep it covered," he said after a moment. He lifted the glove with his left hand and started to pull it on again.

She stepped toward him quickly and pulled the glove away. "No. Absolutely not." Then she took his distorted hand in both of hers and bent her head, pressing a kiss on it.

"Julie..."

"Just shut up, Trace. Stop lying with your mouth and try lying with something else instead."

"What?" The word emerged, short and sharp with astonishment. "I've made every effort not to lie to you."

"Really? Then how about the desire I see when you

look at me? The way you instantly bury it. Is that being truthful?"

"You don't want to get mixed up with me."

Dang, this guy had a talent for lighting her fuse. "Don't tell me what I want. I can figure that out for myself. Somehow I got to be over thirty without your advice."

What the hell was she doing? She listened to herself with amazement, then understood. Without a word, she dropped sideways on his lap, one leg dangling over the chair arm. "This is all about what *I* want," she said honestly. "Now how about you, spy man?"

She defiantly met his gaze and saw those dark brown eyes harden, then soften even more quickly. Against her hip, she felt him hardening in response to her, and it encouraged her. "Quit protecting me," she said, raising her hand to cup his stubbly cheek. Three days without shaving had left the stubble feeling soft, and she liked that.

"Maybe I need to protect myself." She could tell he was trying to joke, but it was just another provocation as far as she was concerned.

"Not doing a very good job of it, are you?"

Something like a stifled laugh escaped him. "I guess not."

"So do you need protecting from me? Just say so."

"I can't," he said, his eyelids growing heavy, his breath speeding up. "Damn it, Julie, I can't."

"Can't make love to me, or can't say you need protection?"

"Oh, I can make love to you," he said huskily. "Oh, I can. I'm just worried about you."

"Last I heard we could all be dead soon, so shut up and deliver."

A smile spread over his face and a quiet laugh escaped him. God, she liked that smile. She'd have stood on her head just to see it. "You're quite a pistol, Julie."

"I've heard," she admitted. "Life is full of do-si-dos we can't escape. The things we have to do and say to keep everything smooth. But sex is one place we ought to just be honest. No pleasant white lies, no pretense, just raw, the way we feel it."

She was leaning back against his right arm, but his left hand settled across her thighs and began to rub gently. The warmth between her legs grew and began to hum with need.

"The thing is," he said, "it's not without consequences. You know that. People can get attached very quickly by making love. How will you feel if I'm gone in a few days?"

She caught her breath as his hand moved upward and began to brush across her breasts. "Like I seized an experience I didn't want to miss." The world was rapidly spinning away as anticipation and excitement began to fill her. Aching need had become the center of her universe.

His hand squeezed her, drawing a faint groan from her. "You sure?"

Before she could answer, her doorbell rang. She stiffened, her mind crashing back to the other reality. She felt Trace tense beneath her. Desire vanished like a balloon popping, replaced by shock.

"Expecting someone?" he murmured.

She shook her head, staring at the door as if beyond it a dragon waited. At this hour of the evening with a storm raging outside? Her heart skipped into top speed. Then she felt a gentle push from Trace and slid off his lap to stand. "Everyone would know I'm home. Who the heck would even be out in this? Ryker?" Fear completely swept away the last web of desire.

"He'd have called first."

"Okay. I guess I have to answer it. Maybe it's the complex management. They could be having some kind of trouble in this storm." She hoped that's all it was. If her life had become the movie she was beginning to feel it had, then she could open that door and find someone standing out there with a gun. Her mind nearly skittered at the image.

Alice's rabbit hole sounded positively cozy by comparison. Her mouth had turned dry, and her heart raced as if she'd run a couple of miles.

He stood, too, and nodded. "I'll slip into my room, but I'll leave the door open. Be careful."

She waited until Trace had disappeared around the corner of his door, the only place he could remain out of sight in this small apartment. What would they do if trouble was out there? She hadn't seen a gun anywhere near him.

Heaven help them if they had to depend on the self-defense classes she'd taken over the past few years. She hadn't taken them because she felt she needed them, although perhaps on some of her travels… *Oh, dang it, Julie*, she thought. *You were more interested in physical fitness than fighting off an attacker. You should have paid more attention!*

She reached the door and peered out the peephole. Was she shaking? She could hardly tell as a million ants of uneasiness crawled all over her. She could see the blowing snow out there in the glow from her porch light, but not a soul in sight. What the…? Then she caught a flash of strawberry blond hair.

Relief left her knees weak. For a second she thought she wasn't going to be able to move. At last she found some strength and worked the dead bolt, opening the door. "My God, Ashley, what are you doing here?" Dang, she sounded cranky. But she was. All that adrenaline was still pouring through her with no useful purpose.

Ashley regarded her from bright blue eyes and grinned. "Cabin fever. I decided to ski over and meet the mystery man. Can I come in or do you want me to ski away?"

A gust of wind slapped Julie in the face with ice crystals, overcoming her astonishment. She stepped back and let Ashley enter. The cross-country ski shoes Ashley wore sounded stiff, which of course they were.

"You're out of your mind," Julie said bluntly. "If you had an accident out there, they wouldn't find you under that blowing snow for weeks." Another horrific image, this one too realistic. She had the worst urge to shake her friend.

"It's okay. I told a few people I was coming to see you. So Connie and Kelly know which way I would have traveled, and they want an update on Mystery Man. If I don't call soon enough, they'll raise the alarm." Ashley pulled down the zipper on her jacket and shucked it, hanging it on one of the pegs by the door. "Besides, it's not like I had that far to come, and I was going stir-crazy."

"Crazy with curiosity, more like."

Ashley grinned again. "Like you, you mean?" She turned to tuck her gloves into the pocket of her jacket along with her ski mask. "Hot chocolate would be nice. It *is* cold out there. Then I want to meet your wilderness guide."

Julie hesitated, feeling caught betwixt and between. Trace might not want to meet anyone else, but Ashley had been her friend for many years and she couldn't just shove her back out the door. Then she saw the sling on the chair where Trace had left it. Double dang!

"Let me see if he's awake," she said, grabbing the sling and heading toward the guest room.

"Keeping him up all night?" Ashley teased.

"I wish. Hang on while I see if he's napping, then I'll make some cocoa." Unreal, she thought as she walked down the very short hallway that had two doors, one on each side. Trace's was wide open, and she immediately saw him waiting.

"You're up," she said with forced cheer, and handed him the sling. "Come meet my friend. Consider it a command performance." Command performance indeed, and at the worst time possible. She'd been getting somewhere with Trace and then Ashley had shown up. The universe must have a wicked sense of humor.

"Don't use my real name," he muttered. "Just call me Race."

From back in the living room she heard Ashley still laughing at her remark. But she didn't miss the concern in Trace's face as he struggled into the sling. Now someone else was involved. Oh, he must be loving this, but she didn't know what else to do.

"First name only," he murmured. "Let me handle most of the explaining, okay?"

Sure, she thought. He probably had loads of practice at this. Feeling a bit sour, she returned to Ashley, who had settled at the bar, still wearing her bibbed snow pants. "So cocoa, right?"

"Anything hot," Ashley answered. "I won't be able to

stay long. The forecast is getting worse, but after being cooped up for two days I had to get out. Skiing a few blocks seemed safe enough."

"Well, you'd better call me as soon as you get home. I'll be worried."

Ashley waved her hand. "It's not like I don't do this all the time."

"In a whiteout? At night?" Julie retorted.

Ashley laughed. "Not usually. But I can actually see where the streets are, thanks to the lights, and while the houses almost disappear, I can see the glow from the windows. No, I'm more worried about the plunging temperature, so one hot drink and I'm out of here."

Julie would never have believed she'd be glad to see Ashley leave. Then she had another thought. Under any other circumstances, she'd ask Ashley to stay the night. Until it was safe to go out.

Oh, dang! Was she going to fail to do the right thing because Trace was here? No matter the circumstances, she couldn't needlessly expose a friend to danger. Except that for the first time in her life, she didn't know where the true danger lay. In the storm? In the man who was hunting Trace? Saying the guy wouldn't be able to reach them in this storm, or find Trace, had just been proved a comforting fiction by Ashley's arrival.

"Something wrong?" Ashley asked. Her expression conveyed real concern.

Some spy she'd make, Julie thought, realizing she had stalled somewhere in the process of making cocoa. She was setting off alarms in her friend. She looked around and realized she'd gotten out the instant mix. Heat water, find the cream… She started moving again, feeling strangely stiff, as if she no longer belonged in her own body. "You shouldn't go back out in this," she said, hoping her internal turmoil wasn't evident. "Stay tonight at least."

"No way," Ashley answered. "I'm still not done wearing off my excess energy. Relax, Jules, I can make it the short distance. I have my phone in case anything happens. Now where is this mystery man?"

"Right here," Trace said.

Julie swung around from the stove to see Trace stepping out of the hallway. He'd tousled his hair a bit as if he'd just awakened and the sling was firmly in place, concealing his hand and his arm up to above the elbow. And looking awfully good in a navy blue flannel shirt and jeans as he approached. "Hey, I'm Race."

"Ashley." Ashley smiled back. "So you followed Julie all the way here from Oregon?"

"*Followed* isn't exactly the word," he said pleasantly as he slid into one of the stools. "We emailed a bit since her trip to the Cascades. She was kind enough to invite me to visit while I'm laid up."

"Cocoa?" Julie asked Trace, growing tenser by the moment. How many lies was he going to give Ashley? How many did he have to? *Cover story*, she reminded herself, but she really didn't like lying to her friends. In fact, she lied as rarely as she could. She'd learned from kindergartners that lie detectors seemed to be built in at an early age, and one falsehood could sacrifice trust forever. Adults might become deadened to them, but not kids. And since she'd learned never to tell lies, not even innocent ones, in the classroom, she'd extended it to most of the rest of her life.

But Ashley wasn't shy about making conversation. "So do you believe in bigfoot?" she asked.

"Me?" Trace's eyes widened a hair.

Of course, thought Julie. The one story she was sure her friends would remember about that trip. She hoped Trace could manage it.

"You, of course," said Ashley. "I know Julie mentioned those huge footprints she found and you thought they might be from a bear."

"Well, they could be. I track a lot of stuff. Bears have a way of walking where the back paw lands almost exactly on the spot the front paw already hit. So you can get an overlay that looks like a really huge five-toed print under some circumstances." He looked at Julie and smiled. "Just coffee for me, please."

She busied her hands, making the cocoa, pouring the coffee, waiting for the bombs that must be incoming already.

"But you spend a lot of time in the wilderness," Ashley argued. "No opinion?"

Yeah, wilderness. Only Trace lived in a different kind of wilderness. Tensely, Julie gave Ashley her cocoa.

"My opinion, if you really want it, is that enough people have found tracks, have seen things, well... There's at least a reason to seriously check it out. Scientifically. But belief? That's a whole different realm. I'll reserve judgment until there's scientific proof."

Ashley sighed, clucked, then laughed. "That's exactly the kind of advice I'd give my fourth graders. So you've never had the kind of experience that made you wonder?"

Trace smiled. "Of course I wonder. I'd have to be deaf and blind not to. I've heard things I can't explain or identify. I've seen footprints that might be bear, but then again... So yeah, I wonder. Julie saw that wilderness. There's even more of it up in Canada. It's within the realm of possibility that a large primate lives out there and keeps hidden. But I need proof, not stories."

Ashley nodded and thanked Julie for the cocoa. "Some stories have led people to species no one believed existed."

"True," Trace agreed. "So are you a believer?"

Ashley laughed and shook her head. "Not yet. The stories, the legends, make me wonder. They go back a long way, and sometimes they turn out not to be just legends, but recountings of things people have actually seen. Anyway, it's far from a settled thing. I was just wondering what you thought because of that story Julie told us."

Julie glanced at Trace and found his smiling brown eyes on her.

"I can't afford to lose my head," he said, then returned his attention to Ashley. "My job depends on being practical and levelheaded. I'm paid to keep people safe, not fill their heads with fear."

Ashley laughed. "I bet you could tell a good campfire story. Not even one little spooky one?"

"I can," said Julie, intervening swiftly. "Just before I hired Race to guide me into the wilderness, I *did* have a spooky night. I was all by myself, too. In fact, that's when I decided I needed a guide."

Ashley's eyes lit up. "Tell."

"Not much to it. I'd been following a logging road and decided to camp about twenty feet to the side of it. While I was cooking my dinner, I heard some howls. Probably mountain lions. They can sound almost human, like a man in pain sometimes. Anyway, it creeped me out, so I hurried up and got into my tent as soon as I could. Later, when I was sleeping, something woke me. It sounded like something hitting my tent. I didn't dare go out, but I didn't sleep much after that. It happened once more, and then the night went quiet."

"Ooh," Ashley said. "What was it?"

"Pine cones probably falling from the tree over me," Julie said drily. "If I hadn't been spooked by the mountain lions, I probably never would have been scared by them."

Ashley laughed. "Well, there goes a good story." She lifted her mug and drained it. "Okay, all warmed up." She stood. "Nice meeting you, Race. Maybe I'll see you again."

"Are you sure you don't want to stay?" Julie asked.

"I'll be perfectly safe. Besides, I don't want to be a third wheel." She winked at Julie and went to don the rest of her outerwear.

Trace spoke. "I hope I'm not making you uncomfortable."

"Nope," Ashley answered as she pulled down her ski mask, then zipped up her hood. "I wanted to bug her mostly because I needed to get outdoors. Besides, who could pass up a chance to meet the guy that Julie actually asked to visit her? Now there's a red-letter event. Anyway, if I'm too late getting home, people will start looking for me. I wouldn't want that."

With a wave, she went out the door and closed it behind her. Julie could faintly hear the sounds as she stepped back into her skis, and then silence returned.

"That was a whirlwind visit," Trace remarked presently.

"Just checking you out, I guess."

"So I'm okay because I don't believe in bigfoot?"

"Maybe so." Julie took a deep breath and exhaled

the tension. "I hope she gets home safely, but I'm glad she didn't stay. I don't want her exposed to this mess."

"Me, either. And so much for your idea that we'd hear the dogs barking before someone got here." His face had grown still, almost stony, and she could tell he was worrying about the problem again. Why wouldn't he? Someone had just shown up unannounced and silently. Crossing the room, she locked the door again and thought that a dead bolt was pretty flimsy security.

The nascent experience they had shared just before Ashley arrived had escaped them. The room was filled with a different kind of tension now. She wanted to resent it, but couldn't.

Maybe just as well, she decided. Yeah, she'd been reaching for an experience, something she often did because an adventurer existed somewhere inside her. But perhaps this time it would be better if she just left it alone. Maybe her own cabin fever had been pushing her as hard as her attraction to Trace.

However, it remained that the likelihood she'd meet another man who attracted her as much as he did was pretty slim, given where she lived. Unless "State" regularly started dumping agents in Conard County…well, it was enough to make her laugh at herself.

What did she feel drawn to, anyway? He was a good-looking man, but that had never been enough. The fact that he was in trouble? She should know better by now. That the danger excited her?

That wouldn't surprise her at all.

Chapter 8

The weatherman assured them on the increasingly poor TV signal that the storm was still worsening. Poor guy, Julie thought, watching him. Some of his cheer had vanished.

"This storm shouldn't be happening. Not to this degree or size. None of the usual signs we look for were there and we're reviewing our models to find out what happened. Regardless, now we're looking at another full day…"

She turned down the volume, letting him continue quietly in the background. Her phone rang and she reached for it, hardly surprised to find it was the teacher above her on the phone tree. "We're sending out emails, too," Lou Tolliver said, "but schools will be closed tomorrow. In case internet service to some of our outlying faculty is down, please make your calls."

"Sure thing, Lou. Weird or what?"

He laughed. "It's not often we close school. Or that we do it before the last minute. You watching the weather forecasts?"

"Who wouldn't be?"

"Yeah. I just hope the emails to parents get through. We need that automated phone system that would call every household."

"Good luck getting that in the budget."

"I know. Anyway, the notice will also be popping up on all available TV and radio stations soon. I just hope someone living in a cave doesn't drop their kid off at school tomorrow. Debbie Meacham and a couple of other teachers have volunteered to be there in case."

"I can't imagine anyone moving in this mess."

"I know. But you also know someone will. Anyway, Debbie and the others live right next to the school. They can get there safely."

After she hung up, she sighed, put her chin in her hand, and stared out the window. "People," she muttered.

"What's wrong?" Trace asked.

"Nothing yet. I have to make a couple of phone calls."

She flipped to the back of her assignment book and opened up the folded paper that held her section of the phone tree. A beeping sound drew her attention to the TV, and she saw the crawler begin announcing the school closings. The list seemed endless, and would probably go on for a long time since their cable provider covered a wide area. She tried to remember the last time this had happened. Well, she knew it had, but it had been a while.

Reaching for the phone again, she called the two

teachers below her on the tree and passed along the message, making sure they'd make their calls. If she'd missed either one, she had some of the names they were responsible for. As it happened, both said they'd reach out immediately.

"Snow day," she said, closing her lesson book and swiveling around.

"I'm kind of noticing," he remarked, indicating the TV.

"I didn't realize how late it's gotten. I need to find us something for dinner."

"Something simple? Can I help?"

"Let me check the pantry. Honestly, I'm in no mood to cook."

"Then don't," he said, rising. "How about sandwiches? You have some of that ham left?"

She had a ton, mainly because she'd bought a spiral ham and had her friends over to dinner a few weeks ago. The leftovers, of which there had been plenty, had been carefully frozen in packets about the size she'd want to use to make a sandwich or dinner for herself.

"Good idea. I'll pull some out of the freezer. The thing about dinner is that I need to think about it early in the day, when it is the last thing I want to think about."

He laughed.

"Well, it's true," she admitted. "Don't ask me about dinner at breakfast." She opened the freezer and looked in. "I also have some mac and cheese I could heat up."

"Sandwiches," he said firmly.

So she pulled out three packets of ham and started them running under cold water. "It shouldn't take long to thaw. How's your thinking coming?"

"My list of possible problems is shrinking. I'll check them out tomorrow."

"How can you do that, exactly?"

"By accessing some very classified files. Trust me. That's all you want to know."

"But…" She turned from the sink. "Does everything get recorded somewhere?"

"Oh, yeah. Butt-covering galore. Truth, even. Reports are made. And by compartmentalizing everything and putting it on a need-to-know basis, in theory nobody but the right people get to see anything they shouldn't. Assuming I haven't had all my clearances canceled, I should be able to see anything that happened on my watch as operations chief."

She chewed her lower lip. "But you don't want anyone to know you looked."

"The most important thing is that they not find out I looked from *here*." He smiled faintly. "There'll be audit trails and they'll find out I looked, but I know how to evade them for at least a while." He sat on a stool and leaned forward. "I need time, Julie. More than anything, I need some time. I have to have some idea which direction the threat will come from, and then some time to get ready. This snowstorm has been a blessing for me. I appear to have reached Denver. When I start looking into files in the morning, I'm going to appear to be somewhere beyond Denver. I think I mentioned that. Anyway, the longer I can postpone them backtracking me, the better a position I can get into."

"How will it help you to know who's after you?" She hated this whole situation, she realized. After diving in for the excitement and to protect Marisa, she had to face the fact that the tension wouldn't completely go away.

She couldn't hide from it, couldn't bury it, couldn't tell herself that nothing could happen until that storm settled down out there, not after Ashley's visit. Trace's life was at risk, and by extension her own. She couldn't just blow it off until the weather cleared.

"Because I'll have some idea of his capabilities. And that'll tell me how dangerous he could really be, and in what ways."

"So you deal with people like that?" Her stomach turned over a bit.

"When I have to, yes. In fact, some of them are the people we can least afford to ignore."

"But how will you know?" she asked, her heart aching for him. Her major concern here had become him, and what might happen to him. "Trace, how will you know?"

"Know what?"

"Who he is? What he can do? I mean…" She didn't know exactly what she meant. "Someone who can just come into this country and come after you? Someone who maybe has the backing of the…your agency? How can you be sure?"

"By what came before. By what kind of work he does for us. By how important he is to protect. It's got to be somebody who's been working for us for a long time, someone who's worth more than I am."

She hated that and felt a spark of anger. "Don't say that. You're worth as much as anyone else."

"Depends on what measuring stick you use," he said flatly. "It always has." Then he said, "Let's talk about something else."

"I'm having trouble thinking about anything else."

"I can tell." He rose and came around the bar to slip

his arm around her and give her a gentle squeeze. "I'm sorry I got you into this."

She shook her head. "I told you already, I got into this myself. Big adventure. Although it's not seeming as much like an adventure as a trip to the executioner now."

His gentle, one-armed hug was proving to be a distraction, though. It eased her apprehension and began to send her thoughts spiraling in another direction. Unfortunately, she figured it wasn't going to last long.

It didn't. After a moment he let go and put the bar between them again. A safe distance. He was quite good at creating those. She wondered if she should try to break through those barriers, then wondered if that would be the worst thing she could do. He had a lot to think about—his life was on the line—and now he was worrying about protecting her as well. Distraction might be welcome, but it also might be deadly.

There was, she realized, absolutely not one normal thing about this situation, not even making ham sandwiches. Tension infused every single moment and action. Walking a high wire must be like this, she thought. Like that guy who had crossed the Grand Canyon. One slip, one moment of inattention, one misjudgment…

In an instant she understood all the way to her bones just how unforgiving life could be. Trace sat there ruminating by the hour with few answers available to him, if any. Working a problem with dimensions he couldn't see. Yet he had to be aware with every breath that making a mistake could cost him everything.

"How do you handle it?" she asked abruptly as she put the sandwiches on plates and moved them to the bar.

"Handle what?"

"This constant tension. This constant thinking about a problem with so little information."

One corner of his mouth lifted, and his gaze gentled. "I'm sorry it's so hard on you."

"I'm not looking for sympathy. I'm asking how you do it. This can't be the first time you've been faced with a box you know nothing about."

"No, it's not."

"Well, you're sitting there ruminating. I can barely imagine the kinds of things that must be running through your head, and you have no one to talk to. You can't even brainstorm. You must feel very alone."

"I'm used to it."

He was used to it. A very sad answer. Coming around the bar, she sat beside him and reached for a piece of her sandwich. She felt helpless, but she supposed that wasn't true. She *had* given him a place to stay where he wouldn't inadvertently endanger Marisa and her baby or Ryker. That was important, and that's why she'd done it.

But right now she needed to do more. She hated being passive, and not knowing when or how she might have to react. That just didn't suit her at all.

"The waiting game can be hard," he said after he ate a couple of bites of sandwich. "I'm used to it. Sometimes I had to wait months, or even years to see if an asset would yield any fruit. After a while, you get used to the fact that there are no quick answers to most things. That everything comes in its own time. That events have to coalesce in a certain way, that everything has to come together to get a result. It's not a job for the impatient."

"I guess not. Am I being too impatient?"

"From whose perspective?" He turned his head and

smiled at her. "I told you this storm has been a blessing for me. They have no idea where I am right now. They last pinged me in or near Denver. They've probably heard by now that I wrecked my car, and from the way your sheriff set things up, they assume I hitched a ride into Denver just ahead of this storm. If I'm still in that area, I'm pretty well nailed down. Right now they're probably waiting for some action on my bank account or credit card, or for me to pop up looking for financing for a new car. When the storm blows out, I'll get maybe a day before they get uneasy. My guess is that first they'll check hospitals to see if I'm laid up from the accident. Once they clear that…well, then they have to decide in what direction to look. That's going to take time, Julie."

"I get it. And that's good, right? But how much good? Are you getting anywhere thinking about this? Why don't you just go on my computer now and do your magic?"

"Because I'll leave an audit trail. No way to avoid it. It won't trace back to here, I'll make sure of it. But sooner, rather than later, someone's going to note that I've accessed certain files. At that point they'll pretty much guess I'm onto them. I'm in no rush to pass them that message."

She sank into thought as she ate, considering all that he'd just shared. So while he hadn't mentioned it earlier, had even made it seem like it wouldn't be dangerous at all, because he could conceal where he was when he entered those files…it would send a message. Why? Well, she didn't need him to explain it to her. Hell, no. Once he started snooping around, they'd know he no longer believed they merely suspected that someone was after him, and no longer believed they were trying to protect him.

She couldn't eat any more. She pushed her plate aside. "If you're still hungry, eat my other half. How long will it take them to figure out you've accessed those files?"

"Depends on whether they're looking for me to turn up. If I've been flagged, it won't take long at all."

Well, she could certainly understand why he was taking all this time to think. Once he had to go after hard information, he might as well call them on the phone.

"This stinks," she announced.

"No kidding."

She sighed and went to make more coffee. The guy drank it as if his life depended on it, and right now she could use a cup, even if it interfered with her sleep tonight.

"Are you getting anywhere at all?" she asked after she started the machine, then caught herself. "I'm sorry. I must sound like a nag." She changed the pitch of her voice to complaining. "What are you thinking? What are you going to do? Why is this so difficult?" Then she let her voice return to normal. "Yeah, a nag. Or maybe a whiner."

"Neither one," he answered promptly as she returned to her seat beside him. "The thing is, I could feel every bit as frustrated as you, but it would get in the way. Like I said, right now is not the time to let anger take over. I need a clear head."

"And I'm not helping. I should just get a book out to read."

"No, you're fine." He once again surprised her by slipping his arm around her waist, this time his right one. His glove was back in place, and she sat looking down at it. She guessed he felt more comfortable with it on, even though she'd already seen his hand.

Then, again to her disappointment, he let go of her and rose, carrying his plate to the sink. She watched as he pulled down two fresh mugs, one after the other, and filled them with coffee. He gave her one and put the other in front of his seat.

"I'm going to take a pain pill," he said. "Just one. Thanks for making the coffee."

The pain, of course. How could she have forgotten that he was suffering so much? Because he didn't mention it, of course. He didn't wander around this place groaning and grimacing.

He pulled a bottle out of his breast pocket. Without asking, she took it from him and opened it, tipping one out. "Just one? This must be one of the things that isn't easy with a single hand."

"At least they didn't give me childproof caps. I can use my teeth if necessary."

"Does that happen often?"

"Not usually." He swallowed the pill with some of the water left from dinner, then held up his damaged hand. "I can't close it completely yet. No fine motor coordination at all. But for opening a pill bottle? Adequate. It'll even shift a car."

"Uncomfortable?"

"Very."

She put her chin in her hand and simply gazed at him. While he didn't say a whole lot, what little she had seen and learned about him suggested that he was a remarkable man in many ways. An extraordinary amount of patience, an endurance that she thought might be almost superhuman. Yeah, he took a half dose of meds from time to time, but she suspected his description of the pain wasn't hyperbole. He didn't at all seem like a man prone to exaggeration.

"What?" he asked finally as if her unwavering stare bothered him.

"I'm staring," she said without removing her gaze.

"Yup."

"Sorry. I like looking at you."

"Me?" That seemed to astonish him.

"You," she said. "I realize you're probably used to passing unnoticed. You have that kind of appearance. How many times have you been mistaken for someone's long-lost friend or relative?"

His eyes danced just a little. "Occasionally."

"I bet. You have one of those faces. Must be very useful to you. But…as far as I'm concerned, you don't blend into the woodwork at all. You're very attractive. But I think I let you know that."

At that his lips quivered as if he were trying hard not to smile. "Just a bit."

"I am not," she said deliberately, "a desperate spinster."

At that his eyes widened and the laugh escaped him. "Not a chance," he retorted. "I'm just surprised you're not married to the handsomest guy around here, trailing a kid or two on your apron strings."

She waved her free hand, her chin still propped on the other. "I'm a little pickier than that. My taste for adventure gets in the way. I may settle down someday, but it's not going to be with anyone ordinary."

"So it has to be someone willing to jaunt around the world with you?"

"At the least. Or willing to go hiking off-trail in the deep woods. I'm not looking for someone extraordinary, just someone with a few surprises and a taste for trying new things."

He didn't answer, but now his gaze seemed locked with hers. Then, almost as if he needed to put the space back, he said, "Ashley's arrival was a little worrisome."

Well, heck, she thought. He'd done it again. "Yeah," she agreed. "The fact that she got here without warning. Could your guy do that?"

"Depends."

"Everything depends." Giving up, she rose and carried her own plate to the sink. At least cleaning up gave her something to do. It wasn't enough, but it was all she had right now.

"Julie?"

She had bent to put the plates in the dishwasher. "Yeah?"

"I'm sorry."

That brought her upright. "For what?" she asked, facing him.

"That I'm not your extraordinary-ordinary guy."

With her hip, she closed the dishwasher. "I don't remember asking you to be. You ever heard of this thing called dating, Trace?"

He nodded, looking wary.

"Dating is the process whereby people try each other on. You know, like shoes or a pair of pants that catches your eye. How can you be sure one way or the other if you don't slip them on?"

Smiling, she sashayed into the living room and sat on the couch. She'd had the pleasure of taking the spy by surprise again.

* * *

Trace remained at the bar, staring into the now-dark kitchen. When all this had blown up on Friday morning, he'd had one singular problem: an assassin on his tail. Now he had two problems, one of them a sassy school-teacher who was gorgeous beyond words and seemed intent on "trying him on."

He couldn't understand that at all. Was she getting high on the danger of the situation? Because there was certainly nothing about him that demanded this kind of attention. As far as he could tell, he was trouble of the worst kind, and crippled besides. What could any woman see in that? Even for a fling?

His mind had run the race circuit of possibilities so many times he was sure there was a groove in the track. Not good. If he got locked in, he could miss something. Already he was planning tomorrow's attempt on the files he needed, figuring out various ways to give himself permissions. He'd had to do that over the years when he'd required information they seemed reluctant to give him. He operated a lot in a relative vacuum, which sometimes had to be pierced for his safety and the safety of those who worked for him.

How else could he discover if someone might be a double agent? How else could he gather background information on an asset that might already be in the files?

Which brought him back to his racetrack. Sighing, he turned on the stool and looked at Julie. She seemed pleased with herself, as if she knew she had rattled him.

Well, she had. He had absolutely no idea what to do in a situation like this. She was interested. So was he. And if he were just any other guy, there'd be no question. But he was a guy with death stalking him.

Somehow he suspected that reminding her of that wasn't going to have an impact. It's not as if she didn't already know. But every time he tried to place a safe distance between them, she punctured it. Apparently she didn't like vacuums any more than he did.

"How's your hand?" she asked.

"Hurting. One pill reduces it to a tolerable level."

"That really stinks," she said bluntly. "I find it hard to believe they can't do any more for you than that."

"Well, they could amputate it."

Now he had the dubious pleasure of knocking her off balance the way she kept doing to him. He waited, wondering how she'd react.

Her response was subdued. "They suggested that?"

"It's still on the table if the pain doesn't subside. I can't go through the rest of my life half doped."

"If you have a life," she retorted.

God, he loved her fire. Everything about Julie was up-front and bold. "I'm going to have a life if I have to rip it out of this tiger."

Her eyebrows lifted. "Murder?"

"Self-defense. Does that shock you?"

She shook her head. "Actually, no. It's the only response when someone wants to kill you. Unless you can take them down another way."

"Well, I hope I can."

"With one arm?"

"It may not be able to grip small things, that hand, but it can still do a lot of damage." He flexed it, feeling a sharp new wave of fiery pain, but the pill caused it to subside quickly.

"You're not afraid of pain, are you?" she said.

"No. I'm not. I'm not crazy—I don't like it, but sometimes you just have to deal with it. Fearing it only makes it worse."

She tucked her legs under her and folded her arms. "There are probably a lot of things in life you could say that about. Fear is a prison."

"It's also good protection."

She tilted her head, studying him again. "I won't say that's not true. Fear's a good warning. A heightened response to a threat. But it can also paralyze you." Then she said, "I was afraid to open the door earlier when Ashley came over. I was so relieved when I caught sight of her hair. I'm not sure I could have opened it if I hadn't seen that."

He was surprised by her admission. "I think you would have."

Her smile was crooked. "So sure?"

"You took me and all my troubles on to protect a friend. If you thought it would protect me in some way, you'd have opened the door. Yeah, I'm sure."

She'd drawn the curtains on the living room window, but they barely muffled the sounds of the raging storm. The TV, on low volume, occasionally offered static along with the voice of a weatherman who was beginning to sound less excited and a whole lot more exhausted.

Trace indicated the TV with a jerk of his chin. "That guy local?"

"Pretty much. I only subscribe to what would be called local channels. Basic service. Why?"

"Just wondering. He doesn't seem to have anyone to spell him."

"I could change to a different station."

"For what? More of the same?" He shook his head

and stood. "Do you mind if I use your computer? I want to make sure I can still access my VPN." Just an excuse to do something rather than think about problems that had no solutions, like a killer. Like Julie. Of course he'd be able to access his VPN. But maybe he could use it as a diversion, explain it better to Julie.

"That's the program that will make it look like you're logging in from somewhere else? Be my guest."

Hers was a standard desktop, a couple of years old. He sat in her chair to face it, aware that she had moved to the nearer end of the couch. "No laptop?" he asked.

"On my salary? One computer is enough. If I need a laptop for some project, I can borrow one from the school, but I stopped buying them. More expensive and less durable. Why? Do you need one?"

"No. I just wondered. I thought everyone was on laptops and tablets these days." With a touch of a button he booted up the system.

"I'm a holdout, I guess. Even my kindergartners know their way around a tablet. Next year, a lot of them will be using them some of the time in class."

He glanced at her as he waited for the boot-up to complete. "So you're a back-to-the-basics sort of teacher?"

"That depends. But it seems to me that you ought to be able to write and do simple arithmetic before you turn it over to a machine."

"I agree. So what kind of internet service do you have?"

"Broadband, believe it or not. The county and city had to fight with the provider, but we've finally climbed out of the Dark Ages. Of course, taxpayer money helped pay for some of the improvements."

"Of course. Hey, here's an interesting tidbit if you don't already know it. Landlines, like your old phone here? They never got built in most of Africa. Too expensive. So in a very short space of time, they went from having to hike ten or twenty miles to talk to a relative to being able to do everything on a smartphone. Cell towers got built instead of phone lines. As for electricity…there are places where one house will have a generator and people will stand in line to charge their cell phones. It's their window on the world and it's speeding up development."

Her eyes brightened. "I think that's a story my students would love to hear."

"I still get a charge out of it." He turned his attention to her computer again and checked her upload and download speeds. Even in this storm they were adequate for his purposes. But when he tried to log in to his VPN account, he cussed.

"What?" she asked.

"They canceled my VPN account," he said. He closed down the browser immediately, wiping the screen of the "invalid login" message. What if they had been waiting for him to log in? "Hell."

He hit the button, shutting down her computer instantly. "If I just broke your computer, I'll replace it." Eventually. If he lived long enough.

"Trace? Would they know where you tried to log in from?"

"I don't think I was there long enough for a trap to work. Anyway, this VPN provider doesn't record that info. They don't record *anything*. Damn! I wonder if my timeline just got shortened."

He stared at her blank monitor, trying to get handle

on this. He hadn't shared his VPN information with anyone. In theory, the agency didn't even know he had it. In theory. It might just be a mess-up because of the storm, but he couldn't afford to take the chance. On the other hand, part of the VPN security he'd purchased was a guarantee that they wouldn't record the ISP he used to enter their tunnel. He'd made sure of that, and given the business the VPN company was in, and given he'd chosen one based in another country, there was little likelihood his account could have been diddled with in some way, other than to shut it down.

He blew a long breath. No, probably no information had been recorded.

"What now?" Julie asked.

He glanced at her and didn't like the pinching around her eyes. He'd like to erase that tension for her. "I've got to get a new account."

"But you can't use your cards."

"No."

"Well, then, use mine." Without another word she popped up. She retrieved her wallet from a backpack beside the door. "I've got plenty of plastic. Let's go."

But still he hesitated, thinking it all through again. Somehow they had learned about his VPN account. That wasn't necessarily good. All the agency's communications ran on its own VPN on secure government servers, but the fact that they'd figured out he had his own on a different service meant someone was too damn interested in him. He used his credit cards mainly to pay necessary bills when he was out of country, like the storage room he maintained for his few odds and ends, and his car payment. And the annual charge on his VPN.

So someone had been delving into his background, which left him all but certain he was more than a blood offering. Somebody else, someone in the agency, wanted to settle some kind of score with him. Or maybe they had just been looking for some vulnerability to pass along to the guy who was after him.

The picture, far from getting clearer, seemed to be getting cloudier. He sat there blindly staring at the computer, and now a gold credit card sat beside the keyboard. He needed to be sure he wouldn't put Julie at more risk.

"Trace? What's worrying you?"

"I must have really messed in someone's corn flakes."

"Meaning?"

"It's one thing to keep an eye on my whereabouts so a guy with a grudge can find me. It's another to be going into my credit card files, which they would have had to do to find my VPN company. And to shut me down, they'd have had to reverse the charge on my credit card. I think it paid automatically two months ago. But I can't go and check what happened."

He swiveled the chair slowly, noting that tension seemed to be ratcheting up the pain in his arm. He flexed his damaged fingers and everything screamed. This time the discomfort had a salutary effect, focusing him, demanding he pay close attention. He started speaking aloud, no longer caring whether any of this might violate anyone's security. He was past that point now. They had violated *him*.

"Assuming that wasn't just some glitch because of this storm," he said slowly, "then they must have known I had my own VPN. Either that or they discovered it by looking through my credit card statements. Now why the hell would they do that? To check where I am now? Maybe. But to look at past statements?"

She nodded. "Something else is going on." Once again she wrapped her arms tightly around herself, a self-protective gesture that made him ache. He felt like a devil for bringing this all into her life, but now he had to just deal with it all, including what he might have done to Julie.

"So it seems." Turning, he reached for her phone and passed it to her. "Ryker?"

She nodded and dialed. Soon she spoke. "That doesn't sound good," she said. "Baby still cranky? I'm passing you to my friend." She handed the receiver to Trace.

"Hey, man," he said. "We may have something else going on here. You got some time? Okay, thanks." He turned and hung the phone up. "He'll be over in about an hour."

"Poor Marisa," Julie remarked. "A cranky baby and a husband who keeps running out."

Trace didn't answer. He sat staring blankly at the room, wondering if he should just walk out of here now, steal a car and get as far away as he could.

Because hell had just taken on a new dimension.

Chapter 9

Julie checked the coffee and was startled to see how much of it Trace had drunk. It was as if it was his fuel, and he'd said something about how it kept his head clearer when he took his pain meds. He was probably wishing now he hadn't taken even that half dose earlier.

Pulling a tube of cinnamon buns out of her freezer, she separated them and arranged them in a cake pan while the oven preheated. She suspected this night was going to require another kind of fuel as well.

She had no real idea why he was so disturbed, and hoped that when Ryker arrived she'd learn more. She was getting awfully tired of wondering what he knew, what he didn't know, and what he hoped to do about any of this.

Getting information from agency files could help, but it could also be very dangerous to him. She got that part. And she certainly didn't want a hack of government files being traced back to her, regardless of what might happen.

She chewed her lip as she made another pot of coffee, baked the sweet rolls, and wished she had something to compare all this to so she could evaluate it. Offering Trace a place to stay had been an obvious, instinctive thing: it would protect Marisa. The things that had been happening since were neither instinctive nor intuitive.

Crap, she was just a small-town kindergarten teacher. What she knew about Trace's business came from books and movies, and she was swiftly discovering they were a poor measure of reality. All those fancy tools of the trade, if they even existed, had come down to her computer and a hardwired telephone. Not cool.

She was quite sure his bosses had considerably more at their disposal, and she hated them for turning it all on him. One man. One maimed man who had served them well for quite a long time. How dare they?

All along she'd been uneasy about his situation, worried for him, for herself, even for Marisa and her family. But now she was getting truly angry. She stood in the kitchen while the coffee brewed, watching Trace pace. He'd put the sling on again, perhaps seeking some relief, but it was clear he couldn't hold still and clear he was impatient for Ryker's arrival. This whole holding pattern was starting to wear thin, yet at least a couple more days of it remained.

He was working pieces of a puzzle. Like one of those really complex puzzles with 1,500 pieces and no picture on the box to even guide him. All he had was a vague idea, an outline. What if it turned out that the guy they'd set loose on him had no connection with his past? What if it was somebody who worked for the agency as well? What if it was one of his colleagues?

He certainly must be wondering those things now. She'd seen how fast he'd moved to back out of that log-in page and shut down her computer. He hadn't even turned it on again. Useless for the moment, it sat on her desk and the credit card remained beside the keyboard.

Stalled again. Neither of them liked it, but she suspected he liked it even less than she did, and her stomach was already churning with acid. If she had any more coffee, she'd have to lace it heavily with cream. It felt as though she was working on an ulcer.

Finally there was a single sharp rap on the door. She glanced at Trace, then went to peer out the peephole. Ryker stood in plain view.

"Ryker," she said as she worked the lock.

When he entered, a whirlwind of stinging snow and cold entered with him. She closed the door swiftly, locking out the night once again, then waited while he removed his jacket and gloves.

"It really sucks to be out tonight," he remarked.

"Something to drink?" she offered.

"Coffee. I'm gonna need it."

Trace had stopped pacing, standing in the middle of the living room near her desk. "We got problems."

"So I heard. I checked in with Bill before I came over. A certain level of tension is growing with some folks at the agency, but he can't localize it. So someone sure as hell is worried about what you're up to."

More acid flooded Julie's stomach with fire, and she wondered if she should just drink cream without coffee.

"Bill doesn't know I'm here?"

"No. He may guess, but he doesn't know."

Trace nodded. When Julie handed him his coffee, he sat at her desk. She perched on the edge of the couch, folding her hands tightly, and waited. Ryker finally settled on one of the armchairs.

"What lit your fuse?" he asked Trace.

"I tried to log in to my VPN. My account's been locked or closed. I may have damaged Julie's computer by shutting it down so quickly."

"I doubt it. They recover," Ryker answered. "So what are you wondering?"

"They shouldn't have been able to scoop up Julie's IP address, given that my VPN provider doesn't record those, but…it still makes me reluctant to try again, even with a new account. And it makes me wonder what's really going on here. "

Ryker nodded, obviously thinking about it. "I doubt they'd go to all the trouble to try to scoop an IP address from a log-in. Anybody could attempt to log in by accident. Where's your VPN service located?"

"Germany."

"Good luck to them, then. Germany isn't too eager to help us out with things like this. My guess is they just wanted to shut your tunnel down so if you try to get into files, you'll have to do it from their network."

"Well, I'll have to do that anyway. I just don't want them to know where I am, and I don't want them to follow it back to Julie most of all."

"Easy." Ryker frowned into his coffee mug. "They expect you to open a new account. Your credit cards and bank accounts are probably flagged. They'll know within minutes if you spend money."

"He can use my credit card," Julie said. "I can open

an account in my name. If he gets into files from that account, they won't be able to tell anything, will they?"

Trace smiled faintly at her. "That's the whole idea of VPN."

"Then let's just do it."

"No," Trace said quietly. "There's something else going on here. Something beyond just hanging me out to dry. This is way too much effort to just allow one assassin to ease me into the next world. There's a cover-up much bigger than me."

Ryker blew a long breath. "It's beginning to look like it. So what was the screwup they're trying to hide? Does this tiger even realize he's being used? Because I'm beginning to think he is."

"They're trying to end something by ending me," Trace said. "Damned if I know what it might be. I'm not aware that I screwed up, so somebody else must have, and I'm the goat."

Blood sacrifice. The term drifted across Julie's mind once again. Unable to hold still, needing something to quiet her stomach, she headed for the kitchen and got a bottle of liquid antacid. She didn't even bother measuring it with a spoon, but instead took a long swig. "Lovely," she said as she screwed the cap back on and wiped her mouth with a napkin. "Just lovely."

Both men twisted to look at her.

"Well, it is, isn't it? What you're suggesting here is that Trace's being offered up to cover up the misdeed of someone else. Probably someone else higher on the food chain. That's ugly, but it's also frightening, because how the hell is he supposed to discover who's behind it? If you catch the hunter who is after him now, then what? Another move to accomplish the same end?"

"No," said Trace. "No. They can't pull this again, and I don't know about Ryker but I intend to use this as a way to clean things up afterward."

"I'm with you on that," said Ryker. "Okay, I got an idea. Let me at the computer."

"Why?" asked Trace, standing.

"Because I have a personal VPN myself. Let's see if we can reach it. If we can't…"

"Then we have an idea if our suspicions are right," Trace finished. "No reason they should interfere with you."

"None at all. Unless they know more than we think they do."

Julie was ready to bite her nails. None of this sounded good; all of it sounded very dangerous, and it was happening in her living room. Maybe she should head for Denver as soon as the snow lifted and take a sabbatical in the Bahamas. Except she couldn't just leave her job and her students. She could almost feel the net tightening until it might strangle her.

But the truth was, she wasn't a runner by nature. All her life she'd planted her feet firmly and faced whatever came. If she ran now, she'd never forgive herself.

"My service runs out of Serbia," Ryker remarked. The reboot took longer than usual because the blue screen appeared to tell them the last exit hadn't been normal. Julie feared they were about to have another one of those.

What would it mean if Ryker found his VPN shut down as well? Or if he didn't? The two of them seemed to think this was important information.

Ryker finally tapped an address into her browser.

"I'm using a proxy server this time. No one will know this came from the same IP you used, Trace."

Then a log-in screen appeared, and he quickly typed the information. Faster than Trace had working with one hand and one finger.

Login invalid. Please retry. An instant later, her computer underwent another hard shutdown.

Nobody said anything, then Ryker reached for her phone and dialed. "Marisa, honey? I'm going to be later than I expected. Are you and Jonni okay? I love you, too. Of course I'll wake you when I get home."

He hung up the phone and swiveled the chair to face the two of them. "It's bad," he said calmly.

Julie soon started another pot of coffee just for something to do and stood in the kitchen while two men paced her small living room, filling it to overflowing. Occasionally they tossed out a word or two, and the other one would grunt an acknowledgment. She couldn't imagine what they were thinking, but they seemed to be on the same wavelength, whatever it was.

Finally it burst out of her. "Can one of you please tell me what you think is going on?"

Trace kept moving, but this time he came around the bar and slipped his good arm around her. "You've earned your spurs," he said and looked at Ryker, who nodded. "Julie? Do you think you can sit? Three of us pacing over there would create a traffic jam."

She heard him trying to be light about all of this, but she couldn't even summon the faintest of smiles. "Yes," she said finally. She went to the couch and sat at one end. To her surprise, Trace sat right beside her and draped his arm over her shoulders, tucking her to his side.

"You or me?" he said to Ryker.

"You go for it. If I hear any gaps, I'll jump in."

"Okay." He squeezed Julie gently. "What we're thinking is really quite simple. We assumed from the outset that some asset wanted to get to me because he'd been burned somehow. Probably by one of the operatives working under me, but he wasn't content to stop there."

She nodded. "I got that part."

"Well, to judge by this, there's more going on. Our guess is that an asset was burned all right, but not by someone lower on the chain. Someone higher. Someone whose career and maybe life could be on the line if it gets traced to him. So he, and maybe a friend or two, are trying to cover his sorry mess by making me the scapegoat. Once I'm dead, the asset is happy and that's the end of the story."

She looked at him, her insides feeling hollow. "But why *you*?"

"Because I'm disabled now. Nothing gets broken if I die. But I was evidently working in the right area of the world to be blamed for having said or done something I shouldn't. And they've got a red-hot asset who's too important to lose, so…"

"You're the blood offering."

"Exactly."

She nodded, understanding it and hating it. "But what about Ryker? Why should he be involved, too?"

"Because," said Ryker, "they're not entirely sure I didn't help Trace in some way. Or that I might not be able to figure all this out and bring down someone in the process. He came to me. Of course they'd distrust me, no matter how many times I said I sent him on his way. But in my case it's just distrust. They don't want to drag me into this mess. There's not much cover when a retired agent gets killed, especially one who's been making a lot of local contacts and friends. I'm a big mess they don't need on top of their current one."

"But I'm no mess at all," Trace said. "When I'm gone, I don't even have any family to raise a ruckus. You could say I'm erasable."

"Quit talking that way," Julie snapped. "You're not erasable. You're not expendable. You're a human being. I don't care how many cost-benefit analyses tell them they can do without you, it's all a lie. Don't buy it, Trace. Please don't buy into their calculus."

"Their calculus," Ryker remarked, "is even simpler— Trace's life or their own."

She shuddered, whether with anger or revulsion she couldn't tell. She turned her face toward Trace. "Just tell me you're done with this. That you'll never go back to this. It's soul-killing."

He nodded, but didn't answer directly. "You know, Ryker, when they killed your VPN, they made a big mistake."

"I know."

"How?" Julie demanded.

Trace's gaze settled on her. "They may have just been trying to keep Ryker out of the way. Sidelining him briefly in case he should try to get information for me. But what they did instead was announce themselves."

"How?" Julie repeated. "You don't have their names!"

"But now we know they exist, and we've guessed why. I'm no longer looking at this as a mistake I must have made with an important asset. Now I'm wondering who *actually* made the mistake and hung me out here to cover his own butt. That guy is on only one mission—to save himself. We're going to take him down."

Julie leaned into him even more closely and rested her arm across his waist. "How can you be so sure, Trace?"

"Because I've had to do harder things than this. Intentionally or not, this guy has left a trail. He started laying it when he checked my credit card statements, when he canceled both our VPN accounts."

"Exactly," Ryker agreed. "And I'd be willing to bet he's a political appointee or someone else who's never worked a day in the field. He's sloppy."

Sloppy sounded good to Julie. She also noticed that for the very first time Trace wasn't trying to place a distance between them. Maybe he felt protected from her by Ryker's presence. Under any other circumstances, she might have been amused.

"Okay, so let me see if I'm understanding this," she said. "You think some guy higher up in the agency burned an essential asset. Revealed something he shouldn't have revealed. And now there's a very angry, very important asset who wants some revenge. Rather than facing the music himself, this guy picked Trace because he's disabled and nothing else will get disturbed if something happens to him, and under the circumstances it was possible to get Trace as far away from wherever this higher-up is as possible?"

"That about sums it up," Trace said, giving her a squeeze. "If anything happens to me, it'll be blamed on something that has nothing to do with the agency. I'm on pain meds and far enough away that I could get myself into all kinds of trouble, like a car accident. An overdose. I'm not at my best right now. Plus I don't know the lay of the land out here. My ducks, instead of being in a row under my control, are scattered all over the place and very much not under my control."

She nodded, but inside a full head of steamy anger was building. They'd picked Trace because he'd been in the right general vicinity when the bad stuff happened, and now, being disabled…well, it all fit the way he said it had.

Trace and Ryker were no longer the only ones who wanted to get this scum. "I will never understand people who can do things like this."

"I hope you never will," Trace said quietly. He ran his hand along her arm. "Okay, we need some kind of operational plan. I think the first thing is to find out who could be so freaking important in Eastern Europe that someone's willing to cooperate in letting him kill me, so important that someone's afraid for his own butt if he gets revealed."

"There couldn't be very many of them," Ryker answered. "Yeah, we protect our assets, but to this degree? This is someone special. It shouldn't be hard to suss out a few of them, the ones we can't afford to lose."

"That's my thinking. So tomorrow we build a new tunnel and get inside."

Julie had an idea and wondered if she should mention it. Then she decided to go ahead with it because she couldn't possibly be any more in the woods than she was now, and both these men knew she had no experience. "I suggest," she said, "that we sign me up for VPN right now. Through that proxy thingy Ryker used earlier. If the account doesn't get closed overnight, we'll know something."

Trace looked at her. "That's an excellent idea. And if it disappears, we'll also have an idea how closely this guy is sitting on us."

"Or maybe," Ryker said, "we should just tunnel in right now. We're still protected by the storm for another day."

Trace lowered his head, thinking about it. Absently he continued to stroke Julie's arm. Contradictory waves of pleasure and apprehension ran through her. She didn't want to leave Trace's embrace, but she wondered how much longer she could hold still.

"First," he said, "we should look at links, at the tree. Not even try to access files. Just see who's connected to whom. The chain. Then we look for where the ends of the chains are."

"Maybe I could have more than one VPN account," Julie offered. "On different services. Then we could come at it from different angles, yes?"

Trace turned his head, and the smile he gave her nearly took her breath away. "She's good at this, Ryker."

"Yeah, it's scaring me. God knows what she'll teach Marisa."

The bubble of tension popped briefly, and Julie was able to smile. Just a kindergarten teacher? Hah. How about a woman with a brain? Yeah.

Trace glanced at his watch, a basic affair that wouldn't catch anyone's eye. "We're seven or eight hours behind Germany and Serbia right now. Give it another hour or so for the world to start waking up over there, so our internet traffic gets lost in the flood as people start their days. Then we'll set up one service."

"Only one?" Julie asked. She'd liked her idea of two.

"Only one, at first. Then we'll see if anything happens if you try to set up another one."

Her heart lurched. "You want to make sure they aren't watching me, too."

"I'm sorry," he said quietly. "But yes. If you set up a VPN and then another couple of hours later set up another without any problem, we'll know they haven't homed in on you."

It made sense. It also made her queasy again. Where was that backbone she was so proud of? Of course, never before had lives been hanging in the balance. Never before had death been peeking over her shoulder.

"Okay," she said. "I've got some cinnamon rolls I baked before Ryker arrived. Anyone hungry?"

They were. She wasn't.

A pan of cinnamon rolls and two bowls of microwave popcorn later, it was finally time. During the hour or so, they'd chatted casually about Ryker's baby, about her school and teaching. Oh so casual, Julie thought, when she could tell both men's minds were multitasking and thinking about the problem they faced. Ryker said only one thing of true significance.

"Don't go sniffing around anything to do with Johnny Hayes."

Trace's eyes narrowed, and Julie felt her heart skip a couple of beats. Marisa's late husband?

"Why not?" Trace asked.

"Because Bill warned me that I made them nervous as a cat on a hot stove when I tried to get past the wall. They stuck to the official story, and finally I let it go. If there was anything hinky about it, you can be sure it's been buried even deeper. Don't waste your time. You won't have much of it."

Trace turned to Julie. "Once I start snooping, there's a possibility that security will shut me down fast. Every second is going to count."

She nodded, wondering why her mouth was so dry. "It's okay. Some things are better left alone."

"No kidding," said Ryker drily. "Anyway, it won't be safe for any of us if we snoop in that area. I rang all those alarms before. That alone could get them to hook me to you."

And if they hooked Ryker to Trace, they could connect Marisa with all of this. Julie was prepared to walk over hot coals to prevent that. She stood. "Let me do the typing. I'm faster than either of you. Just write down any web addresses you want me to access, then tell me what to do."

She sat at her computer and rebooted it, navigating through the blue screen that warned her the machine hadn't shut down normally before. No kidding, she thought sourly. And it might not do so again.

Trace handed her a slip of paper on which he'd written some web addresses. As her computer rebooted, she scanned them.

"That first one is a high-anonymity proxy server," he said. "It's the first layer of protection and it changes your IP address. It won't, however, encrypt anything. That way, when you go from there, no one can trace back to you unless they're really looking. The next two are the VPN providers, which give a much higher level of security and encrypt all information. Just use one of them on this trip. You'll have to download software, though."

"If I'm spending money," she said, "I'm glad to know I'll get a download for it."

Trace laughed quietly and laid his hand on her shoulder, causing her to feel a pleasurable shock. "I'll pay you back as soon as I can."

"Do I look worried? I was just being sarcastic." She turned her head until she could meet his gaze. "I'm also nervous. Don't mind me. I pop off at the mouth a lot when I'm uneasy."

"Pop away."

She called up her web browser. Then she typed in the proxy address and a second later she was at a screen asking her the URL of the site she wanted to go to. "Any preference, guys?"

"Either one."

A few moments later, she said, "Um, fellas? I don't read whatever language this is." The site clearly wanted information from her, but it wasn't asking in English.

Trace leaned closer and pointed. "Click on this for a thirty-day subscription. Then, down here, type in your credit card information."

Well, that was easy enough. So was downloading the software. As soon as it was installed, Trace showed her how to use it. "Pick a country."

"Any country?"

He laughed again. "Where do you want to be coming from?"

"Any place I can read."

That caused both men to laugh. "You don't have to go anywhere at all," Trace said. "Right now we're just going to make sure they don't shut you down, remember?"

"Right." She'd forgotten that part. "Should I wait to do the other one? You said an hour, right?"

Trace hesitated. "Part of me thinks you should be perfectly safe. You're behind a proxy server. You went to a VPN company that won't record any information about you except the card to bill. The only thing that could flag you is that you'll have an international charge on your credit card, and those take days to show up."

She bit her lip. "Trace, I only have international charges when I'm traveling. Is that enough to be suspicious?"

"Your credit card company might call you to see if you authorized the charge, but it's so small they probably won't."

"I've never had to be this suspicious before," she admitted. "It feels weird." Especially the butterflies in her stomach that now refused to settle at all.

"I'm so sorry," he said quietly. "I never meant to bring this stuff into anyone else's life."

She shook her head quickly. "I seem to remember volunteering. It just feels weird. I mean…my apartment is now spy central!"

Then without another word she faced her computer, selected the United States and chose the city of San Francisco. "Okay, I'm signing up for the other one. I'm behind this wall, right? Then nobody should catch it because nobody's watching my credit card, right? In fact," she continued, pushing back from the desk, "I'm going to get my other credit card. Then nobody at all will flag me for having purchased a duplicate service."

"God," said Trace as she went to get her wallet.

"What?" she asked.

"I'm changing you."

She put on a smile. "Only temporarily." But she didn't fail to notice the way he continued to frown at her, as if he was disturbed.

Well, this whole thing was disturbing. Stuff like this didn't happen in her life. Even with all her adventures, she'd never felt like this before. But even as she was evaluating the way all this was affecting her, she had to face the fact that it was Trace's way of life. What changes had it wrought in him over so many years?

From missionaries' son to spy? The transition was almost breathtaking in its scope.

She experienced no problem in purchasing the second service. The software download and installation went smoothly.

"Now hit the kill button." He pointed.

"Why?" she asked even as she did it.

"It's going to take you off the internet until we tell it otherwise."

She swiveled around and looked at the two men. "Okay. I guess we wait and see if both my accounts remain active."

"That's it for now," Ryker said, rising. "Can I use your phone? I need to call my ride."

Fifteen minutes later, he stepped out her door, leaving her and Trace alone.

Far away, the clerk couldn't sleep. Rising finally, he decided to take his husky for a walk to the all-night coffee shop that allowed dogs inside, and get one of their creamy hot chocolates to bring home with him.

He didn't like that general, and he didn't like the way he was being put in the middle of something that he sensed could turn into a very big bomb. Even his imme-diate superior didn't seem to know what was going on.

And while secrecy was part of life in the agency, this time it felt wrong to him. Very wrong. As if with just one piece of information the entire picture would change.

His dog, Chinook, was delighted by the unexpected late-night walk along quiet streets. Everything must smell different to him, the clerk thought. Scents must be clearer, less muddied. The husky pranced with a grace-ful stride and paused often to sniff at shrubs that poked out between the iron bars of fences that enclosed the yards. At corners, he found even more of interest, and the clerk often thought it was as if Chinook were read-ing email from other dogs. The husky probably had a better idea of what was happening in this neighborhood than any of the humans did.

Cheered by the thought, he stepped into the coffee bar and placed his order, adding a slice of banana bread for himself and a bagel for Chinook. As he sat waiting to be called, an older man brushed by his table and sud-denly coffee spilled.

"Oh, I am so sorry," the man said, immediately pull-ing napkins from the dispenser and throwing them on the spill. "Did I get any on you?"

"I doubt it," the clerk answered, as he too started cleaning the spill. Not that it mattered; he wore old clothes he didn't care about. Chinook watched with an interested gaze.

Then the clerk looked up. Recognition niggled at him. "Do I know you?" he asked the older man with thinning hair.

"You've seen me around, I'm sure. I know I've seen you."

The café seemed to grow still. The clerk froze, and a quiet whimper escaped his dog in response to the sudden tension.

The man finished wiping up his spill, then smiled at the clerk. "That's a beautiful dog. What they haven't told you is that the target is one of our own operatives."

Then the man walked out of the shop, leaving the clerk in shock so profound he couldn't move. All he wanted to do was vomit.

Chapter 10

Trace studied Julie as she sat staring at the screen saver on her computer. Remembering the woman he had first met, he felt just awful. Right now her shoulders seemed a little slumped and she was so silent it didn't feel right. Not that she constantly chattered, but rarely was she this still, as if she'd crossed a bridge too far tonight.

It was all his fault and too late now to fix it. He'd wandered into this town, basically blind to the real danger he was in, thinking of looking up an old friend. After all, they'd told him they weren't sure anyone was after him. He certainly hadn't suspected his own people were involved in hunting him down.

But regardless of what he had known or not, it remained that he'd allowed apparent voices of reason to persuade him to stay, that everyone would be safer if he did. He didn't question Ryker's motives, or the sheriff's. They had made a lot of sense.

But Julie in the middle of this made no sense at all. Ryker had honestly thought that if they told Julie this was dangerous, she'd just back off. It turned out the sheriff had known her far better, as he'd said. Julie wouldn't take no for an answer.

Now here she was, in it up to her neck. Tonight had given her an education on the seamier side of the world. She looked as if she had been sideswiped.

He could never restore to her what she had lost since meeting him. Somehow she needed to knit it into her world and make peace with it. Life was like that sometimes. He just wished he hadn't been the one to bring the changes.

The phone rang unexpectedly, and he saw her jump. God, he'd made her react that way. A phone call could make her leap out of her skin. Of all the things he'd done in his life of which he wasn't very proud, this ranked near the very top on his list of shame.

She hesitated visibly before answering. No sooner had she said hello than she turned to hand him the phone. She looked pale. "Ryker."

Of course it was Ryker. What now? He doubted there'd be much useful.

"Yo," he said into the phone.

Ryker's voice answered him. "A friend called. He apparently made a contact with someone very low level that he thinks is involved. He's hoping the guy will want a way out. He's going to make himself available to the contact tomorrow."

"So should I hold off?"

"Your decision. My thinking is, you don't want all of your eggs in one basket."

"I read you." He passed the receiver back to Julie, who replaced it in the cradle.

"I suppose that wasn't good news?" she asked quietly.

"Maybe, maybe not. We'll see how it pans out tomorrow."

"Okay." She turned back to her screen.

Trace hadn't known Julie for long, but she didn't strike him as the type to pull into her shell. He wouldn't have thought she had one at all. Disturbed, he rose and went to stand behind her, resting his hands on her shoulders.

She astonished him. "Don't touch me unless you mean it."

He dropped his hands immediately, wondering how to interpret that. He'd thought his situation, the danger she was in, was eating at her. Was it something else? "Julie?"

She didn't look at him, but continued to stare at the screen saver making its endless ribbons of color. "I can't figure you, Trace. You slip your arm around me, you hug me, and then you back away as if I smell bad. You're really good at creating distances, aren't you? Well, just keep your distance. You live in some kind of bubble. I haven't seen you anywhere else, but you turned to Ryker, and I gather you don't know him all that well, either. So, do you ever let anyone close?"

Ouch. That question hurt, because even as she asked it, he realized it was true. Painfully true. In his world, connections and relationships could be dangerous to everyone involved. They needed to be controlled, kept superficial, ready to discard if the need arose. The less he cared personally or allowed others to care about him, the safer they were, the safer he was.

He gave no one a lever to use against him.

He perched on the end of the couch and studied her profile. "What is it you want of me?" he asked quietly.

"Apparently something you're incapable of giving."

"Which is?"

"Just about anything real aside from your job."

"Meaning?"

Now she turned to face him. "You're using me. I agreed to be used because of Marisa. But somewhere in the last two days I started caring about what might happen to you. Maddening as you can be, much as you're the chameleon you claim, I still care what happens to you. I get that you don't care about me, except that I not become collateral damage, but that's all you care about. I'm willing to be used to protect you and my friends, but that doesn't mean I have to like the way you shut me out."

He nodded because he didn't know what to say. She was right. He was using her. And he was trying like mad to keep her as safe as he could, but he wasn't allowing himself to feel one other thing. Feelings were dangerous.

"You live in an awfully cold, ugly world, Trace Archer. Now you're about to escape it, but will you ever change? I doubt you can. I doubt you can cut the job out of you enough to ever be like the rest of us."

"I haven't been off the job long enough to know what I can become. Hell, I'm still *on* the job."

"Obviously. Well, I want you to think about what this job has cost *you*. How much it has stolen from you. You might have been doing important work. Well, clearly you were. But not important enough that the people you work for aren't as willing to see you physically dead as they've made you become emotionally."

He tried to tell himself she was just reacting to all the strain of the last couple of days, but there was truth in what she said. Enough truth that it hit him like a gut punch. "I made my choices. Now I live with them."

"Each little choice added up, apparently. And you never counted the cost."

It was true, but now he was getting angry. "This is no time to pick apart my life. Here we are. Unfortunately you're involved. If you want, I'll leave right now. But what I can't do is change what's already done. The past is fixed."

"But the future doesn't have to be," she said quietly. "Right now you have two friends who really care about you. Try caring back, just a little. I know I'll feel better."

"You think I haven't been sweating your involvement? You think I haven't been worrying about you? I care more about what happens to you than what happens to me. From the minute I saw you putting smiley faces and stars on those papers in the diner, I've thought you were a beautiful human being. The world would be a poorer place without you, and I never wanted to drag you into the middle of this."

"I'm sure." She didn't sound sarcastic, merely weary.

"But there you were at Ryker's house before we'd sorted everything out. Ryker was hoping once he told you how dangerous this was you'd back away. But you didn't, did you? So here we are, and I'll do whatever it takes to keep you safe."

She looked down, and he thought he heard a small

sigh escape her. "I know you will. That scares me, too. I don't want anyone to die, least of all for me."

Something deep inside him felt as if it were cracking. Feelings better left caged were beginning to bend the bars to get out. All of a sudden the pain in his arm and hand seemed minor compared to what was trying to erupt inside him. Yes, he'd made his choices, and to this day he would stand by them. They'd been his best options at the time. But some…some might follow him to his grave.

He realized that Julie was rising, moving. Going to bed to escape him and all of this? He wouldn't blame her. For the first time he was facing just how much concrete he'd packed himself in, how many times he'd refused to evaluate himself and what he was doing. He'd believed he had a mission, a higher purpose, that he was serving his country. Right now, all of that seemed like so much dross layered over reality. Because the reality, however essential, had often violated him and others. Yes, it was a job that had to be done. But now he was wondering about the people who had given him his missions. What had they intended? Had he merely been a tool for purposes he would have hated had he known them?

How could this not make him wonder?

Julie sat beside him on the couch. "I'm sorry, Trace."

"For what?"

"For being so… I don't know. You need your head in the game right now and I'm going on about feelings. I have no right to question you or criticize you. I've never walked in your shoes."

He responded with bitter humor. "Under the circumstances, maybe you have a better right to question me than anyone else. I cast my shadows over your life. I never should have done that."

"Like you said, the past can't be changed." She surprised him again, this time by reaching out to rest her hand on his thigh.

At once his thoughts shifted downward, to his groin. She had lit his fuse once again with a single touch. She did that so easily that he wondered if he should be terrified of it. Everything she did seemed to ease past walls he'd built over many years. The throbbing in his loins did *not* make him feel any easier.

"Do you feel safe tonight?" she asked him.

"Pretty much, thanks to the storm." He figured tomorrow morning would be soon enough to tackle this problem again. A Monday morning, unfortunately, when even the CIA offices at Langley would be in high gear for the start of a new week.

"Then let's look for those files you want to see, if my accounts haven't been shut down."

Startled once again, he looked at her. She had an odd little smile on her face. "What?"

"Take a look," she said. "Even if you don't want to backdoor your way into classified files tonight. Make sure my accounts are still good."

"You know, you're bouncing all over the place."

"Not really." Her smile broadened a hair. "I want you as relaxed as you can get tonight."

"Why?"

"Because, spy man, I want you to be thinking about nothing but me for a few hours. Because I want you to take me to bed."

Well, he could do that right now, he realized. At her words, every pleasure nerve in his body leaped to life, and he felt his erection begin to throb. That easily, she turned him on like a blast from a furnace. Yeah, he could put it all on hold for a few hours. No reason not to. But as he tried to read her expressive face, he understood that she needed to be able to put it aside for a little while, too. They wanted each other, and right now he didn't want to resist for another instant. She had routed his defenses with a surprising frontal attack.

He was not the only one in this leaky boat. Finally he nodded. "You can check your two accounts and see."

"I suppose I could, but if you want to go further..."

"I'm not sure I do, not just yet. But I might take a peek at a few things."

"Then peek away. Something's got to give us a few hours off. I don't know about you, but I think I'm ready to go nuts with wondering."

Typing proved painful for Trace, and he was doing this only so she could shove this off her plate. So she would be thinking of nothing else when he gave in to his pounding desire and made love to her. Damn, he wanted her so badly he might as well have had five thumbs. Her honesty had made it impossible to hide from himself any longer, but he kept at it. He didn't want her even wondering about this for the next few hours.

He was essentially operating with one working hand and one finger from the other. Julie waited patiently while he turned off the internet block and selected a city from a menu. He reached it without any trouble. "Okay, so far."

"You want me to type for you?" It seemed the least she could do. She knew she was pushing him on several fronts, but she was becoming frustrated, and not just sexually. So much she didn't know, so much he wouldn't say, death lurking around some invisible corner… Yeah, the desire to make love with him was only a piece of the picture. Something inside her was pressing to get to know the real Trace, but she'd begun to wonder if there was one, apart from his job. He'd warned her that he was a chameleon, but she didn't think that was what she was seeing.

She was seeing a man who'd pared himself to the bone emotionally to do his job. Maybe he could act any part he thought he needed to, but she was fairly certain he wasn't acting with her. Why would he? He could push her away as easily as he'd pushed away so many people in the past. He wasn't trying to be charming, or persuasive, or to manipulate her in any way she could detect.

So for all he could change and adapt as needed, she figured she was seeing the real Trace Archer. The things he said sometimes made her ache for him. He didn't seem to have a very high self-opinion. Mephistopheles? That was a bit over the top, she thought. But if that's how he thought of himself, he needed to undergo a major renovation. He needed to find the part of him that he was still proud of, the man who had set out on a mission for his country, probably with the highest of ideals.

Considering that she devoted her life to making youngsters feel good about themselves, she knew she was inclined to do that with others as well. But would she even have time? Likely not.

"Trace?"

"Yeah?"

"How did your parents make you feel about yourself?"

"Just a sec. I want to back out of all this and shut your internet down quickly. To be extra safe."

"Are both accounts working?"

"Believe it. If I can remember how, I may even piggy-back them and use them both at once." He clicked on the kill button, then turned to face her. "You were saying?"

"How did your parents make you feel about yourself? Truthfully." Her heart pounded a little at her temerity, but she had a great need to know.

He shrugged his good shoulder. "Like most kids, I guess. The only thing that griped me was…" He caught himself.

"What? Just say it."

One corner of his mouth twisted upward. "My dad used to tell me to give glory to God every time I succeeded at something because it was God's doing."

"But?"

"But everything I did wrong was my own dang fault."

She caught her breath. "That's awful," she murmured.

"I don't think he intended it that way, truthfully. He wasn't a cruel man. But I kinda grew up thinking my successes were God's and my failings were my own."

That would sure ding any kid's self-esteem, she thought. No pride in doing something well, but all the blame when something went wrong? Inside her, something clicked.

"So how about this?" she said. "Stop blaming yourself for me being in the middle of this. I put myself here. I won't say I'm enjoying every second, but I didn't have to ask you to stay here. I didn't have to insert myself. That wasn't your fault."

"Thanks. But maybe at its root, it is. Maybe I did something wrong without knowing it, and now it's catching up to me."

That did it. She jumped to her feet. "The only thing I see here is some major butt-covering by some people who are probably responsible for all this." She knew she was talking too loudly, too emphatically, but didn't care.

"I hope we find out," he said.

"We probably will, one way or another. Has it occurred to you that you're not responsible for ensuring that everything in the world goes right, that the planets continue to revolve around the sun?"

"Do they?" Then he amazed her by laughing. "You're a beautiful woman, Julie Ardlow. Your students are blessed to have you."

"Don't make fun of me!" Tension, tension of all kinds, was making her irritable and edgy. She was shocking herself because she wasn't generally a snappish person. But she was snapping now.

"I'm not making fun of you," he said flatly. "I was telling the truth as I see it. Isn't that what you want from me? Truth?"

"Yes, dang it. Truth."

"Then I've been giving it to you. I've explained why I can't let feelings take over. Maybe I've had to do that enough over the years that I've become crippled in some ways, but it's still important. It'll remain important until I deal with this mess. I need my head to be clear. But you keep distracting me."

God, that made her feel awful. She was distracting him with her whining, her criticisms, her demands for his attention, even with her inexplicable need to have sex with him. What the hell was happening to her? She couldn't even understand herself, and usually she felt pretty comfortable with who she was. It was as if this experience was turning her into someone else.

"Julie?"

"I'm sorry. I have no business giving you a hard time like this. I should shut up." And go crawl away into her bedroom and just leave him alone. Didn't this man have enough on his mind right now?

"No, don't shut up. Express yourself. This situation is difficult enough without you bottling everything inside."

"But you have enough on your mind. You don't need me adding to it. It's just that…" She finally turned to stare at him, realizing that she was devouring him with her eyes. Somehow the man she had once thought looked ordinary enough to pass anywhere unnoticed no longer looked ordinary to her.

Crazy thoughts were seeping into her mind. Memories of his brief hugs, of the way his hard body had felt against hers. His scent, uniquely his own, yet utterly masculine. The brush of his flannel shirt against her cheek. The way his skin had felt when she seized his hand to kiss it.

How long had it been since she had felt like this, as if she stood on the cusp of a wonderful experience, as if every cell in her body was crying out for this man's touch? Everything else was slipping away as her body called out. She needed strong arms around her. She craved this man's hardness against her and inside her. She hardly dared hope he would give her what she wanted. He'd ignored her blatant invitations so far. But oh, how she ached for him, for his skin against hers, his weight on her, his mouth and hands exploring her.

A drumbeat of desire began pounding in her body, seeming to fill her ears until she could hardly hear. The ache between her legs consumed her universe. Nothing existed except her hunger for Trace. Suspended on the knife-edge of anticipation, hoping against hope, expecting rejection, fearing rejection, she waited. Helpless, defenseless, so very vulnerable.

"Ah, God, Julie," he whispered.

She thought she saw the flare of recognition in his gaze, a flare that might reflect his own desire. But what if he didn't want her? What if all his evasions had been because she'd thrown herself at him and he just didn't want her?

Just as fear began to conquer her desire, just as she felt she might shatter into a million pieces, he came to her. Cradling her cheek in one hand, he looked directly into her eyes. Reading her, she supposed. Seeking her certainty.

She had never been so certain in her life, at least not for years now. She needed this. As her desire seemed to suck the last air from the universe, leaving her breathless and shaking, he wrapped his left arm around her and drew her up hard against him.

Then his mouth swallowed hers, feeling as if it swallowed her entire being. His tongue, with absolutely no gentleness, plunged into her mouth, claiming her with his demand.

Oh, it felt so good to be wrapped in his embrace, so good to feel a man's strength surrounding her once more. It had been so long, and she hadn't realized how much she had missed this.

But it wasn't just a hug. It felt supremely important that it was Trace hugging her. She wondered if he felt the same, and wrapped her arms around his waist, trying to get him even closer. They'd both been alone too long, she thought hazily. Too long.

Then the world spun away as heavy heat focused in her very core, demanding more, demanding answers from him, answers only he could provide.

When he tore his mouth from hers, they were both panting. She opened her eyes to a slit and saw him through her eyelashes. He looked different, as if some deep tension in him had let go. Relaxed.

"Trace…" She whispered his name, afraid he would withdraw.

He touched a finger across her lips. "Shh," he murmured roughly. "We'll talk later. For right now…heaven."

Heaven, indeed. When he pulled back a little, a shaft of fear pierced her, then vanished as she realized he was tugging her toward the bedroom. She didn't care which one. His sheets would smell of him now, and that appealed to her.

Inside his darkened room, he drew her close once more for a feverish kiss. "So sweet," he muttered.

Sweet? It felt hot, his mouth like fire on hers. With each plunge of his tongue, he seemed to drive the fire deeper into her until she burned everywhere.

Then he eased back a bit. She wanted to snatch him closer, and opened her eyes reluctantly. "Trace?"

"I can't be graceful about this," he said, his voice husky. "Not now. It's hard enough to get my own clothes off."

So he wasn't getting ready to change his mind. Far from it. Her personal imp sprang to life, reminding her that despite everything she still had one. "Well, I can do something about that, gorgeous."

Odd, but she had never undressed a man before. They'd been the ones in a rush to pull clothes away, and then when the relationship had become less fresh, undressing had been something she'd done for herself.

This was new. She smiled and reached for the buttons on his shirt. She'd had no idea what to expect, but what she found deprived her of breath once again. A smooth, expansive, well-muscled chest, as if despite all he'd been through he was taking care of himself. She felt a little shudder run through him as she began to ease the shirt off his shoulders.

She froze. "Did I hurt you?"

"No!" He sounded almost winded, and she smiled inwardly. Clearly she was not going to take this ride alone.

As the shirt fell to the floor, she answered another craving by running her hands over him, feeling him against her palms, savoring his warmth and surprisingly silken skin. As her palms passed over his small nipples, hard now, he shuddered again and a groan escaped him. Delighting in the power he was giving her, in the ability to make this self-contained man give himself up to her, she returned to those nipples again and again until finally she leaned in and sucked on each. As she did so, his arms snapped around her, pulling her as close as he could.

"Tease," he muttered.

Then, inexplicably, a happy laugh escaped her. "Can't take it?"

"I'm about to erupt."

So was she. She could feel it coming, building, like the hum of a generator ramping up. Want, need, passion were becoming a storm inside her. *Dally later*, she thought with the last bit of her brain, and bending, she tugged his sweatpants and undershorts down until he could step out of them.

Then the world froze again for one crackling moment while she drank him in. Every line of him struck her as perfect, the long, leanly muscled legs of a runner, the chest and arms of a man with strength. Even his injured right arm remained strong, as if he had kept working it through all the pain.

And his erection. A thing of male beauty, stiff and proud. She dropped to her knees and ran her tongue over him, then cupped his testicles in her palm.

A groan escaped Trace, then with surprising strength, heedless of the pain it must have cost him, he pulled her up and pushed her back. "Witch! It'll be all over before it starts. And don't you dare laugh."

But she did, and watched a grin start to spread over his face. How had she ever thought him ordinary?

"Strip," he said, as if it were the most natural thing in the world to demand.

She guessed it was at this point. She wasted no time pulling off her sweat suit and underclothes, figuring from the sound of him that he'd about reached his limit. Next time she'd tease him more. Next time…

But next time vanished as he urged her onto the bed. "Damn. Condom."

She waved to the bedside table. "A kindergarten teacher is prepared for everything," she said, listening to her voice crack with eagerness. She wanted him in her and on her right now. No more dallying. She almost hated that condom, but pushed herself up enough to help him with it.

"Sexy," he muttered, then he fell onto the bed beside her, propped himself on his elbow, and began to drag his good hand over her, finding every hill and hollow, teasing her nipples to eager, exquisitely sensitive nubs. But it was amazing how quickly her patience died. Not now. Now she just wanted culmination the fastest way she could get it, as if this moment had been building in her forever.

As if she had been waiting for this man forever, like some Sleeping Beauty who was now only discovering that she had never been truly awake before.

"Trace, please…"

So that's how she wanted it. Delight exploded in him. No finessing lover, just hard, quick and right now. Holding himself back had been almost impossible from the moment he'd given in to her, but now he simply wanted to bury himself deep within her. Raw, as she'd said. Basic. Need. Now, while there was still time.

The urge for life, to live, had been growing in him. After all the years of thinking of himself as expendable, he no longer wanted to be that way. He wanted to taste the mysteries, the fruits, the joys of life, lived to the fullest without being on an adrenaline edge.

He wanted the fantastic normalcy of making love to this woman, of sharing the ultimate pleasure with her. Of carrying another person with him to the greatest peak a human could reach.

But he paused just a little longer, filling himself with the beauty of her lying there. Even in the dim light he could see how superbly she was formed. Breasts, just the right size, begged to be kissed and touched. Large nipples seemed to reach for his mouth, erect and ready for his tongue and teeth. Her waist tapered down to hips that flared invitingly, a cradle to hold a man. Auburn hair grew thickly at the apex of her thighs, a nest concealing her most sensitive places. Below, her legs might have been created for a dancer, exquisitely formed with pretty knees, tiny ankles, and feet that could not have been shaped any better.

There would be time to adore all that later, he promised himself. But the hammering of passion pushed him, so strong now that he was barely aware of the pain that still pounded him.

Then she raised a hand, gripping his shoulder until her nails dug in a bit. The message was clear as she parted her legs, giving him the oldest of all invitations.

Her body begged for him, and his cried out, *Now!*

Propping himself on his elbow, he slid over her. At once her legs rose to lock around his hips and draw him in. Electric shocks ripped through him, driving everything else far away as he slid into her. She was damp already, and so, so warm. He felt her clench her muscles around him, pulsing in an ancient rhythm that drove him to the edge of madness.

Lowering his head, propped on his elbows, he found one of her nipples, drawing it into his mouth and sucking on it in time with the pumping of his body. The universe had shrunk to their points of contact, yet expanded so much he felt he encompassed all life with his hunger and passion.

Pressure inside him built. He lifted his head, gritting his teeth to hang on just a little longer. He wanted her with him in that perfect instant of complete union. Images of her body floated through his mind, driving him harder and harder. Feeling her arms close around him as her legs had brought them so close he could no longer tell they were separate beings.

The tempest swept him along as if he were a leaf, carrying him where it would, but always higher and higher until he felt as if he were nothing but a huge ache, the prisoner of its winds.

Then he heard her cry out, felt the paroxysm take her body, stiffening her. Only then did he give in to the consuming storm, finding release and peace all at once, an explosion that deafened him and blinded him, then left him feeling as if he floated in the darkness of space among an infinity of stars.

Julie didn't want to let it end. Lying beneath Trace's damp body, she had found a place she had dreamed of but had never quite reached before. After a sundering lance of pleasure so strong it almost hurt, she had found a gently throbbing peace, a complete relaxation, a sense of repletion she wished she could hang on to forever.

Trace curled beside her, lying on his good side, his painful hand across her middle. He seemed to have melted as much as she had, everything about him soft and still. He might have fallen asleep.

But soon she felt him press a light kiss to her shoulder. Then a momentary spear of guilt struck her. "Are you okay?" She had forgotten his hand and how much pain he suffered.

"Never better," he said, sounding a bit hoarse. "You? It wasn't too raw?"

"I think," she whispered, "I have become crazy about raw."

A quiet, short laugh escaped him. "I think I was beyond anything else."

"Me, too. That was…that was incredible."

Another kiss followed the first on her shoulder, but

then she felt him stir a bit, and he no longer felt quite so relaxed.

"Pain?" she asked immediately.

"Sorry. I somehow managed to forget all about it, but…"

At once she pushed the covers away. When had they pulled them up? She couldn't even remember. She remembered very little, actually, that didn't have to do with what her body had been feeling and experiencing. Wow.

"Let's get you a pill," she said, much as she didn't want to move. "I'm not going to relax any better than you if I keep thinking of your poor hand being hammered by a blacksmith."

Refusing to give in to her own desire to just savor the experience, she pushed herself upright and hunted up her sweats. "Coffee, too?"

"If you want me awake for a little while to tell you how fantastic you are."

"I can always handle a bit of that," she answered lightly. She found her sweat suit, skipped her underthings, and quickly put on her slippers. She left Trace to manage for himself because she suspected that at this point he might not like being cared for. Right now a ding to his ego could be awful.

Nor did he deserve one. In the kitchen, she gripped the edge of the counter and closed her eyes, letting lingering aftershocks roll through her. She thought she'd been well-loved before, but this had gone far beyond that. She didn't even want to think about why, just to hang on to it as long as she could. Life had just delivered her a miraculous experience. All she could do was hope that another might come her way, and feel grateful for what she had just known.

At last, reminding herself that Trace had to be hurting pretty badly and that he wouldn't take his pain meds without coffee to keep his head clear, she started the pot going. It seemed too late at night for espresso, but she'd ask him if he wanted one.

It took him a while to emerge from the bedroom, and when he did she saw that awful sheen of perspiration on his forehead again. Pain. Lots and lots of it. He gave her a faint smile as he entered the living room, then immediately picked up the bottle of meds from the coffee table where he'd left it. She watched him work the cap loose, then bit her lip as she saw him pour two into his gloved hand. Two? She hated to think what he must be suffering since he usually avoided taking more than one.

"That isn't too much?" she asked.

"It might barely be enough."

At once her heart and stomach tumbled. "I'm sorry, Trace. I should never…"

"Don't say it," he interrupted. "Please don't say it. No amount of pain could have made me miss that experience with you."

Her heart lifted and she was able to smile at him. He popped the pills dry, then sipped at the hot mug of coffee she handed him.

He settled on the couch and extended his right arm in invitation. She curled up beside him and rested her head in the hollow of his shoulder. His arm lay comfortably heavy on her shoulders, but his hand didn't caress her at all. She hoped the pills worked soon.

He spoke. "I'm so glad I met you."

That lifted her heart even more. He'd been constantly

apologizing for dragging her into this, frequently suggesting he should just leave, but now, at least for now, he was simply glad to be with her. "I've been difficult," she admitted.

"No, really you haven't. This is such a mess, and I can certainly understand your frustration with knowing so little. I haven't been much help, staring off into space and pacing, traveling mental pathways I simply can't share with anyone."

"Are they getting you anywhere?"

"Maybe." He shifted a little. "Right now, I'd rather talk about you. About that storm outside. About anything else."

"I forgot about the storm," she admitted.

"Me, too." He gave a little laugh. "Somehow it was easy to forget what was going on outside." He set his coffee down and reached for her hand, raising it to his lips to kiss. "You could make a man forget everything."

She snuggled a little closer. "That might not be good."

"At the moment, I think it's just fine." He released her hand and reached for his coffee, downing half of it.

"Should I have made you espresso?"

"No, this is fine. I may drink the whole pot by myself, though. I hate the way these pills cloud my mind."

"Are you sure it's your mind you need right now?"

He laughed and gave her a little squeeze. "I will, very shortly. Sorry."

Then, in a horrifying moment that froze both of them, there was a knock on the door. Given the hour, she didn't even want to look out the peephole. Straightening, she looked at Trace. He nodded toward the door, but she noticed when he followed her, he stood right behind it where he couldn't be seen. Everything about him said he was ready for an attack.

She didn't blame him. Ryker hadn't called, so it couldn't be him. Shaking now, she peered out and saw a man standing back from the door. As he turned, she recognized him.

"Thank God," she whispered, then wondered what was going on. Micah Parish, long a deputy in this county, had no reason to be standing at her door in the middle of the night.

She quickly worked the latch and opened it. The storm still raged outside. "Micah?"

"Sorry to scare you," he said. "Gage sent me over."

"Did something happen?" she asked as she let him in.

"Not yet. But Gage has been gnawing on the problem and wanted to offer some reassurance."

Once inside, he shucked his jacket. Julie thought he still looked almost like the man who had arrived in this county more than two decades ago, except for some gray streaks in his long inky hair. His Cherokee ancestry was stamped clearly on his face, and had caused him to meet a little initial resistance when he arrived here.

He accepted an offer of coffee, then introduced himself to Trace who, she noticed, offered only his first name. Micah didn't seem troubled by it.

"So what's going on?" Julie asked as they settled in the living room, Trace on a chair, Julie at her desk, and Micah on the couch.

"I wish something was going on," Micah answered. "It always helps to have some kind of movement to let you know where to look. Right now we're in a holding pattern partly because of the storm. Travel right now is pretty much restricted to snowplows, and even some of them are getting stuck all over this state and Colorado."

"Well," said Trace, "I guess it helps to know nothing is moving."

"Air traffic pretty much ground to a halt overnight on Friday and it's still not moving. I pity all the people stuck in airports." He smiled faintly. "But mostly I'm to let you know…you met Seth, right? Seth Hardin? One of the guys who got rid of your car?"

Trace shifted uneasily. "How many people know what's going on?"

Micah's smile broadened. "Let's just say there are a group of us in this county who've had some experience in classified missions. Highly classified missions. Seth's one of them, and so am I. We know how to keep our yaps shut. Anyway, Gage has been worrying about the problem, and in the process drew some of us in on it. We're keeping a watchful eye that's going to get even more watchful as the ability to travel returns. We've got an eye on Ryker's family, and now we've got one on you. You won't know we're around."

Julie instinctively looked toward the window, even though she knew she couldn't see through the curtains. "How long?" she asked.

"Can't say for sure, but according to the latest forecasts the worst should be moving out late tomorrow. The airports are hoping to start moving again tomorrow afternoon. Then the roads. So not long."

"But everyone believes Trace is in Denver."

"But for how long?" Micah asked rhetorically. "Anyway, you're not sitting here alone, much as it may seem so. And the sheriff sent a present for you." He stood and pulled what looked like a black brick off his belt, handing it to Trace. "I'm sure you know how to use a satellite phone."

"I sure do," Trace said, accepting it.

"It's working now," Micah said, "but it'll work even better after this storm blows through. It's set up so the instant you key it, you'll be in touch with our group. If you need more help, dial two-one-one. That'll reach everyone in the department."

"You realize I don't know my way around here."

Micah nodded. "That radio has GPS on it. You won't even have to report your location."

Trace studied the radio a moment, then said quietly, "I can't tell you how much it means to know I have backup."

"I reckon I already know. Well, hell, any of us who've ever gone on a covert op has a pretty good idea of what it feels like in your shoes. No backup, no one willing to claim you if things go sour…no, we get it. And that's the reason you're not going to be alone unless you want to be." Then he smiled at Julie. "You, either. Mind if I have some more of that coffee?"

She went to refill his mug while a strange silence settled over the apartment. Something was happening at a level she didn't fully understand, but she could almost feel the strands of an alliance forming right now.

For her part, she was glad to know friends were keeping an eye on Ryker, Marisa and the baby. From the start her biggest concern had been her best friend and her family, but Trace had risen to a position right alongside them.

"I'll be fine," she told Micah as she gave him his coffee and refreshed Trace's cup from the pot. He smiled his gratitude to her, but his eyes seemed to say more.

Once again she felt the drizzle of desire running through her. A ridiculous case of bad timing, she thought wryly.

And how unusual that a simple look from him could affect her that way. With effort, she dragged herself back to the matters at hand. Life and death were far more important. She shouldn't even need to remind herself of that.

Carrying the pot back to the kitchen to place it on the warmer, she kept her ears open, waiting to hear something. Anything.

She guessed pieces she couldn't imagine were beginning to click into place. Pieces of protection? Understanding?

"You know," Trace said slowly, "it occurs to me that they may already be backtracking me."

Julie stiffened. "But…" She remembered clearly that they had ditched his car, making it look like an accident, that Ryker had sent his phone on to Denver. Surely no one…

"We were wondering that," Micah drawled. "Hence the satellite phone in the middle of the night. Ryker's been getting increasingly antsy, along with Gage, and while neither of them has likely shared that with you, they're not so sure anyone fell for the diversion. At least not for long."

Pills or no pills, Trace was suddenly on his feet, pacing. "Yeah. It's an obvious diversion, the kind of thing I'm capable of pulling off without trouble. And after I got Ryker's address…" He stopped suddenly and faced Micah. "You make sure that man and his family are well-covered. I had no idea when I got here what was going on, but now that I know I'm not betting he's safe."

"Neither are we," Micah said. "Neither are we. This

was your last known location. They may interpret the rest as an evasion. We can't afford to overlook the possibility."

Then, rising, he carried his cup into the kitchen and put it beside the sink. "I'm off. Don't use the sat phone for anything except an emergency. Conversation isn't encoded. Just know a number of us are out there and we're not far away."

The entire night changed because of Micah's visit. Adrenaline and coffee seemed to be holding Trace's pain pills at bay. He had settled at her computer desk, but hadn't turned it on.

Now it was Julie who paced, weariness a long way away, memories of their lovemaking pushed into the background because right now they, too, were a diversion.

Neither of them spoke, but soon she was starting another pot of coffee.

Then, out of the blue, Trace spoke. "It's someone here on a diplomatic mission."

She froze. "How can you know that?"

"Because no one else would be important enough for this kind of response. No one. It has to be a high government official. And since it seems clear the agency is helping someone but not yet taking action that could be traced back to them…my guess is the tiger is in this country. It's not enough to remove me, or that would have been done already. No, this guy wants to take me out himself. And that means he has to be here with a really good cover. Being on a diplomatic mission would be the best."

Her heart skipped several beats. "Any way to find out?"

"Yeah, maybe. The question is, do I want to look right away? Anything I do could set off alarms."

She wasn't liking this at all. Her stomach turned over and started burning again. She headed for the antacid, something she usually needed only rarely. "I'm still trying to grasp why knowing who it is will help."

"Because then I'll know just what he's capable of. What kind of threat he'd pose."

She still didn't really get it. Did he mean he needed to know what kind of murderer the guy might be? How he was capable of achieving it? "But if he's a high-level official, wouldn't he have sent someone else to deal with you?"

"Maybe he already did." He held up his hand. "Screwup. So maybe now he wants to do it himself. I've known egos like that. Amazingly, they tend to rise high in some circles."

"Well, that's an appalling thought." She swallowed some antacid and wiped her mouth again. "So how can you find out?"

"Well, just generally speaking, I can find out which diplomatic missions are in the country from State. It's not like it's a huge secret, usually. And it would be great cover for this guy. He's here for a good, innocent reason for some kind of talks. If he disappears for a few days, who will report it?"

He punched the power button on her computer. It began revving up and made a few beeps.

"This is safe to look at?" she asked.

"This part, yes. Any reporter or citizen should be able to access it. By and large, secret diplomacy happens behind closed doors, but you can still find out who is in the country. Delegations are usually in the open."

That fascinated her. It wasn't like she ever turned on the news and heard about it. Well, once in a while, when it was some really big deal, but most of the time, unless the issue under discussion was huge, she never heard a thing. "They must be coming and going all the time."

"All the time," he agreed. "Most are minor, managed by lower-level functionaries at State. They wouldn't make any news. This guy might be different. In fact, he should be considering what they're willing to do to clean up some mess."

He moved her mouse so that he could manipulate it with his left hand, then put her back online through one of the VPNs. It was painful to watch him type with one hand, even though he was doing pretty well, and she had to bite back an offer to do it for him.

Translating English to English probably wouldn't make this go any faster, she thought sourly. Even if he wrote everything down for her, typing odd internet addresses didn't come naturally to her. She supposed a search engine, her usual recourse, wouldn't work at all.

"What are you looking for specifically?" she asked.

"Lists of current diplomatic missions, most especially from Eastern Europe."

"Because of your work in Bulgaria."

"Yes."

Soon a list popped up on the screen. She was kind of relieved to see that nowhere did it have a label that said it was classified.

"Three missions from Eastern Europe," he said finally. "Slovakia, Ukraine and Romania." He clicked on one, and a small information box popped up. "Nothing unusual. Aid funding." He clicked the rest and found the same thing.

"No Bulgaria?"

"Not recently." He backed out of the page. "I guess I should try to see who's in the delegations, whether any of them are recognizable to me."

But instead of doing anything more, he clicked on the "kill" button to take the computer off the internet. He leaned back, rubbing his eyes. "I shouldn't have taken those pills."

"Maybe you should sleep." Nervous or not, she was beginning to feel the urge.

"I guess so," he said after a moment. "Can you set an alarm? I want to get back to this in a couple of hours."

"Sure," she answered. She guessed that put paid to any hope of making love again tonight. But then, after that dose of painkillers, he wouldn't be in the mood anyway.

She washed up quickly and found him waiting in the doorway of his bedroom when she emerged from her bath.

"Stay with me," he said.

So she climbed into the rumpled bed with him, the scents of their lovemaking still perfuming them, and felt a whole lot better when he spooned against her back, settling his arm over her waist.

"We'll hear the alarm in here?" he asked.

"Can't miss it. A Klaxon would be quieter."

He laughed wearily. "Good. But don't let me sleep late. Micah's right. We can't count on anything."

"I promise."

She was just dozing off when she heard him murmur sleepily. "Kiev. John Hayes. I wonder…"

He drifted off then, but she was left suddenly wide-awake, staring into the dark room. John? Kiev?

Then she remembered. He'd said a Ukrainian delegation was in the country.

She squeezed her eyes shut tightly. *Oh, please, don't let this have anything to do with Johnny.*

Chapter 11

The alarm woke her as she promised it would. Even from her own room across the hall, the noxious noise reached her, and she was trained enough to it that she popped her eyes open and stirred. The sun had still not risen, but it didn't matter. Her eyes felt grainy and she had to battle an urge to simply close them and return to sleep. She had promised.

"Trace?" She spoke his name loudly.

At once he jerked into wakefulness. "Julie," he murmured, and ran his hand over her waist, her breasts.

"Keep that up, spy guy, and we're going to be here for a while." Her voice, foggy from sleep, at least managed to sound light, not disappointed.

He groaned. "After this is over…"

"Yes?"

"A month alone with you on a desert island might just about iron me out."

At least he still made her want to smile. She eased away, trying not to jar him. "I didn't set this wake-up rule. I'm going to make more coffee."

"Espresso, please. Four shots. I'm going to need it."

Well, she could do that. She took time to wash the sleep out of her eyes, brush her teeth and pull her hair back into a ponytail. Shower later, she thought. He hadn't wanted to sleep for long, so that must mean he wanted to get going on something.

She had just finished pulling the last of his four shots of espresso into a large mug and was able to hand it to him when he joined her. He'd changed into a dark fleece shirt and pants, but she didn't fail to notice that he also wore his boots.

She pointed to them. "Getting ready to go out?"

"Getting ready for whatever."

Comforting answer. Not. She almost hesitated, but she'd never been one to keep thoughts to herself unless she thought they were hurtful or ridiculous. "Last night as you were falling asleep, you mentioned John and Kiev."

He stiffened. "I did?"

"You know you did. Why?"

"I don't know. Maybe because there's a delegation from Ukraine in the country. I seem to remember you didn't want to pursue that avenue. The honest truth, Julie, is that nobody at my level knows what happened to John. The story is that he was caught in cross fire. Plenty of that in Kiev these days. And you heard Ryker warn me not to push at those walls again. He tried."

She felt him closing in on himself, withdrawing into the person she'd first met, the self-contained operations guy. God, she had an urge to shake him out of that. "No more secrets," she said sharply. "I need to know what I need to know, and there's no reason Marisa will hear any of it. In fact, she'd better not. So what about John?"

"Nothing really. It was just a confluence of thoughts in my head."

She wanted to believe him. But one more question had to be asked. "Did he work for you?"

At last he looked at her, and she hated the way he seemed to have hollowed out. "Several layers removed." Then he turned away and carried his coffee to the computer.

Several layers removed? What in the world did that mean? Was this all tied together somehow?

For once she cursed her own innate curiosity. Some things were better left alone, she reminded herself. How difficult would it be to meet Marisa's gaze again if she knew anything about Jonny's death? Impossible. She bit down until her teeth ached and battled her characteristic desire to have every question answered. And he was right, Ryker had warned him not to touch it. God, she hated these secrets.

"Last night..." He paused.

She waited, feeling torn in a million directions. A threat was moving toward them, whether fast or slow, they couldn't guess. Maybe they'd relied too much on the snowstorm. Maybe the guy was already somewhere around here. Even Trace had questioned last night whether they'd relied too much on the protection of the storm.

"Last night," he repeated. "It was wonderful. Incredible. I want you to know that. Precious. But I can't promise any more."

She didn't recall having asked for any promises, but

there he was, pulling back into the safe enclosure he'd apparently built over the years. Did he mean he'd had all he wanted from her? Or was he telling her he was in no position right now to promise anything beyond this mission?

The whole life-and-death situation made long-term thoughts out of the question. She got it, but she wondered why he'd felt it necessary to say so.

"You know, Trace, you are a pain in the butt."

His eyes widened. "Just stating the obvious. What can I promise you? Not even that I won't be dead in the next few days."

"Funny, nobody can. And I don't remember asking for anything." Determined to remind him, she brushed past him, then wiggled her hips.

"Julie, what the…?"

"Just remember, secret agent man, that you wanted it, too."

Once again she had the delight of stunning him. "Now get to work. Save the world or save your life. I'd really like you to accomplish both."

His jaw clamped shut, then his eyes danced, taking her by surprise. "You're too much," he said. "More than a handful. I like it."

Then without another word, he settled at her computer and went to work.

She turned on the TV quietly. The weather was improving. Time had just grown very short.

The Virginia morning dawned clear and warmer. As the clerk got out of his car at Langley, he thought again of the cherry blossoms and he figured they'd be gorgeous by the weekend, especially with the weather warming.

Then he looked at the iconic CIA buildings that held so many secrets and half wished he'd called in ill that morning. He didn't want to be here, didn't want to be sent on another mission to see that disgusting general. He wanted no part of whatever was going on here.

But he didn't know how the hell to get out of it.

His phone rang before he was halfway across the parking lot. He glanced at the caller ID and seriously considered not answering it. He'd taken the advice to keep it off all weekend, but now it was his boss. Time to get back to work, whether his superior was happy about it or not.

He answered, giving only his first name. In theory the phone was secure, but anything traveling over the airwaves and via cell towers was anything but. He'd long since learned to avoid saying something that could cause trouble.

His boss's voice poured into the phone. "No control," he said.

"Sir?"

"Whatever we were doing, our dog slipped the leash. You and I are off this mission."

"Yes, sir."

"Be grateful," his boss said. "There's a line about company and old fish...anyway. I have a meeting, so clear my morning when you get to the office."

"I will."

By the time the clerk cleared building security, stopping at the cafeteria to pick up a bran muffin and coffee for his breakfast, questions were rising in his head like a tsunami pushing hard on a seawall. He knew he should just let it go; he'd been around long enough to know that when he was off something, he was really *off* it. As soon as his involvement ended, he needed to forget he'd ever been a part of it.

But he kept remembering that familiar older man who'd spoken to him at the coffee shop. The target was one of their own operatives?

That seemed so wrong he still didn't want to believe it. But he knew that man, and he was pretty sure he knew him from this building. But how could he find him again without drawing attention? And worse, what would he tell him? He was presuming the dog was the general, but he couldn't be sure. And after their attempts to keep the man from leaving town, he'd apparently taken off anyway. To where?

That storm… Maybe it hadn't been enough to stop the target. Or maybe someone higher up had changed the parameters. He could only wonder. He'd never know.

But he kept a sharp eye out for that older man. An hour later, he was almost relieved to run into him in the washroom.

"I need a cigarette," the older man said. "Join me?"

The clerk had been nervous before, but now he was more nervous than ever. "I…"

"I know you don't smoke. I like company when I stroll, though."

Then, drying his hands on the towel, the other man left him.

The clerk remained at the sink, hoping the shakiness he felt didn't show. Maybe he didn't want to become an operative after all. Judging by this experience, he ought to be happy to spend his life safely pushing files around the bowels of this building.

He should just ignore this. Maybe meeting this man would be an act of disloyalty. Or maybe he'd be saving a life. He'd heard the vitriol in the Ukrainian general's voice as he spoke of needing to clean up this mess. What mess? The clerk was quite sure he didn't want to know.

Outside the restroom, he turned toward his office, his mind nearly made up. Then, before he took two paces, he changed course. Stepping outside for a walk with a fellow employee would hardly raise any suspicions. People did it all the time.

"I think I've got it," Trace announced. "Holy mother of…" He trailed off.

Julie hopped off the couch and went to stand beside him. "What?"

"There's a Ukrainian general who's in Washington. He's part of a formal delegation. Are you aware of the fight going on over there? Russia trying to reclaim parts of Ukraine?"

"Yes. I don't follow closely, but there's been a lot of fighting, right?"

"Right. Anyway, this guy is a former Russian army officer. Now he's with the Ukrainian army. I wouldn't even venture to guess which side he's really on."

She licked her dry lips, the butterflies once again flapping frantically in her stomach. "So how can you know it's him?"

"Because I recognize his name. Because I know…" He hesitated.

God, she hated this secrecy. "You can't tell me, can you? Okay, I'll put it together myself." If Trace was aware of him and thought it might be him, then the guy must have worked for Trace or his superiors at some point. A very important asset. From the beginning Trace had said there were assets they couldn't afford to lose. To her it seemed a general with connections on both sides of a war might fit the bill perfectly. A general who was part of a diplomatic mission.

"Anything else?" she asked.

Again he hesitated. "Well, I can tell you he's got an ugly past. A violent man. Not afraid to do his own wet work, and totally capable of it."

"Wet work?" But understanding hit her like a punch. Of course. Killing. The guy was able and willing to kill. "So…is this someone you should be afraid of? Seriously?"

"If it's him, anyone should be afraid of him."

"Great." Her knees felt rubbery, but increasing agitation made her want to pace. Trace wasn't minimizing the guy's capabilities. He was in the best position to judge.

Reality was hitting her hard again. Really hard. This wasn't a spy game. Trace could really die. And if Ryker somehow became involved, Marisa might… "Women and children?" she asked, her voice cracking.

"He has no lines."

She closed her eyes, not sure how much more she could take. "Is he still in Washington?" she asked, a whisper.

"I don't know. If he's staying at the embassy, I have no way to find out. If he's staying elsewhere…well, how many hotels are there in the area? I could spend a day calling them all and asking for him. Hacking into the hotels' databases would probably take as much time."

"You've got to find out more." Suddenly dropping to

her knees beside him, she looked up at him. "Trace… Marisa. Ryker. Whatever it takes. Please."

He grew so still he might have turned to stone. Then, as if recovering his ability to move, he cupped her head with his hand and pulled it to his side. She could hear his heart beating, and it amazed her it wasn't hammering as fast as hers.

"I'll protect them," he said, his voice like steel. "I'm the one this hunter wants. There's no reason for him to take out anyone but me. He'd only get a bigger mess."

She hated to hear him say that even if it was true. He sounded like a man who was willing to go to the guillotine rather than let anyone else get hurt.

But she didn't want him thinking that way. That was dangerous. "You've got to save yourself, too," she begged. "Please, Trace. Don't just give yourself up to this madman."

The steel remained in his voice. "I may have been sidelined, but I am not inoperative."

The clerk and the older man, who identified himself only as Bill and didn't ask the younger man's name— probably because he already knew—took a stroll along one of the walkways around the buildings. Most led to the parking lots, but some were just pleasant to walk on a nice day. Occasionally, when the pressure cooker grew to be too much, a handful of employees would stroll or jog out here. Lunch hour was a favorite time. Usually, however, they remained at their desks.

Overall, the place looked like a sterile campus, but with none of the older architecture that would have lent it grace. No one was much interested in grace except at the visitors' entrance and central courtyard. The two of them strolled toward a parking lot, away from the buildings.

The clerk remained edgy, and a whole bunch of new reasons for it were rattling around in his brain. How had Bill identified him? How was it the man seemed to know what was going on? He could only imagine that Bill had a massive network of informants in the CIA. Or possibly, that Bill was behind this, whatever it was. In which case the clerk figured he was about to lose his job. But he kept remembering the words from the coffee shop. He didn't feel right about any of this.

"So, you've been thinking?" Bill asked.

"Too much or not enough."

"Let me assure you, the target was not responsible for what's going on here. There's a cover-up. You got caught in the middle."

The clerk wished he were anywhere else on earth. "I'm out of it now."

"Why's that?"

"The dog slipped the leash I was supposed to put on him."

At that, he felt Bill's eyes bore into him. "When?"

"Since sometime on Saturday morning. That's the last time I saw him."

Bill lit a second cigarette, even though he'd barely finished the first. The discarded one wound up in sand on the top of a concrete trash bin. "Do you think that was accidental?"

Things inside the clerk felt as if they were shredding. How much security was he violating with this conversation?

"Look," said Bill, "no one will know you told me anything. But I can tell you this much. An innocent man is being targeted to cover some expensively up-holstered rumps."

The clerk swallowed hard. Loyalties clashed within him. "My boss only did what he was instructed by his superiors."

"I know that, sir. You and your boss are being accused of nothing, not by me or anyone else. Unfortunately you're being used as cover. So what do you know?"

Through a mouth as dry as sand, the clerk answered. "Very little. I got the feeling this morning that my boss thinks a plan was changed, that this wasn't a mistake."

"And who were you leashing? Who?"

"A Ukrainian general." The clerk would have given anything for a bench right then. His legs felt like spaghetti. What had he just done?

Bill blew a cloud of smoke. "I'll be a better patron for you than the man you work for. Trust me. Futures are built on relationships here. You just did me a favor. Now I'll see that you get one in return."

The clerk finally faced him. "Frankly, I feel so sick right now I might puke. I don't know what I've done."

"For now," said Bill, "just know that you did exactly the right thing. I guarantee it. And you know it, too. We don't throw our operatives to the wolves. Let that be one of your most important lessons."

The storm was blowing out. Trace stood at the window in Julie's apartment and watched as the white-out simply vanished. Occasionally a little whirlwind of snow would blow through the open space between the buildings, but that was it.

While he hadn't told Julie much about this general,

he knew a lot about the man, enough to make his gut twist. A torturer, a murderer with an iron fist. He'd been smart enough to navigate himself to the upper echelons of two armies, which meant he wasn't stupid. Certainly not stupid enough to think Trace had gone off the map in Denver.

The trick might have misled many, but not this guy. And probably not his contacts within the agency. Oh, there'd probably been some brief consternation, but when Trace hadn't crossed their radar again for three days? No, they were already backtracking him. They'd probably already figured he was here. Ryker was too obvious as a link. If they were applying any brains at all, they'd know that Trace had passed through the town where Ryker lived. Looking back at it, once Trace disappeared, it must be as bright as neon, even if they hadn't intercepted any calls.

So, because he hadn't known that he was being pursued, because it had seemed so unlikely, because all he'd heard was an unverifiable rumor, he'd come here. Thinking what? How much had those damn pain pills affected his brain?

Too much, evidently. He'd been a fool. He'd put a whole bunch of people at risk.

He closed his eyes, feeling it. Putting aside his own anger with himself, he let intuition and experience guide him.

He knew this General Andrepov. Not personally, but by reputation. He'd been part of the arsenal of assets who had occasionally passed extremely useful information.

As it suited him, of course. The guy was always working an angle, all of it designed to protect and improve his positioning. For men like the general, life was a huge chessboard, and the pawns didn't matter a damn unless they were useful.

Sinking into intuition born of years in the field, he felt tension gripping him. The agency knew where to look. In fact, given the support the general was presumably receiving, he might already be in the area. How had he allowed himself to be lulled into complacency? Why had he ever allowed himself to believe the agency was trying to protect him? Because that was what they usually did?

Because he hadn't ever dreamed this was the man who wanted him dead. He'd never done anything to expose this general. He was no fool. He had dealt with all kinds of assets over the years, and had protected them all insofar as he was capable. But when it was a man like the general... Not only was he a necessary asset, but he was a dangerous one who had to be handled with kid gloves.

So who had upset the man? Who had put him in a position dangerous enough that he wanted revenge, a desire so urgent that someone at the agency had named Trace as the cause of all his problems?

He closed his eyes, facing the likelihood that he was being offered up to protect a man who honestly didn't deserve to breathe the same air as decent people. A man whose offerings of information had been extremely useful over the years, but one who had also carefully chosen the bits he would share. A man perfectly capable of playing countries off against each other if it suited him.

It could be someone else, of course, but any way he looked at it, it was unlikely anyone else would get this level of help, or be able to hunt Trace down. It was also highly informative that the general was now in the country on a diplomatic mission, a great cover for whatever else he might intend.

Instinct, intuition, experience, they were all solidifying inside Trace. He didn't even want to turn to look at Julie, who was dozing on the couch finally.

He felt ashamed and foolish. Between the pain in his hand and the meds he'd kept on taking to control it, he'd mistakenly thought he'd been functional enough, given that all he was supposed to do was keep moving. Clearly he was not up to par.

Gritting his teeth, ignoring the hammering in his hand and arm, he faced himself squarely. He'd been on meds when he'd called for Ryker's address. Stupid, stupid, and worse. The rumors had just started to reach him, and while he hadn't believed them…

His jaw tightened even more. It was unthinkable that the agency wouldn't protect him as much as it would protect any asset. He'd been swamped by disbelief, had been able to brush it aside, especially after they told him they were watching over him. Would let him know if a real threat arose.

It had never entered his numb brain that they might be hanging him out to dry. Never entered his mind that he was worth so little. Not before he headed for Ryker. Not before he dragged others into this nightmare with him.

When Ryker and the sheriff had made him "disappear" and assured him it was better he stay here rather than risk bringing unaware innocents into his mess, he'd bought it. Freaking pain pills.

But no matter how he battered his brain, he couldn't find a better solution. Moving on, as Ryker had pointed out, would simply have drawn others into his shadow. He wouldn't have been able to hide indefinitely. His resources were limited, and sooner or later he'd have needed cash, or bought gas, or somehow otherwise revealed his whereabouts. How long could he go like that, just barely skipping ahead of his hunter?

Not long. Not when the agency was helping the general. He'd have had to make a stand somewhere.

But going off the grid had been a big mistake in its own way, one he should have thought of. By disappearing for three days, he'd let his watchers know that he was onto them. Not good. Now they were warned, just as he was warned.

Slowly he turned and looked at Julie. She was curled in a tight ball around a book she'd been reading, her beautiful auburn hair trailing over her face.

He had to get out of there. He had to make sure she wouldn't be part of whatever was coming.

But then he remembered that visit from her girlfriend. Being snowed in for several days…what else was there to do but talk on the phone? How many people in this town now knew that Julie had a man staying with her, a man from somewhere else?

Damn, he might as well have staked a flag on this whole town.

He hadn't downed any meds since those he'd taken during the night. His hand shrieked at him, battered at him, told him he needed more pills, but he refused to take them. Better the pain that wouldn't let him rest than the painkillers that had evidently turned him into an idiot.

The roads were being cleared even now. He'd almost bet the general was on his way here from Denver. The question was, would he go for Ryker? Or did he know more?

Feeling sickened, Trace looked at the phone and the computer and honestly wondered how well all their evasive maneuvers had worked.

Maybe not at all. A tap on Ryker's phone line could quickly identify the calls he'd made to this number. Hell, these days, finding that out wouldn't even need a warrant. National security. Yeah.

So calls from Ryker to here, possibly tapped. And while they'd been circumspect, voice identification could place Trace at this end of the line.

He didn't know all the technology available to the agency because he hadn't needed to. But he suspected they had a lot more than he'd ever dreamed. How long had the three of them been located and watched in their ignorance?

He paced a little, forcing his brain to ignore the insistent shrieks of his hand. Okay, assume the worst. Assume the general was already on the way. There was at least some hope he wasn't here yet.

But he couldn't count on them not knowing exactly where he was. At Julie's apartment. He had to get the hell out of here quickly.

He looked at the satellite radio they'd left him and knew he couldn't use it except in a dire emergency. It wasn't encrypted. Anything he said would be picked up by a number of agencies monitoring satellite transmissions.

But staring at it, a thought was born.

Returning to the computer, he went to the State Department's public information and clicked on the Ukrainian delegation. While he was certain not everyone involved or meeting with them was named, he might see something.

Twenty minutes later, he looked up, his chest so tight that he almost couldn't draw a breath. He recognized one of the contacts the delegation was supposed to meet. Listed as an undersecretary for State, he was in actuality a high-level director at the agency, a political appointee.

Someone who, if he slipped, would be able to press the levers of power in a way that would offer Trace Archer up as an appeasement. A way to settle one very unhappy, very dangerous man.

Now he knew. And what he knew filled his head with a red rage.

Andrepov drove into the small town in a four-wheel-drive vehicle with chains on the tires. He hated the noise the chains made, but he knew they wouldn't draw attention on these roads. No need for stealth yet. Nor would he, after Bulgaria, trust anyone else to deal with this problem.

He had an address. He had a map. What he didn't yet have was a way to lure his quarry out. The stupid US agents had warned him not to make a big mess because they would have trouble cleaning it up. He didn't much care how much trouble he caused them, because they had created a near-catastrophe for him. Only years of experience and wisdom had allowed him to tamp down the fires they had awakened, to quiet those who wanted to throw him into a bottomless hole forever.

But he'd dealt with them. Now he needed to deal with the man who'd caused all this. Once he departed the country, he didn't care how much trouble he left in his wake, but he was experienced enough to know that a clean job would be best for him as well. After he was done with this Trace Archer, he'd have to get out quickly. It was a long drive from this town to Denver to catch the flights he needed, so he had to ensure he had time for his escape.

It was the one thing that made him unhappy. The fools should have just kept this man in the Washington area, but he understood they had to protect themselves as well. He knew that if he burned them, they would become useless to him and his goals.

So keep it as clean as possible.

He's got to surface soon, they had told him. He would need a phone, a car, some way to move again. The storm had merely stalled him, and he had taken shelter with some woman.

The general suspected there was something else they weren't telling him, but he believed it would not interfere with his mission. Why should it? They'd handed him this agent after a long fight and a lot of threats from him, but they'd agreed to help. If they were protecting someone who wasn't involved, that was not a problem.

But if there was one thing the general knew for certain, it was that the CIA needed him more than he needed them. He had access to information they could get no other way, the backroom information, the whispered information. The secrets. So yes, they'd given in to his demands.

He had one goal and one goal only: to make it clear that no one, absolutely no one, had better screw with him again. Even now he figured that message was coming through loud and clear.

And of course, taking his vengeance would be sweet.

Revenge was necessary to a man in his position. He needed to be feared. That he also enjoyed it was merely an added benefit.

Because he would definitely enjoy it.

Chapter 12

Julie awoke to gentle fingertips brushing her cheek. Opening her eyes, she found Trace bent over her, smiling. Then he bowed his head and kissed her deeply on her mouth. Fire poured through her almost instantly, but when she raised her hands to pull him close, to begin another adventure in his arms, he drew back.

"Time to rise," he said quietly. "The road outside has been plowed. Can you get to your friend's place?"

"Ashley?" Confused, then suddenly frightened, she sat up. "Why would I go there?"

"Because I need to pull out of here quickly and I don't want to leave you alone."

He might as well have dropped a brick on her head. Emerging from gentle sleep and surprisingly sexy and happy dreams, he had just thrust her back into the reality of all this.

"Trace? What?"

"I'm growing increasingly paranoid," he said flatly. "I can't run the risk that I'm not right. I think things are about to go south in a hurry."

She passed a hand across her eyes, trying to wipe away the last sleep, trying to connect with his sudden urgency. "What happened?"

"Nothing yet."

"The storm…"

"Is over. And I think with a little help from our friends, the bad guy might already be here. And he might know where I am. I want you out of here now."

Her heart was sinking rapidly, faster than fear was rising. This was it? He was sending her away?

"I don't have time to explain," he said. "There may not be any time now. Get dressed and get out. I'm leaving, too."

"Leaving," she repeated, hearing the dullness in her own voice.

Suddenly he moved in close again, seizing her shoulder with one hand. "If I get through this, I'll be back. I promise. Now get going. Don't even call. Just get over there."

Not call? Pieces began connecting in her head. She looked at the phone and realized he thought it might be tapped. She didn't question whether that was possible; she accepted his expertise as being far better than her own.

She pushed to her feet. "What happened, Trace?"

"I stopped taking pain meds and used my brains. We didn't fool them this long, Julie. *I* wouldn't have been fooled for this long. The storm bought a little time, but not as much as I imagined. Damn pills. They likely figured out it was all a ruse. And if they knew I came here, they probably figured out who I was going to see. So you get out of here. I'm going to meet Ryker and take care of some things. Make sure he and his family are safe. But I can't do any of that if I'm worrying about you. So please, go to your friend's house."

She nodded. "Okay. Marisa will know how to reach me after it's over. But, Trace, please…be careful. I don't think I could stand it if anything happened to you."

But he'd withdrawn again, his eyes hard as chips of brown glass. He nodded, acknowledging her, but didn't answer.

Game time.

"Meet me," Trace said into the phone. "Make sure your family…"

Ryker answered. "Sheriff's. They're safe."

"Got it."

Julie emerged from her bedroom with a tote and began to pull on her outerwear. "Where are you meeting him?"

"Sheriff's."

"I can drop you there," Julie said. "It's on the way to Ashley's."

"Like this place was on the way to the motel?" The essential focus he needed was taking over, and he heard the edge in his own voice but refused to apologize for it. There was too much on the line now.

"No," she retorted sharply. "For real. I have to drive right past it. Hurry up, and let's go."

He pulled on his outerwear as quickly as he could, ignoring the fiery poker in his hand. No time for that, no room for that, and it might not matter much longer.

At the door he paused. He hated to step outside, making targets of both himself and Julie.

"Let me go first."

She looked as if she would balk, but then nodded. "You know where my car is?"

"Right out front."

"Okay."

"Don't pause to lock the place up."

"I rarely do," she admitted. "Let's go."

"Me first," he insisted. Pulling his ski mask down took a few seconds, and he didn't object when she helped. Then he pulled his hood up.

"Don't follow me until I tell you. Promise."

She promised, her eyes looking suspiciously bright, with creases of tension around the corner. He could almost smell her fear. Fear for him, he realized. All he had was the brick of the satellite phone in his pocket and a knife he had taken from her drawer and tucked into his boot without letting her see it. He was useless with a gun, and he knew it.

All he could count on was coming up against this guy face-to-face.

Outside, he felt the bite of the cold, but saw that the clouds were lightening. No more snow fell, and the whipping wind had settled down quite a bit. He forced himself to wait, to see if anything moved or happened. Nothing did. He walked out more into the open and waited, every sense straining. The world remained frozen in place.

Good. He could at least get Julie away. He checked her car, then went back and opened the door. "Come on."

She had her car key ready in her hand. She had good instincts, lots of them. She walked straight to her car, unlocked it, threw her bag in back and climbed in. He wasn't far behind her with his duffel.

The motor started without any trouble. She had backed in to her parking place, which turned out to be a good thing as the front-wheel drive grabbed the accumulated snow and pulled them through the lot to the recently plowed street.

She drove with the expertise of a long winter behind her, carefully but quickly. "Just let me out at the sheriff's office," he said. "Then keep going straight to Ashley's. I'll tell everyone where you've gone, okay?"

Occasional cars passed them, apparently folks who'd had enough of being locked indoors. None of them caught his attention or seemed out of place.

"Why didn't you want me to lock my door?" she asked.

"Because I didn't want you standing in the open any longer than necessary."

She murmured something under her breath.

"Julie, I'm sorry. I'm sorrier than I can say. I never should have taken those freaking pain pills. I thought I was keeping them under control with coffee, but when they started wearing off early this morning, as I was reaching for the bottle to take just one more, it was like my brain truly kicked into gear again. Probably for the first time since I was wounded. I should have been thinking more clearly."

"You were thinking clearly enough, it seemed," she argued firmly. "You weren't acting stupid."

"I acted stupidly the instant I decided to look up Ryker."

"Maybe not. If you hadn't, you would never have

been sure you were being hunted. That wouldn't have gone well."

No, it might not have, not when he considered the soothing promise that they were keeping an eye out for him. And why on earth would it ever have occurred to him that they weren't? It was an unwritten rule. *We take care of our operatives.*

"How's the pain?" she asked.

"It's keeping me wide-awake."

"Not distracting?"

"Not right now. I can't let it."

As they pulled up in front of the sheriff's office, he reached for the door release and his duffel all at once.

"Listen," he said before he climbed out, "I'll find you once this is over. Okay?"

"Sure."

He didn't like the look on her face. He was certain there were a million things she wanted to say to him, things he probably deserved, and maybe some things he wasn't ready to hear. Regardless, she bit them back, and it saddened him that Julie, who always spoke her mind, was refusing to speak it now.

"Straight to Ashley's, okay?"

"I promised."

Then he climbed out into the cold day and strode toward the door of the office. He didn't want to look back, but he did anyway, making sure she was disappearing down the street. If he survived this, he supposed he'd have plenty of time to hate himself later for what he had brought into that woman's life.

The general had seen them leave the woman's apartment. It had been easy enough to stay out of sight. In fact, he favored snow for his operations. It splintered light, messed up shadows and provided a lot of cover each time the wind stirred when the powder was this dry.

So from a block away, his white vehicle almost completely hidden behind a snowbank, dressed all in white, he had watched. Where were they going? As soon as they pulled away, he decided to follow. Besides, he hadn't liked the look of the building in which the woman lived. The possibility of too many neighbors to hear or see something, no cover in the parking lot except for a handful of vehicles…no, it was not a good place to take Archer down.

Nor did he especially want to take the woman down. She probably had no idea what she harbored. A man like this Archer was perfectly capable of seducing a woman to help him out. The general knew it to be true because he had done so, many times. Women were weak, and they became very stupid when a man smiled and flattered them. They had an urgent need to be liked by the opposite sex.

But he would use that woman if it became necessary. Nor would he shrink from killing her. It was just that he had decided his CIA acquaintance was right: clean would be better. One man dead, no more.

So he followed at a distance. Among the other cars passing, while they were few, he would not stand out at all.

He got a jolt, though, when he saw the car stop at the sheriff's office. He had thought they might be going for food or something similar. But no, Archer got out there and headed inside.

The general hesitated. He believed Archer knew

someone was coming for him, but to break security by speaking to the local law?

This was something he needed to think over quickly. Matters might have become more complicated than he had thought. Clearly Archer knew someone was coming. Even his CIA friend had admitted that when he dropped off the grid. Nor had it taken them long to locate him. By yesterday morning, they were able to tell the general where to look. By yesterday afternoon they had given him an address.

And while all that was going on, they'd had one of their planes fly him to Denver, despite the storm, to bring him close to his target. Casell, his contact, was doing a fine job of making amends for the slipup that had nearly cost the general everything. When this was done, they would be even.

A new relationship, now that the agency understood the general's importance. How essential he was to them.

As the woman drove off, he decided to follow her. He needed to know where all the pieces were. Archer was at the sheriff's and Andrepov was fairly certain he'd be there for a while. Breaking protocol, sharing secrets, perhaps trying to convince someone to protect him.

But he couldn't afford to count the woman out yet. She might have been sent on a mission for Archer. Andrepov had persuaded many women to do things for him in his time. No reason to think Archer was any less ruthless.

Because the only way a man could survive in this game was through sheer ruthlessness.

Trace was sent to the sheriff's private office the instant he entered. He'd barely had time to greet Gage

Dalton and take a seat before Ryker arrived carrying two trays full of tall coffees. At once the door was closed and for a few moments silence fell.

"Where do we begin?" Gage asked.

"How about we start with my stupidity?" Trace began. "I was more doped up than I realized until this morning when the last pills cleared totally out of my system."

"Let's not run over that," Ryker said. "Pointless. We're here now. Tell us what you're thinking."

"I'm thinking that a very high-level party in the CIA is behind this. I'm fairly sure a certain General Andrepov is the guy they've sent after me, and he's one dangerous man. And I realized this morning that our little ruse probably didn't throw them off my trail for more than twenty-four hours."

"Andrepov?" Ryker repeated, and swore.

Trace looked at him. "You know him?"

"By reputation. I'd rather face Lucifer."

"Great," said Gage, drumming his fingers. "I've run into the minions of hell before."

"This guy is more than a minion," Trace said.

"You worked with him?" Ryker asked.

"Not directly. Some operatives below me did. Several layers down."

"Layers and more layers," Ryker remarked. "Safer for everyone."

"Right," said Trace. "More layers, more deniability for everyone, including assets. Even Andrepov understood that. But now…"

"What makes you think it's him?" Gage asked.

"He's part of a Ukrainian delegation that's been in town for the last week. And one of the people he was meeting with is listed as an undersecretary of State. But he's actually an assistant director at the CIA."

Ryker stiffened. "Who?"

"Casell."

Another cussword filled the air. "That dirty son of a…"

"That's not helping right now," Trace said. "I think time is limited. Look at it. I went off the radar on Friday. By Saturday night they could be fairly certain I wasn't in a hospital somewhere. I didn't access my bank or credit, so they could safely assume that I didn't buy a car, and I didn't stay in a motel. Which direction would you look, Ryker? Especially if they heard me call for your address? I wasn't on a secure line. I told you that."

"But you were on a burner, right?"

"What the hell difference would that make? I thought they were covering me. So when I bought the burner, I pulled out the credit card."

"Well, double damn," said Gage. "So you're thinking he's on his way here now?"

"I'm thinking he could already be here."

"But the storm…"

Ryker interjected then. "I had a friendly phone call from someone we know. A certain diplomat hasn't been seen by anyone since Saturday morning."

"So your contact knows?"

Ryker nodded. "He wasn't sure, but he talked to a clerk who got shoved into the middle of this. The guy mentioned a general."

"Then it's him," Trace said. If he'd had time, he might have exploded, but that was a luxury for later. Right now he needed every unclouded, objective brain cell he had. His hand was pounding again, but he drew a breath and used the pain to clear his head.

"Where's Julie?" Ryker asked. "Not at home?"

"Of course not. I'm assuming it didn't take them long to put a tap on your line. They know who you've been calling. Maybe they even listened in. I told her to go to her friend Ashley's place and stay put."

Gage picked up a radio and keyed it. "Twenty-one, this is Dalton."

"Twenty-one here," said a woman's voice.

"Connie, where are you?" The voice gave him a street intersection. "That's near Ashley's, right?"

"Less than a minute."

"Get over there right now and stay with her. Julie should be there soon, if she's not already. You stay with them, but make it seem like a friendly drop-in. I want you on alert."

He received an affirmative response and put the radio aside.

"Who's Connie?" Trace asked.

"One of my deputies. Daughter-in-law of a guy you met, Micah Parish. Anyway, she's part of that circle of friends. Ashley, Julie, Connie and a couple of others. Connie can show up at Ashley's without scaring them and keep an eye on them, okay?"

The radio crackled. "I'm at Ashley's," Connie's voice said. "No sign of Julie yet. I'm going inside."

Trace looked at the sheriff. "Is that a problem that Julie's not there?"

"Not yet. From here to Ashley's might take a couple of minutes longer, especially if she ran into an unplowed street, which is possible."

"Thanks. Julie's been my biggest concern." Then he looked at Ryker. "And you and your family, of course."

"Me and mine are fine. Gage has given us enough protection to hold off a squad, never mind one guy. But what's the plan?"

"You're going to stay close to your family. Julie's going to stay with Ashley. And I'm going back on the grid. Where can I get a phone?"

Ryker tucked his hand in his jacket pocket. "You know, I figured that was coming. Paid cash for a burner when I was out on Saturday. But why do you want to get back on the grid?"

"So he can hunt me and leave everyone else alone. I want everyone else out of sight and out of mind."

"You're going to need to be able to get around," Ryker added, and tossed him a key that he caught with his good hand. "John Hayes's car. It runs reliably, but not much more than that."

"Not Marisa's, though."

Ryker shook his head. "I wouldn't risk that. No, it's John's car, and we were thinking it was time to let it go. This seems as good a way as any. It's parked outside."

Trace looked at the two men, feeling everything inside him deadening, all unnecessary systems shutting down. Right now he needed to be an automaton with a brain. No room for anything else.

"I mean it," he said again. "Everyone stays away, including the people you told to watch me. Have them watch Julie. Not me. I need to lead this guy away from here."

He looked at the number on the phone, memorized it, then dialed a number he knew too well.

"Hey, this is Archer. Got any news for me?"

* * *

The general saw a huge wrinkle as he watched Archer's woman friend pull up at a house. There was a sheriff's vehicle parked out front. Something was being planned, and he had to interrupt it before matters grew more difficult.

Without another thought, he put his car in Park and climbed out. As the woman eased out of her car, holding a cloth bag, he approached her with his most charming smile. She glanced at him, then froze. "Can I help you?"

"Please," he said, then took one strong swing with his fist.

Julie came to with a head that felt as if it were being jackhammered. Without opening her eyes, she assessed what she could. She was in a moving car. She was probably concussed, to judge by the headache. And she felt fairly certain she was with the general.

Moving very cautiously, a millimeter at a time, she realized her wrists were bound. Then terror slammed her. She'd been kidnapped by a man Trace had described in the ugliest terms imaginable. There could be only one reason: to draw Trace to him, away from any possible safety. Oh God, she had to do something.

But she couldn't imagine what. As her head jolted against the car's window, she opened her eyes just a bit and saw nothing but empty, snowy countryside. From the way the vehicle was jolting, she suspected they were off-road. Each bounce made her head hurt worse.

Fear was clogging her throat, causing her heart to hammer wildly, creating a desperate need for oxygen.

"I know you are awake," said a heavily accented, deep voice. "But do not fear. You will be all right."

Julie turned her head slowly to look at the driver. She supposed most would consider him a handsome man, with gray hair and a deceptively young face. A strong nose that balanced a heavy brow. "Who are you?"

"You know that man who has been visiting you? I am an old friend."

"I'm supposed to believe that when you knocked me out, kidnapped me and tied me up?"

The man laughed as if he was enjoying all this. "Oh yes, you can believe. He will come for you and then I will let you leave."

"If he's a friend, you could have just called him."

"So sad," said the man, shaking his head. "But he seems to have lost his telephone."

"But who are you?"

"If I tell you that, I will not be able to let you go."

The words struck her like an icy shaft. She dragged her gaze from her abductor and stared out the windshield. Headed for the middle of nowhere, somewhere closer to the mountains. Nothing in sight for miles and miles.

Despair filled her heart. Trace would have to come alone. No one else would be able to get within visual range. But Trace had only one good hand.

She needed to think, she realized. Think hard. There had to be something she could do to interfere with this guy. She fell silent again, and let her eyes close most of the way, testing her wrist restraints, testing her body with minuscule movements. She had to be ready when an opportunity presented itself. And if it didn't she'd have to make one.

For Trace. For the first time it occurred to her that

she was as willing to die to protect him as she was to protect Marisa and her family.

Where the hell had that come from?

Gloomily, she watched the countryside pass, knowing they had probably moved out of range of her cell phone. No one would be able to track her now, and Ashley hadn't even known she was coming. No one would even wonder where she was.

Trace's attempt to protect her seemed to have put her in some serious trouble. But she didn't blame him for that, she realized. No, she blamed the man beside her. How the hell had he figured out she was linked to Trace?

Despite her pounding head, she turned her thoughts back to the drive from her apartment to Ashley's. She *had* gone out of her way, so she'd lied to Trace about that, but she didn't want to leave him on his own to walk to the sheriff's. So…had this guy followed them? Had he seen Trace get out at the sheriff's?

Had he decided that Julie was the only way to draw Trace out?

The thought sickened her, and she was already feeling nauseated enough from the blow to her head. Trace might be the goat, but she was being used as the bait for him. Desperation filled her.

God, she needed to figure out something.

Fast.

Trace made the phone call last longer than it needed to. They fed him some flimflam about having been worried when he dropped out of sight, some crap about how glad they were he was all right after his accident, and yes, the threat appeared to be real and they were on it.

He didn't bother telling them anything. The guy he was talking to probably didn't know what was going on. Just a mouthpiece. Anyway, the stories didn't matter anymore. Nobody believed anyone else now.

He gave them enough time to locate him and determine the number of the cell he was using, then pushed their hand a bit. "I got another car. I'll be hitting the road soon."

"Denver?" asked his contact.

"I don't know. Haven't decided yet. I spent a nice weekend in this town, but I gotta head out now the storm is over. You know that. You told me to keep moving. I just don't know where yet. Yeah, I'll let you know."

He was certain his number was already being relayed to the general. He was back on the grid, and they'd track him now. So it was time to hit the road. For real.

Then the radio crackled again. "Sheriff, this is twenty-one."

Gage picked up the radio. "Go, twenty-one."

"We have a problem. Julie never arrived, but her car is out front. No sign of her except the contents of a tote bag scattered on the ground."

Trace felt as if a fist had punched him in the chest. How in the hell?

Chapter 13

Julie suddenly knew where they were headed. They weren't on the road, but in the end it didn't matter. She began to recognize her surroundings and knew they were headed for an unoccupied ranch, a place that had been empty for years after it had been foreclosed. Nobody would think to look out here, and there would be no one around for miles.

The place had a tragic past. A father and son had worked it together, eking out a living. Then one day the father had gone to look for his son and had found the twenty-five-year-old had been gruesomely killed in an accident with machinery. The father had had a heart attack on the spot, and by the time the mother had found them both…well.

No one knew where the woman had gone after that. She had sold off the livestock and the equipment she could in a quick auction, where her neighbors had been as generous to her as they could manage, and then had vanished. She'd packed up clothes, a few keepsakes, and taken the best of the vehicles. No one had ever heard from her again.

Just looking at the place made Julie shiver. Abandoned now for so long, as if it were cursed. No one seemed interested in buying the farmstead, and she could understand why. Some neighboring ranchers leased the grazing land from the bank, but nobody went near that house anymore, except possibly drifters and squatters. Neglect had left its mark all over the place. Tumbleweeds, some buried in snow, others just dusted with it, lined the whole house, even covered the porch. Rusting hulks of large equipment looked as if they might crumble at a touch.

Perfect setting for a nightmare, she thought acidly. Her nightmare. Perhaps Trace's. She squeezed her eyes shut and hoped Ryker and Gage persuaded him to just clear out of town. Convinced him that he could do nothing.

This was a big county, and there was no way it could be rapidly searched. She could be anywhere, and they had to make that clear to him. That there was no hope of finding her.

Because if they failed to, she feared what might happen to Trace. She didn't even begin to believe this man had any intention of setting her free.

Gage was putting helicopters into the air, possibly a dangerous thing to do given that the storm still occasionally gusted, and the winds had to be worse aloft.

Pointless, probably, when they had no idea who they were looking for, or what kind of vehicle.

Trace couldn't hold still. He paced the hallway, up and down, waiting for his phone to ring. If Andrepov wanted him, then he was going to have to call him and tell him where they'd meet. Taking Julie got him nowhere, except as a means of ensuring Trace would show up. Hell, maybe he'd even seen the deputy's car at Ashley's and had concluded there was a plan hatching.

So the man would call. Trace clung to that certainty.

"Go home," he told Ryker.

"I'm not letting you face this guy alone."

"What makes you think he'll face me any other way? You could endanger Julie. Worse, you could put your family at risk if he figures out who you are. Go home. Please."

But still Ryker hesitated, and Trace could understand that. It went against his grain to leave Trace uncovered. Hell, it would have gone against Trace's grain, too.

But some things mattered more.

"We've got Trace's back," Gage said. "Go take care of your wife and family. That's the biggest help you can give both of us right now. No additional concerns."

So Ryker departed, extracting a promise they'd keep him posted and call on him if needed. Then Trace was left alone with the sheriff.

"You have to stand down, too."

Gage shook his head. "I can't let you go alone. I have men…"

"I know about your men. You can bet Andrepov does, too. He's probably got the agency's full four-one-one on this place."

Gage's face darkened. "They're not supposed to…"

"Oh, give me a break, Sheriff. You know reality is often very different. Everybody in this county is cataloged somewhere, and your men, as you call them, are apt to be of special interest to Homeland Security. No secrets."

Gage nodded and sighed. "I'd like to feel more shocked than I do."

"We all would. And while it wouldn't ordinarily be a problem for anyone, this time it is. This time the bad guys used to be the good guys. And I no longer believe that they'd hesitate to call on all that information they're not supposed to use. How could it possibly be traced back to them anyway? My point is, if they know, then they've let Andrepov know because it's in their best interests to ensure he takes me down and then clears out swiftly. They don't want him caught. They don't want a diplomatic incident, and they sure as hell don't want to be caught pulling a stunt like this. So get your guys to stay back. I'll have to handle this."

Gage nodded slowly.

"So tell your men to stand down. Use the sat phone. Whoever's been paying attention to transmissions from the area will hear the order."

"You know," Gage said slowly, "I'm not used to feeling this naked."

"Who is? Better not to think about it. Most of the time, nobody cares at all what's going on around here. Blame me for your change in perspective."

Gage stared at the radio for a few minutes, as if pondering. "All right," he said finally. "But you give me one promise."

"What's that?"

"That you'll carry the satellite phone we gave you in

your car. When you get out, leave the window or door open so there's a strong signal. We'll stay out of the way, but you owe that much to Julie. If she needs help, we need to know where to look."

Trace hesitated. Gage was right. Julie. She stood right at the heart of this through no fault of her own. What if he managed to take out the general but got mortally wounded himself? She'd be in the middle of nowhere with no way back.

"Okay. But don't act. Stay clear. There can be no transmissions from the time I leave, or they'll warn him."

Gage picked up his own brick and keyed it. "Dalton here. Stand back. You're done except in town."

A series of affirmatives answered him. Trace noted, however, that the sheriff hadn't told them to stand down. Well, he couldn't, not when they were watching Ryker's place. As satisfied as he could be under the circumstances, he waited for the call he knew had to be coming.

This general had apparently already scouted this house. How had he managed that? As they pulled up, Julie dared to say, "Nobody ever comes here anymore. How did you find it?"

"Friends in high places," he answered shortly.

She understood. She wondered how much else the agency knew or could find out about Conard County. If they'd directed this man to this abandoned spot, they must know no one ever came here anymore.

"It scares me," she said, stalling.

"What? Ghosts? Every place has ghosts."

"Maybe where you come from."

He snorted. "Ghosts can't hurt you. I can."

Well, that was clear enough. He pulled the car up close to the house where it would blend better with the drifted snow. Then he urged her out of it at gunpoint.

For the first time in her life, Julie stared down the barrel of a rifle, one held by a man who would use it. For an instant she was frozen in fear, not even sure her legs would hold her. But then he waved the gun insistently and she knew she had to move or lose her chance.

After all, said the remaining part of her mind that hadn't caved to raw emotion, at this point she was still bait, dead or alive. Because how would Trace know if she was dead?

He'd still come. And lifeless, she'd be of no use to anyone.

She struggled out of the car. For the first time she got a true sense of how big and strong this man appeared. She hoped half of it was winter clothing.

Not having prepared for any extended period out of doors, she felt the chill cutting right into her each time the air stirred. It was almost a relief to stumble up the uneven steps and push her way through the tumbleweeds. The guy opened the door for her and shoved her inside. She nearly fell when her foot caught on a rumpled rug.

But at least there was no wind. Somehow the windows had remained unbroken despite all the years.

He waved her into a wooden chair. All thoughts of fleeing dissipated in about two seconds flat. If she ran out here, in the middle of nowhere, he wouldn't even to have to shoot her in the back. She'd get hypothermic before she could hope to reach any help, and she'd be found frozen to death in the snow.

He'd picked a good place for his confrontation. But Trace had warned her. He was a man who was very good at what he did. He'd risen to the top of two armies. Lots of experience and lots of intelligence, however bent he might be.

Then there was a loud *beep*. He lifted the bottom of his white jacket and pulled out a black brick that looked almost like the one Micah Parish had given to Trace.

"Da," he said, then listened. He muttered something, then pulled out a pad and pencil from one of the cargo pockets on his pants. "Yes," he said. "I have it. Now we will complete our business. No one else will come, yes?"

He listened again. When he put the satellite phone down, he smiled. "Your Archer is leaving town. Without you. I think we will stop him, yes?"

Julie closed her eyes, not believing for one second that Trace would simply run. But it was certainly clear that this man was getting intelligence from sources inside this country. No questions remained.

A wave of despair wanted to wash over her, but she refused to let it. Instead she focused on the room around her, seeking any means of protecting herself or taking this man out.

The previous owner had left an awful lot behind. Rats or mice had left their traces all over everything, but she didn't see anything within reach that she could use, at least not while her hands were tied. Thankfully he'd used rope, not one of those plastic cuffs. Apparently he wasn't prepared for everything, and that fueled a small spark of hope in her.

Remembering her belt buckle, she tucked her hands up inside her jacket.

He saw the movement immediately. "Pull your hands out!"

She did so, but immediately adopted the whiniest voice she could. "My hands are freezing. My fingers hurt!"

He hesitated, then must have decided that as long as he held the gun she was really not a threat. "Okay. But not for long."

"Thanks." She managed to make her tone sound begrudging. She tucked her hands up inside against and moved them until the rope was right over her belt buckle. At least the edges of it were thin enough to qualify as an exceptionally dull knife. Then she began to saw as surreptitiously as she could. She encouraged no delusional hopes that she would free her hands any time soon.

But then the guy made a phone call, and for several blessed minutes he didn't even look her way. She hurried her movements, prepared to stop the instant he started to turn back to her.

There was no time to waste. As she sawed, she kept looking around for items she could use for self-defense. At last she noted a poker lying on the floor by the wood-stove, covered in dust and ash. If she could get to it...

Then her heart froze. The man was talking to Trace.

The call didn't come quickly enough to suit Trace. He was geared up, ready to go. Even though he couldn't use it easily, a pistol was now tucked in his jacket pocket. A deadlier sheathed knife had been added to his arsenal and tucked into his left boot. The one thing he could say about Velcro closures was that they wouldn't hamper him if he had to reach that knife. In his right pocket, he carried a flash-bang grenade, courtesy of one worried sheriff.

"We'll be tracking you from the air. Leave the sat phone on," Gage said. "We'll stay back, but if we need to move…"

Trace nodded. Then at long last his phone rang. He picked it up and answered. "Archer."

"At long last we will meet," said a heavily accented voice. "You say you are leaving town?"

"Climbing in the car right now. Who are you?"

"You do not need to know. I have your friend with the red hair. If you want to see her alive again, come."

"Come where?"

"You have GPS?"

Trace hesitated. "I can get it," he answered finally.

"Then start driving east on the highway. I will give you direction once you are away from friends."

With that, the general disconnected.

"We'll be listening," Gage said. "Radio silence will be observed."

Trace nodded. Rage boiled in him again, and this time he didn't try to tamp it down. "Keep back. I don't care if I die. This is for Julie."

Gage merely nodded.

Trace stepped out into the bracing air and slid into the car that had been left for him. A decade-old model of four-wheel drive, it looked almost new in condition. Apparently John Hayes hadn't used it very much.

But when had Hayes ever been home?

When he was a mile out of town, his cell phone rang again.

"We will not be able to talk for long," the general said. "You will lose signal soon. There is a road to this place. Make sure you do not get stuck. Make a left on CR 480."

"Okay. Then?"

"Ten miles. You will have to walk up to a house on the right. Approach alone. I see one other person, your friend dies."

"I want proof the woman is still alive. Now."

There was a pause, then he heard Julie say, "Run, Trace!" Followed by a *click*.

The barrenness of the land gnawed at him. No cover. No place to hide. It was a good thing he'd told the sheriff to have his men stand down. They'd have had to belly-crawl their way for miles out here in order not to be seen.

But mostly he thought about Julie, prisoner of a madman. Probably certain that, no matter what happened, she was going to die. That realization hurt worse than his hand ever had. If they got through this, he'd never be able to make it up to her. Never.

This, thought Trace, was about to become the longest ten miles in his life.

Julie didn't expect to survive this. How could she when she had seen the man's face? No, he didn't intend to leave a witness. But apparently his plan to use her as bait had worked. She half expected him to shoot her the instant she told Trace to run, but he hadn't. In fact, he sat across the room from her, looking as if he was enjoying himself.

Enjoying her fear. Enjoying Trace's approach. Enjoying what he planned to do.

Rarely in her life had Julie ever felt anything approaching hatred, but she felt it then. He told her to pull her hands out from under her jacket, and she did so. Looking down quickly, she could see she had worked her way through half the rope's thickness. She positioned her hands so he couldn't see the fraying.

"You should have dressed warm," he said.

She didn't believe his solicitousness for a minute. "I wasn't planning to be stuck out here in an unheated house for hours."

"Oh, it won't be hours. He'll come as fast as he can, this Archer, and then he'll have to walk to the house. By the time he gets here, he'll be *so* tired."

Yeah, he probably would, Julie thought. And with his arm screaming at him as well. "What do you have against him, anyway?"

"He revealed me to people who shouldn't know. He endangered my life and my family. And after all I have done for this country!"

Well, he sounded righteously indignant. She didn't know whether it was an act or not, but his fury was real enough. Real enough to want a man's blood.

He revolted her. During all Marisa's suffering, Marisa had never wished ill on anyone. Never called for someone to pay. She had endured the worst of grief without ever speaking an unkind word.

This guy could use a few lessons in something called simple humanity. "I never did anything to you," she said. "I don't even know you or what you're talking about."

"Ah, the innocent." A glare darkened his face. "My family, they are innocent, too. How will that save them? I have been accused of terrible things and have had to fight to keep my family out of prison. It will not be completely over until I completely clear my name."

"How will it protect them to kill Trace?"

"I will have proof I never cooperated with your country. You people think you are so great, but you are nothing. You interfere where you should not. And then when someone seeks your help, you betray him. *Pah* on you all."

Silence fell, interrupted only occasionally by the scratching of tumbleweed against a wall as the wind stirred.

"Let me go," she suggested. "You don't need me anymore. He's coming."

"I could," he said. "You would not get far. But no, I want him to see the cost of his actions before he dies."

And there it was, she thought. She would die, too. The adrenaline, which had never quite left her, resurged now. She slipped her hands up under her jacket again when he went to the front window to watch. Sawing, sawing, would it be fast enough?

When Trace got here, he was going to need whatever help she could provide. It probably wouldn't be much, but she clearly remembered him saying he shot with his right hand. His damaged hand. So an unarmed man was coming to this gunfight. She didn't find that old saying at all amusing just then. It was so true it hurt.

If Trace died, she didn't think she'd care if she lived.

New strength filled her while she scanned the room and the man's back. He didn't expect any trouble from her, she realized. She was just a mere woman.

Maybe she could teach him another lesson.

The drive was precarious. The road hadn't been plowed and Trace used reflectors as his guide, probably much as the snowplows did. There was nothing out here, nothing. Some fencing, almost no trees, no signs of life anywhere. Andrepov had chosen well.

He couldn't help imagining the helpless terror Julie must be feeling, and the burn in his gut grew until it felt close to nuclear heat. He could hope for nothing except that Andrepov wanted him to see Julie die, that he'd keep her alive in order to savor that moment.

Which meant he was going to get to the house. Beyond that…who knew? But when the guy told him to disarm himself, he would at least have a gun to throw in the snow. He silently thanked the sheriff for that.

Would Andrepov suspect a knife in his boot? He didn't know. Then there was the flash-bang, which might cause a few moments of utter confusion if he could get it inside and find a way to tell Julie to close her eyes so she wouldn't be blinded by the flash.

So many questions, and all the answers awaited him in the distance. He couldn't even plan, not knowing what the layout was, who would be where, what items might be useful.

God, he hated this. He'd walked in blind before in his career, but he still hated it. Everything would rest on an instant decision, a decision that could easily be wrong. He hadn't been a praying man in a long time, but he realized he was praying now, praying that Julie would come through this unscathed.

Because if she didn't, he'd hunt Andrepov to the ends of the earth. And if he couldn't, he suspected Ryker would. That man's days were numbered, one way or another.

As were Casell's and anyone who had helped Andrepov knowingly in this endeavor. If the Fates favored him today, he was damn well going to make sure that this never happened again.

At last the farmstead appeared, rising above the snow caught on the fences. This had to be the place. A weathered house, a barn that looked as if it were halfway through the job of collapsing. The house, Andrepov had said. The house.

His heart accelerated now, approaching the rate at which he would be fully ready for whatever lay ahead. At last he pulled over to the side of the road. A driveway, or what had been one once, was marked by sagging fence lines on either side of it. He took the sat phone and shoved it under the seat, out of sight, and climbed slowly out of the car, leaving the door open. This had to be it.

Checking his cell, he found he could no longer make a connection. The middle of nowhere. Open and exposed. Andrepov could shoot him as he plowed his way up to the house.

But he wouldn't. Trace knew that with a certainty born of long experience. Those who wanted revenge also wanted to savor it. Andrepov was going to make him walk that distance unprotected and unsheltered and enjoy watching Trace tire with each step.

Except Trace had never tired easily. He knew how to measure himself the way a finely tuned athlete knew, never pushing himself into the red zone, always ensuring there would be plenty of energy for what came next.

So much as he wanted to race up to that house and do what he could for Julie, he paced himself carefully, and made a show of letting his arm appear to dangle uselessly against his side. Like a bird feigning a broken wing.

Except that arm still had plenty of strength, and

pain or no pain, grip or no grip, it could still do a lot. Like throw a punch. Like wrap itself around someone's throat.

He hoped he got a chance to do that.

He heard a helicopter, but it sounded far away. *Good job, Gage.* He had telescopic eyes on the situation, but kept enough distance that it didn't seem he was following. Then the sound of rotors died away, muffled perhaps by distant woods, making the pass seem merely routine.

But they knew where he was, and that meant they could help Julie if he could save her from this maniac.

Julie. Nothing else on earth mattered except her. Freeing her. Keeping her safe. He'd have cut his own throat to accomplish that.

When he'd covered all but the last twenty feet to the door, the door opened a crack.

"Get rid of your weapons, Archer. Now."

He made a show of hesitating, then stuck his hand in his pocket and pulled out the service revolver. Holding it up so it could be seen, he tossed it into the snow.

"Anything else you have."

"What else would I have? I only have one arm. I can't even fight you."

"Ah yes, so the bullet did at least part of the job. I heard you were disabled."

Trace didn't answer. He simply waited for the man to believe him. If Andrepov pushed it any further, he could ditch the flash-bang, which might be useless anyway.

"So, you know what you did to me?"

"I don't have the slightest idea. I had almost nothing to do with you."

"You gave my name to someone."

"Hate to disappoint you, but that wasn't me. I never compromised an asset. Never. So sure you have the right man?"

"Very sure," came the answer. "Come closer. But drop your jacket outside."

"That's going to be hard to do," Trace said, stepping slowly closer. "I needed help getting into it."

At that Andrepov laughed. "This is going to be too easy."

Julie felt the last of the rope give way. Now she had an additional problem. Andrepov had a bead on Trace, who was approaching the house. If she moved, he might shoot Trace, then turn on her. She couldn't risk that, so she held perfectly still.

A few tears right now might make her look usefully weak, but she didn't cry easily. And the last thing she felt like doing right now was weeping. The anger that filled her consumed everything else, even her fear. This general was a sick man, and he was acting like he was at a shooting gallery. She wondered if he had only that one rifle, or if he had other weapons. No way to know. She eyed the poker again, forgotten in the ashes and dust, and figured that she could reach it in one long stride. But then she'd have to pick it up and face the man who held the rifle.

It wasn't looking good. None of this was.

Then the door opened wider and Trace stepped in. He hadn't shed his jacket, and she saw the unusual way he was carrying his arm, as if it just flopped uselessly. Never before had he done that. Smart move, she thought.

"Let her go," Trace said as soon as he was inside.

"She's never done anything to you. Never. And she has no idea who you are."

"So you say," Andrepov answered, motioning Trace farther into the room, closer to Julie. Not good, Julie thought. She tried to catch Trace's eye and with a slight jerk of her head tried to tell him to put space between them, but he never took his eyes off the general. Anyway, he'd apparently figured it out himself because he tripped slightly on some junk on the floor and wound up on the far side of the old living room from her.

The general waved the gun between them. "Move over beside her."

"Why?" Trace asked. "It's going to take two bullets any way you look at it." He moved a little, however, and soon the man's back was to Julie. She started frantically moving, jerking her eyes toward the poker, and then she took a risk, pulling her hands from beneath her jacket and showing her freed wrists.

Trace's expression never changed, but she saw the spark in his gaze as he got her message. Quickly, she buried her hands within her jacket again.

"Trace?" she said. Her voice trembled. At least it wasn't hard to feign that. "What's going on?"

"Apparently this…man was given some faulty intelligence."

"About what? I don't understand any of this!"

The general spoke. "Your man here betrayed me. Did he ever tell you he was a spy?"

"A spy?" Julie made her voice sound thin, disbelieving. "For real?"

"For real," said Trace, his gaze never wavering. He never once looked at her again. All his attention was on the man who pointed the rifle at him. "And this man thinks I betrayed him. Only he's wrong about that. I never betrayed an asset in my life."

The general snorted. "So you claim it was all lies? I know the danger I faced, the danger my family faced. When I was accused of treason, I not only had to fight to save myself from execution but also to protect my family from prison. You hurt us all."

"I know the dangers," Trace answered, his voice taking on an edge. "Which is exactly why I would never betray anyone. *Never.*"

"Of course you would say that. But sources in your own agency say it was you."

"Of course they would," Trace answered. "You didn't look high enough."

"You were high."

"I worked at a group of embassies. Do you really think that was high up? I never reached the kinds of levels you did. Never reached the kind of level that would let me betray you. Although, right now, I half wish I had."

"Brave words from a dead man."

"I may be dead, but what makes you think you won't be soon, too? Because the betrayal came from higher up than me. Believe it. Some political functionary who'd rather show off his knowledge than protect it. Someone who doesn't get the dangers of exposing those who help us. Someone who told a good story at a party over too many drinks."

Julie wondered if she should move now. Any movement she made would draw the general's attention her way. Away from Trace. The problem was, she didn't know whether she'd get shot for her efforts, or how much Trace could still manage to do. If she died, and he couldn't deal with that man, he'd be dead, too. Biting her lip, she waited, hoping for a sign.

"The problem with you," Trace said to the general, edging closer to the man and his gun, "is that you live a life of lies, but you can't tell when you're being lied to and used."

The general let out an angry string of what sounded like curses, perhaps in Russian. "You lie."

"No, actually, I don't. You're being used right now. Someone is concealing their part in your betrayal by offering me as a sacrifice. Have you never made a sacrifice play, General?"

Words erupted from the man.

"Of course you have," Trace said. "Something goes wrong. It doesn't matter what, but you direct the blame elsewhere. Here, we call it covering your butt. Someone's using me to cover his butt, to keep you in play, and send you home satisfied. But if you kill me, you won't be getting the right man."

A short, sharp sound escaped the general, but his attention was clearly focused on Trace now. Julie started to move, but caught the slightest shake of Trace's head, so she remained on the chair.

"You'll go home, and the man who betrayed you will still be here. Just think, he could make the same mistake again. What makes you believe he'll be able to help you this way another time?"

"Enough," roared the general. "If it is not you, then give me the name. Now!"

Trace answered flatly. "Casell." The "State Department" employee who was actually an assistant director at the CIA. A man who had regularly been meeting with the Ukrainian delegation.

For a perceptible instant, the general froze. As he did so, the gun barrel dropped a few inches and a bit to the side. "Casell? I don't believe you."

"When I found out you wanted me, I made it my business to find out who had betrayed *me*. It was Casell."

"I talk to him all the time." But the faintest doubt had crept into the general's voice.

"Which is more than you can say about me. You were barely on my radar."

Then Trace exploded into action. His left arm swung out like a striking snake, pushing the gun aside. It nearly fell from the general's hand. But then, amazingly, Trace delivered a punch straight to the guy's midsection with his damaged right hand.

The general doubled over as breath escaped him. Blow to the solar plexus, Julie thought in the instant before she leaped into action herself.

In one swift movement, she rose from the chair, took the step and grabbed the poker. When she turned, the general, still unable to breathe, was caught in a struggle with Trace, who didn't seem at all hindered by the pain in his right hand.

She tried to remember what she'd learned in her defense classes, but something else took over. Sheer survival instinct, maybe. Stepping toward the two battling men, she kicked the rifle away and then laid into the general's head with the poker.

It wasn't easy, given how close they were and the intensity of their struggle, but she managed to deliver two good blows. The second caused blood to run from Andrepov's scalp.

Then Trace whipped the man around and closed his

arm around his neck. Julie stood there, watching as Trace used a choke hold, never letting go of the struggling man.

Enough, she thought, and drove the pointed end of the poker into the man's gut. His eyes widened, then he sagged.

"Rifle," Trace gasped.

She grabbed it, having only the vaguest idea what to do with it. The general seemed to be unconscious, but Trace stepped back as he let go of him, watching him sprawl on the floor.

"Give me the rifle."

She passed it to him willingly, and watched as he settled it in his left arm, finger around the trigger, the barrel pointed straight at the man.

"Run out to the car. The sat phone is under the driver's seat. Hit the red button."

"Will you be okay?"

"If he moves, he'll be dead."

The chill in his voice told her all she needed to know. She ran for the car.

Chapter 14

Julie heard the sound of helicopter rotors overhead, but now it was a good sound, a welcome sound. In the weeks since the general had been defeated and arrested, most of life had returned to normal. She sat now in Marisa's kitchen, holding baby Jonni, who was just learning to smile.

Marisa had carried the phone into the other room, but returned now with a smile on her face. "Ryker says they'll be back tomorrow."

"They?" Julie asked, her heart skipping a beat with unwarranted hope. She hadn't seen Trace since the general's arrest and a swarm of federal law enforcement had descended on the town. She'd been questioned about all that happened, then let go. As for the general, his diplomatic immunity didn't protect him from charges of kidnapping and attempted murder.

But Trace and Ryker had set out for Langley a day

later, and she'd been on the edge of her seat ever since. They were taking on some pretty powerful people inside the secretive walls of the CIA. How would that turn out?

Ryker called each evening to talk to Marisa, but she didn't hear from Trace. It was as if he had cut her out of his life, and that gouged at her heart, painful every waking minute. Couldn't the guy at least have said goodbye?

She sighed and cooed at the baby. Another smile answered her, and Jonni tried hard to imitate the sound.

"Both of them, I gathered," Marisa answered. "You want me to take her?"

"I'm fine. I've heard that babies can whistle. I wonder if I should try to teach her."

Anything except think about Trace's return and what it might mean. Or worse, that Marisa had misunderstood and he wouldn't come back at all.

Those days she'd spent with him had taught her that he wasn't a man who opened up easily. What he did share skimmed the surface, and even though she'd been caught up in all of this with him, he'd guarded his secrets carefully. He'd talked about his parents without saying a whole lot, she realized in retrospect. He hadn't even evinced grief when he spoke of them dying in the Ebola crisis in Africa. Maybe most of his emotions were out of reach to him now. Maybe he'd locked them away in a safe place so he could do his job, and simply didn't let anyone past those walls.

Odd to think she'd made love with a man and didn't truly have any idea if he liked her. He'd said some nice things, but that didn't add up to liking. People said those things because they felt it necessary, and she *had* kind of pushed him into making love to her.

Well, if he was coming back here, it was probably

only to say goodbye. She couldn't imagine him staying here in the middle of nowhere after the exciting and widely traveled life he'd lived.

He'd probably die of boredom.

Jonni started fussing, and Marisa took her to feed her.

"It'll all be okay," Marisa said.

"What will?" She certainly hadn't revealed that she was pining for a man who clearly wasn't pining for her. Not even a phone call?

When she finally went home that evening, she was grateful it was a weekend. Because she suddenly had a strong urge for a good cry, an emotional catch-up with herself after all that had happened. A spy had waltzed into her life, saved her from a bad guy she never would have met except for him, and then waltzed away again.

Why should she ever have allowed herself to imagine anything else?

When the doorbell rang late the next afternoon, she almost didn't answer it. She was in no mood to see anyone, and right now she most especially didn't want to see Trace.

But then irritation goaded her and she went to throw open the door. It was definitely Trace, with a fresh haircut, a long wool coat with buttons rather than a zipper and a half smile.

"Well, hello," she said a bit sharply. "Not even a phone call? Like I'm nothing?" She started to close the door, deciding in an instant that she was going to end this herself and not give him the opportunity.

"They wouldn't let me call."

That stopped her just as she started to close the door. Heedless of the still-chilly air, although spring was beginning to make real inroads, she said, "I'm supposed to believe that?"

"It's true."

"Ryker called Marisa."

"Ryker wasn't under the intense investigation and questioning that I was."

She regarded him steadily, thinking that he looked a little tired, and even a bit thinner. Evidently these past weeks hadn't been easy on him. Sympathy began to rise in her, the last thing she wanted to feel for him.

She stepped back, letting him enter, and stood several feet away as he unbuttoned his coat. The glove was gone from his scarred right hand. "There's coffee," she said with less than usual grace.

"Thank you."

But he didn't move immediately, simply closing the door and standing there, looking at her. Just looking at her. As if…he were hungry for the sight of her? She didn't dare believe it.

"We need to talk," he said finally. "Maybe that coffee would be good after all."

"Still taking pain meds?"

"Rarely. They're talking about amputation again."

She froze on her way to the coffeepot and caught her breath as she resumed getting two mugs and filling them. "No alternative?"

"There's always an alternative. Like living with this."

"Have you made up your mind?"

"Not yet."

She carried the mugs to the living room. When he sat on the sofa, she took the chair, the safest place to be. He'd unbuttoned his coat, but still wore it, a sure sign he expected to be gone soon.

This was painful, hurtful. Why in the hell had he come back? She couldn't tell if this was worse than not hearing from him all this time. All it seemed to be doing was strengthening her sense of loss. No amount of telling herself she barely knew the guy was enough to ease what had taken root in her heart. "So," she said, trying to keep the conversation to safe subjects, "did you clean house?"

He smiled faintly. "We surely did. Ryker's friend Bill was a great help with that. Apparently he'd been doing some digging of his own. And then of course I was exhibit A. It helped, too, that when the general started talking, he was mad enough to tell his side of the story."

"So what's going to happen to him?"

"I think he outlived his usefulness. My guess is he's going to be tried and sent to prison. All because he wanted revenge. Or we might trade him for another prisoner."

She nodded, uncomfortably aware that her heart was beating heavily. She could feel it in her chest. What did she want, anyway? For this guy to leave or stay? His departure would return her life to its uncomplicated, normal state. If he hung around…well, why would he hang around anyway?

"And what about the guy who betrayed you?"

"He's getting schooled by some very annoyed FBI agents about revealing the identity of a foreign informant, among other things. His star is rapidly crashing. As it should."

"I'm glad to hear that." Good news, it seemed, except in one respect. "So are you going back to the agency?" she asked finally, her heart thundering.

"Hell, no. And I wanted to talk with you about that."

"Me?" Now she felt confused. "What do I have to say about it?"

"Everything." Then he stood and came toward her, finally dropping to his knees in front of her. "I know I'm not easy. I know I'm a clam and it drives you nuts sometimes. I know I'm probably as crippled emotionally as I am physically. But I also know that I realized I missed you every single moment of every single day I was away."

Her heart was skittering now with both hope and fear. She wanted to reach for him, but for the first time in her life, she didn't dare do what impulse demanded. "What do you want from me, Trace?"

"A chance. I can't ask for any more than that. A chance to grow whatever this is between us. A chance to make it into something lasting and beautiful. Because everything about you is beautiful to me, Julie. Even the way you give me a hard time. I love the way I never have to wonder what you're thinking because you just tell me. I love the way you rarely let me run away and hide inside myself. I think with you I could be a better man."

She was breathing rapidly now, hopeful and half panicked. "You hardly know me."

"I saw you under the best circumstances when we made love, and I saw you under the worst circumstances with the general. Everything in between is bound to be just as remarkable. I'm not worried about who you are. I'm worried about whether you can stand *me*."

"Stand you?" she repeated. Everything inside her was melting with the understanding that she wanted this man with her every single day in the future. He wouldn't be easy, but that wasn't part of bargains like this.

"I know I'm difficult, but you've opened my heart for the first time in years. I'd like to be part of your world, part of a world where you put smiley faces on students' papers and take care of your friends with everything you've got. Just let me try."

Enough, she thought. The answers were exploding inside her, and they were joyful. She slid off the chair until they were kneeling face-to-face. "Just tell me why, Trace. Just tell me *why*."

"Because," he said firmly, "I'm in love with you."

She felt the smile growing on her face. "I could get used to hearing that."

"Then I'll say it until you tell me to shut up."

She lifted a hand to cradle his cheek. "I never want you to shut up. Trace… I love you, too. Let's make this work."

His face lit up like the Fourth of July, giving her a glimpse of the untroubled man he could become. "Really? How do you want to start?"

"You can start by taking me to bed. This time, for a long time. I want to make love with you."

He leaned in to kiss her deeply, and she felt the familiar rush of desire through her entire body. "For hours and hours," he murmured. "I want to make love to you forever."

"Me, too," she whispered, throwing her arms around him and hugging him with every ounce of passion and strength in her body.

A spy had come to Conard County. To stay.

* * * * *

#1899 CAVANAUGH COLD CASE
Cavanaugh Justice • by Marie Ferrarella
Playboy detective Malloy Cavanaugh is on the case when
bodies are unearthed in a cactus nursery. But it's medical
examiner Kristin Alberghetti who poses the greatest threat
to his heart.

#1900 A BABY FOR AGENT COLTON
The Coltons of Texas • by Jennifer Morey
FBI profiler Trevor Colton isn't looking for a family beyond
his recent reunion with his siblings, but when his partner,
Jocelyn Locke, announces she's pregnant, he's thrown into
the role of protector while they chase a dangerous serial
killer.

#1901 DELTA FORCE DESIRE
by C.J. Miller
When Griffin Brooks rescues a computer programmer from
being kidnapped by cyberterrorists, he marvels at his client's
beauty *and* brains. But the classified project Kit worked on
threatens both of them and their burgeoning relationship.

#1902 A SEAL TO SAVE HER
To Protect and Serve • by Karen Anders
A wounded navy SEAL and a hunted US senator run for their
lives in war-torn Afghanistan. Their pursuers: her security
detail. Their mission: get out alive!

REQUEST YOUR FREE BOOKS!
2 FREE NOVELS PLUS 2 FREE GIFTS!

ROMANTIC suspense

Sparked by danger, fueled by passion

YES! Please send me 2 FREE Harlequin® Romantic Suspense novels and my 2 FREE gifts (gifts are worth about $10). After receiving them, if I don't wish to receive any more books, I can return the shipping statement marked "cancel." If I don't cancel, I will receive 4 brand-new novels every month and be billed just $4.74 per book in the U.S. or $5.49 per book in Canada. That's a savings of at least 12% off the cover price! It's quite a bargain! Shipping and handling is just 50¢ per book in the U.S. and 75¢ per book in Canada.* I understand that accepting the 2 free books and gifts places me under no obligation to buy anything. I can always return a shipment and cancel at any time. Even if I never buy another book, the two free books and gifts are mine to keep forever.

240/340 HDN GH3P

Name _____ (PLEASE PRINT) _____

Address _____ Apt. # _____

City _____ State/Prov. _____ Zip/Postal Code _____

Signature (if under 18, a parent or guardian must sign) _____

Mail to the **Reader Service:**

IN U.S.A.: P.O. Box 1867, Buffalo, NY 14240-1867
IN CANADA: P.O. Box 609, Fort Erie, Ontario L2A 5X3

Want to try two free books from another line?
Call 1-800-873-8635 or visit www.ReaderService.com.

* Terms and prices subject to change without notice. Prices do not include applicable taxes. Sales tax applicable in N.Y. Canadian residents will be charged applicable taxes. Offer not valid in Quebec. This offer is limited to one order per household. Not valid for current subscribers to Harlequin Romantic Suspense books. All orders subject to credit approval. Credit or debit balances in a customer's account(s) may be offset by any other outstanding balance owed by or to the customer. Please allow 4 to 6 weeks for delivery. Offer available while quantities last.

Your Privacy—The Reader Service is committed to protecting your privacy. Our Privacy Policy is available online at www.ReaderService.com or upon request from the Reader Service.

We make a portion of our mailing list available to reputable third parties that offer products we believe may interest you. If you prefer that we not exchange your name with third parties, or if you wish to clarify or modify your communication preferences, please visit us at www.ReaderService.com/consumerschoice or write to us at Reader Service Preference Service, P.O. Box 9062, Buffalo, NY 14240-9062. Include your complete name and address.

With the pregnancy test long ago thrown in the trash, Trevor paced from one end of the living room of Jocelyn's condo to the other. She sat on her gray sofa before the stacked gray rock wall, a fresh vase of yellow lilies on the coffee table, reminding him that her chosen profession missed the mark. What hit the mark was what had him pacing the room. Her. Pregnant. Raising babies in a warm, inviting home like this one, in a gated community with a pool and clubhouse.

He knew what he had to do. He just couldn't believe he actually would.

He stopped pacing in front of the sofa, looking at Jocelyn over the tops of cheery lilies. "We have to get married."

That blunt announcement removed her annoyed observation of him digesting the idea of his impending fatherhood. Now shock rounded her eyes and parted her lips with a grunt.

"Will I be at gunpoint?" she asked.

She felt forced into this. He understood that. So did he.

"Love isn't important right now. The baby is what's important. No child of mine is going to be raised in a broken home."

She stood up. "Nothing's broken in *my* home."

She kind of went low on that one. His home was broken. Did she mean him or his dad? Both, probably.

"I won't get married just because I'm pregnant," she said. "I want love. Love is important to me, equally as much as this child." After a beat, she added, "And I thought you didn't mix personal relationships with your professional ones."

"I don't, but a baby changes everything. I won't be my father. I won't tear apart a family and destroy the lives of my children. I'll give them support and the best chance at a good life as I can."

Nothing in the world held more importance than that. He'd do anything, go to any length to avoid turning out like his father. He was no murderer. He had sanity. And he was on the opposite side of the law from his father. That was where he'd stay.

Don't miss
A BABY FOR AGENT COLTON by Jennifer Morey,
available June 2016 wherever
Harlequin® Romantic Suspense
books and ebooks are sold.

www.Harlequin.com

HRSEXP0516

Turn your love of reading into
rewards you'll love with
Harlequin My Rewards

**Join for FREE today at
www.HarlequinMyRewards.com**

Earn **FREE BOOKS** of your choice.

Experience **EXCLUSIVE OFFERS** and contests.

Enjoy **BOOK RECOMMENDATIONS**
selected just for you.

PLUS! Sign up now
and get **500** points
right away!

Earn
**FREE
REWARDS**
HarlequinMyRewards.com
Join
Today!

MYR16R